White Pines

Gemma Amor

White Pines

First Edition March 2020

Cover design by: Kealan Patrick Burke of Elderlemon Designs

ISBN: 9781793845610

There are people I need to thank for making this book possible:

My Kickstarter backers- each and every one of you took a chance on this book based on the prologue alone, and for that you have my unending love and gratitude. There is a full list of backers at the end of this novel. Thank you a million times.

Mr. M, for alerting me to Gruinard Island, and throwing me in at the deep end. I didn't drown (well, nearly).

The people of the Highlands, for being so friendly and not at all like the people in this book, thank heavens.

My brilliant editor (and friend) Dan Hanks, for diligently turning this into a much better book than I could ever have imagined, and being the most exuberant cheerleader a writer could hope for.

David Cummings of the No Sleep Podcast, for being so supportive of everything I do and boosting the Kickstarter so tremendously. You are a true mentor and a dear friend.

Sadie Hartmann, a champion for indie authors, a beautiful force of nature in the world of horror, and, hopefully, a friend. You said you wanted a novel. Here she is!

Brandon Boone, otherwise known as Shit Thom Yorke, for the White Pines playlist and for *not* supporting the Kickstarter, you tight bastard. Timing is everything.

The effortlessly talented Kealan Patrick-Burke for the stunning cover. You're one of my favourite people too!

Eòghainn MacGriogair for the invaluable Gàidhlig advice (I hope I did it justice- the audiobook will be fun!)

My dedicated beta reader Aiden Merchant, a huge supporter and enthusiastic megaphone for my questionable talents.

The Poolewe Hotel, for the peace and quiet,
and simply awesome fish and chips.

And BTP, my second home from home, although
you probably don't realise that. Best coffee
and poached eggs in town.

'One by one they were all becoming shades.
Better pass boldly into that other world,
in the full glory of some passion, than
fade and wither dismally with age'

James Joyce, The Dead

PROLOGUE

This is where White Pines used to stand.

Of the 1,351 people who used to live here, only bare, blackened earth remains. Instead of the self-made town, there is now a scar now upon the land, made all the more horrifying by its proportions, for the charred soil is laid out in the shape of a perfectly proportioned equilateral triangle.

It's been over ten years, yet still it feels as if the Island is waiting for White Pines to return. Time has stopped here. Nature has not reclaimed the land. The ground remains scorched. Nothing grows. Not even weeds. Animals don't forage here, birds don't fly over the big, blank space in the soil where houses used to stand. I can't even see insects flitting around on the breeze. There is no breeze, despite the fact that the sea is all around me.

I reach down, pull my gloves off, touch the dark soil with my bare hands. Nine fingers press down into the cold earth, and I shiver. I was told, years ago, not to do this, but I do it anyway.

I was told, years ago, to stay away, but I come, anyway. Every year I make the journey, across the bay, through the stand of strange white pine trees that encircles the site, underneath the tall barbed-wire fence that marks the old settlement boundary, and I have done so every year since it happened. The event. The vanishing. Every year, just like this, I press my hands to the soil and feel the same peculiar tingle run through my fingers, a numbness which speaks not only of loss, but of a huge wrongness in the natural order of things. I can't keep my hands pressed to the ground in this way for long. After only a few moments, my head and my teeth begin to ache. I rise, pull my gloves back on, and walk away from what used to be the centre of the community. A small square once lay here. In the middle of this square, a cast iron water pump stood, the Island's main source of clean water. Birds used to sit on the roof that covered the pump, chattering amongst themselves and coating it with a white, crusty layer of shit. There was a carved sandstone bench next to the pump. Folk would sit there and feed the birds: seagulls, crows, sparrows, the occasional robin. The birds are gone, now. So is the pump, the square, the shit, and the people. The absence of things is so loud it pierces my brain with loss. What used to be, is simply no more.

But the memories linger like smoke in the air.

It is time to leave. There are no answers here for me, not today. I walk slowly back towards the barbed-wire fence. The ragged remains of a few cards and flowers hang sadly from the wire, long-degraded evidence of a tragedy, of mystery, of a dirty secret. Time has erased the messages on the cards, just as time has erased the days that have passed since White Pines disappeared. But I know what is written in each one. The cards were left by me. One for every year since...it happened.

You see, no-one comes here anymore, except for me. There is no reason to. There is nothing to see, no ruins to mourn over. No visible remains of what has been lost. People need something tangible to attach their grief to. There is no comfort to be taken from wide open spaces full of nothing.

And in a way, it makes things simpler. A secret is much easier to keep safe when there are no signs it ever existed in the first place.

The rigid pine trees outside of the barbed-wire boundary frown upon me as I hunker down onto all fours, preparing to climb under the fence and head back to the south shore, where my way off the Island lies. I notice there is no wind in their branches. There never is. I am, as usual, the only moving thing in this static, frozen landscape. I may as well be standing on the moon.

There is a tearing sound. The fence

catches my jacket, shreds a long strip of the scarlet material right off. It hangs there, motionless alongside the wilted cards, the colour too bright amongst the faded detritus of grief. It seems brash by comparison, garish. And yet, I feel defiant, looking at it. The colour *should* be bright. It is fitting, symbolic, a brightness which proudly shouts that I have not forgotten. It's a small, torn, defiant marker of my remembrance. A tiny red flag challenging the still, dead air.

Besides, I never liked this coat much anyway. It belonged to someone else, once, someone thankfully long-dead. I hadn't liked her very much, either.

With effort, I free myself from the fence, and stand up, panting. I am not as agile as I once was. I am nearly fifty now, and things in my body don't work as nimbly as they once did. I wonder if prolonged exposure to the echo of White Pines has something to do with the vicious onset of arthritis that twists my body in increasingly cruel ways. It certainly always seems worse after my annual visit. Or maybe it's the cold Scottish climate. Or perhaps I'm just getting older, and this is what happens.

I pat myself down, making sure I've dropped nothing, left nothing behind except that single strip of red fabric on the fence. Then, reassured, I take one long, last look at White Pines, as is tradition.

The things I have seen here. Such terrible,

terrible things.

As I think this, I see movement on the scorched soil.

There is a flicker. A change in the atmosphere. A familiar break in the static. Like a light blinking on in a darkened room.

Oh, God. I rub my eyes, wondering if I've imagined the flicker. The air shudders again. I haven't.

Something is coming back.

The atmosphere breaks one last time, a contraction that gives birth to a shadow. And I see...

...I see a dark, limping shape headed down the slope towards me.

Fear fills my heart. Is it the Hunter? It can't be. The Hunter is dead.

The shape moves in the way that a human moves, only more slowly, with a staggering gait. A small noise escapes my mouth. *Not again,* I think. I know how this works. It has been years since I've seen it happen, but every time, it's the same. The air ripples, a shape moves, and something that once belonged to White Pines returns. Momentarily, like a mirage. A building, an item of clothing like a shoe, or a glove, or a dog, or even a person. They appear, and then, before anyone can do anything, they disappear again, blinking out of the world in a matter of seconds, leaving only small flakes of ash in the air, ash which drifts to the floor, and then melts, like snow.

Determination grabs my heart as the figure stumbles across the blasted earth. Maybe this time it will be different. Maybe this time, I can save just one of them, one, single part of White Pines, before the nothing sucks it out of existence again.

Another thought occurs, stealing my breath away.

Maybe this time, it'll be Matthew.

Matthew, come back, from wherever he has been.

I scramble back underneath the fence again. This time, my jacket catches on the barbs and almost comes off entirely, but I barely notice. I wrestle free of it and leave it hanging on the wire, tilting forward, my eyes fixed on the goal, trying to make the silhouette out more clearly. It looks...it's not large enough to be Matthew...it looks...

Like a child!

A child smeared with ash, eyes white and haunted in its face. The child cries, and the sound carries across to me: scared, lost, pitiful.

Run! I think, *run towards me! You don't have long!*

The child runs, and I can see now that it is a small boy, maybe six or seven years of age, judging by his height and build. My stomach lurches with recognition. I know this boy. I know this boy! His cries grow louder as he moves, and the sound of him spurs me into action, giving my feet wings.

Because by now, the ghosts have normally winked out of existence. By now, he should have vanished again. This time, things are different. The boy is still here.

I might just make it.

I might just save one of them.

And I am moving, legs wheeling beneath me, pulled to the silhouette like iron filings to a magnet, throwing my body forward with all the speed I can muster, despite the inherent dangers of staying on the unhallowed ground for too long. I have to get to the boy before the Island steals him back. I *have* to. I have to repair it, somehow. The loss. In ten years, I have done nothing of any use except mourn. This time it will be different. I force my legs to move faster than they have for a long, long time, despite the pain in my joints, despite the awkwardness of my twisted bones.

Finally, gloriously, after what feels like eons of running towards each other, he is within reach. I lunge for him, grasp his outstretched arm, heave him up into my embrace, ignoring the screams of pain my bones make. With the boy wrapped tight to my chest, I make an abrupt turn, wheeling about and almost over-balancing, and then I shuffle back towards the fence, hating my weak body, wishing I was younger, wishing I was faster, desperation and fear urging me on nonetheless. I had been full of power, once. I had been something extraordinary. Beyond human. Where was that power now? Why give me such a gift, only to take it away again? The Island is cruel, indiscriminate.

It deceives.

'Hurry!' The boy shrieks, and I can feel him flickering in my embrace, his form pulsating between solid and...something else. Something less real. Something less *now*. I move faster, sobbing with the effort of carrying him, aiming for the beacon that is my crimson jacket hanging from the fence. It looms brighter and closer, the colour still defiant, and now, more hopeful than I could have imagined possible.

Behind it, tall pines with brilliant white bark watch, impassive. They are always watching.

They can go to hell.

Because we are going to make it. The fence is mere feet away.

'Hurry up, hurry up, *hurry up!*' The boy babbles as we close in on the boundary, and I feel him flicker once again, almost disappearing from my grip completely. I stumble to my knees, and make a decision. I hurl him at the fence, and he coalesce back into solidity, made more real by his proximity to the invisible border that runs parallel to the fence. A border I set in place and sealed, many years ago. Is it still fast? No time for that now.

The boy hits the wire, rights himself, scrambles to his knees and disappears underneath, like a rabbit into a burrow. As he goes, his legs vanish completely, and he wails in panic, but then they reappear, and, against all possible odds, he is on the opposite side of the fence, and he is whole once more. Whole, and *real*.

I hold out a hand, a signal to stop him from moving. The message is clear: *stay still, stay there until I can get you.*

Shuffling and shambling the last few steps, feeling the air snap and wane around me, I wonder if this is my time, finally. My hair stands up on my scalp, as if pulled upright by static. Will White Pines take me where all the others went? Am I ready, after all this time, to follow?

Would I be leaving, or arriving?

I *am* ready. I want to find Matthew. I want to know, once and for all, where he went.

But then there is the boy. And the boy needs help.

Oh, God. I saved one. I saved one!

It is not time.

A red jacket waits, like a flag at the end of a race. I push back underneath the fence, where wire knots scrape my back. I cannot believe what has just happened. Tears roll down my cheeks. A faint breeze picks up from somewhere, the first breeze I have felt in ten years in this place.

The tall, pale pines rustle gently around

us, as if applauding.

I lie down next to the boy on the ground and hold him tightly, soothing him as he sobs hysterically, great, big, wonderful, real sobs.

I've got you, I think, over and over again, as we lay crying on the floor, clutching at each other. The boy is here. He is not a ghost, or a memory. He is real. His tears are hot against my cheek. The stink of ash, and of something else, is rich in my nostrils. I hold him so tightly I fear I may break him.

I have done it. I have saved one.

One survivor. One, of so many lost souls.

I saved one.

I begin to laugh, hysterically. If I can save one, then I can save more.

My courage rises for the first time in years. It rises, and becomes a great marble plinth of resolve, upon which, a small boy stands like Eros, his face streaked with tears.

I am going to find out what happened to White Pines, once and for all.

And this boy is going to help me.

Maybe, together, we can save them all.

PART ONE: ROOTS

1. A HOUSE CALLED TAIGH-FAIRE

Before all of this, there was a house. An old stone and slate house, once painted a pristine white. Now, rather like me, it had faded and discolored to something greyer, shabbier, altogether less attractive, if no less robust.

It was once a guest house. The last guest checked out in 1988, and after that it stood empty for some time, clinging like a weathered barnacle to a lip of stone that juts out above the shore of a beautiful sandy cove called Little Gruinard beach, in Gruinard Bay, on the north-west coast of Scotland. As idyllic and isolated a spot as you could possibly imagine, and once you got used to the breathtaking views, once they stopped being a distraction, you realised there was something wild about the house, too, something untamed, as if it were not built by man's hands at all, but rather formed by natural design. A part of the empty, golden sands of the bay with the deep blue sea beyond, and the impressive hummocking mountains that squatted down around it protectively.

The house was called *Taigh-Faire*, which meant 'watch house' in Gaelic, and it belonged to my Granny before she grew too old and infirm to live there alone. When my Granny died, the house became mine. It was a surprise bequeathment, for I had not seen her since I was a young child. I could barely remember anything about her, and never got the impression, from what I did remember, that Granny had liked me that much. She had been a cold and uncompromising character, according to my mother. The only real, concrete fact I knew about her was that she was missing the little finger on her right hand. Just like I was. I'd lost mine in an accident involving a door, although I didn't remember it. I never knew how Granny lost her finger, but as an adult, I found the shared injury amusing. It was a good story to trot out at parties, at any rate. Not that I went to many of those.

And so, one day, there they were, sitting in a large Manila envelope on my doormat: the deeds to Granny's house. I opened the envelope, and nearly dropped the accompanying solicitor's letter in shock as I read through the details. It was all mine. The stone walls, ancient wiring, wilting wallpaper, cobwebs everywhere and gutters full of moss and sprouting weeds. A house, on a cliff, in a remote part of Scotland where I had once belonged, and now did not. Granny was gifting my heritage back to me from beyond the grave, heaven knows why. Maybe there was no-one else to leave the house to, now that my parents were gone. Maybe there was another, more secret agenda.

Either way, I was at a loss as to what to do with it.

Taigh-Faire was pronounced a bit like 'tie fareh', although not exactly like that, because Highlands Gaelic is a special, ancient language with a very particular form of pronunciation. Although I was from the Highlands, I lost the tongue very early on in my life, and fumbled my way around the native words like a tourist when I first read the deeds anew.

But I liked the name: 'watch house'. It felt apt, considering its location on a cliff overlooking the sea, facing the ocean like a small, squat lighthouse, windowed eyes scanning the waves and all that lay beyond. There was a definite sense, from the photo stapled to the paperwork, of the house waiting for something. Watching.

Watching what, I didn't know, or much care about back then.

Not until later.

Ironically, I had been leafing through the papers and deeds associated with *Taigh-Faire*, and toying with the idea of selling Granny's house, when my husband Tim decided he no longer loved me and ended our marriage.

Just like that, after nine years.

I had just set the papers to one side, and was standing in the hallway, cradling a half-drunk coffee in my cold hands when he came home from work. I heard his key slide into the latch, and wondered, as I always did, where the time had gone. So many hours, all of them creeping slyly past without comment, and I had achieved nothing of note with any of the time I'd been given that day. I waited for my husband, thinking that maybe he had made better progress against the inertia that hits when you reach a certain age, a certain phase of your life. Maybe he was winning, finding a clearer path through the dreary fog of mid-life, because I sure wasn't.

Be careful what you wish for, I thought, later. Because it turned out Tim *was* winning, and *had* found a path. It was just a different path to the one I was on.

He walked in, saw me, and sighed. I could tell something was wrong immediately. My heart sank. I watched as he dropped his key wearily into the porcelain bowl on the hall stand, looked me up and down, and told me, without preamble, that it was over.

And my first fleeting, split-second reaction, one that was quickly squashed down by a subsequent tidal wave of conflicting feelings, was a profound sense of relief.

Thank god, I thought. *Finally. Finally!*

But then the words sank in, really sank in.

'I don't love you anymore, Megan,' he said.

Just like that.

The bottom fell out of my world. I slid down abruptly to the floor, as if gravity had suddenly intensified around me, and I sat there, feeling cold, and numb, and I wondered at the audacity of it, walking in through the front door as if it were any other day of the week instead of the first day of the end of my marriage, handing me the news that he didn't love me as perfunctorily as if he were telling me the weather forecast. I suppose Tim thought he was doing the right thing by being quite so brutally honest with me, but was he doing the right thing for me, or for himself? I suspected the latter. Tim was a canny, business-like sort of person. The idea of a 'clean break' suited his personality better than it did mine.

My second reaction, after gravity had normalised, was to throw my coffee mug at him from my awkward position on the floor. I have a finger missing on my right hand, my little finger, taken by a childhood accident, but I'm still a crack shot. The mug hit the wall immediately behind him and smashed, splattering liquid and pottery shards all over the tiled floor. Timothy just stood there, watching the coffee coalesce into little brown puddles all around him. I searched his face desperately for any traces of the man who had once loved me, and saw nothing there but weariness and unfamiliarity. As if we were total strangers, which I suppose, looking back, we were.

And then, horribly, with an indecent disregard for everything that was happening, my brain threw a curveball into the situation, and Tim's face blurred, and became the face of another man, for only a split second, but long enough to feel as if I had been punched in the stomach.

Matthew.

He smiled, and then became my husband once again.

Did Tim find out? I thought, desperately hoping he hadn't, because I was not sure I could bear the shame of it. It had been a slip, a pleasurable and wonderful slip, but a slip nonetheless.

No, wait.

That wasn't fair.

It wasn't a 'slip.' I didn't know what it *was*, exactly. I certainly didn't want to use the word 'mistake', because it had never felt like a mistake. It defied an easy description. Too brief a thing for it to be deemed an 'affair', it hadn't even felt like cheating, although it most certainly was. Matthew was special to me. I trusted him. I loved him, dearly. I wouldn't have slept with him, otherwise.

Whatever it was, it had only been once, and I had been in knots about it ever since. I had never intended to hurt anyone. I had certainly never meant for it to end our marriage.

But I knew somehow, with a flash of instinct, that this wasn't it. I lacked the courage to ask Tim outright why he was doing what he was doing, but I knew it wasn't my 'slip'.

It was something else. Some other reason why he didn't love me anymore.

My ego cried out, and I realised I was angry. I lashed out, and raged at him. He bore it. Then, I wept. He looked on with pity, but didn't console me. I shifted tack, tried to get a hold of myself, act reasonably, maybe even coax a change of heart out of him. I wheedled and cajoled, hating myself for it, but he remained indifferent. He had locked himself down, tuned himself to a different frequency. I may as well have been trying to appeal to the emotional sanctity of a robot.

Upon realising this, I erupted into one final, frantic tantrum as he looked on, blank-eyed. I threw things out of kitchen cupboards, tore up photographs of us, smashed a fruit bowl onto the floor, watching with wild disbelief as it shattered into a million pieces.

None of it made a difference. It was wasted energy.

Tim stood strong and silent in the face of

the storm.

Exhausted, defeated, I stilled as I thought about what to do next. If he wanted to end things, I couldn't stay here. I wasn't wired that way: I was not magnanimous in defeat. I needed to leave, but to go where? I could go to a hotel, I supposed. Or a friend's house. Trouble was, I didn't have too many friends. Well, I had one, but he was half the reason I was in this mess. My eyes roamed our house, the house Tim and I had bought together, furnished together, renovated together, grown apart in together, and eventually, an answer presented itself to me.

The deeds to *Taigh-Faire*, sitting on the kitchen counter.

Almost as if Granny had known.

Looking at the paperwork, I felt as if something had dropped, somewhere, something heavy and definitive. As if a die had been cast, or a bell struck.

So be it, I thought. *Careful what you wish for.*

I gathered up the deeds, and the keys that came with it, and went upstairs to pack. Tim watched me as I did so, still wordless, still resolute. I found I no longer cared to know what he was thinking.

I loaded up our van with the few personal possessions I could be bothered to pack, and left my husband behind in our house, closing the door behind me without saying another word, not even a goodbye. Nine years of marriage, dissolved in a single evening.

Was I sad?

I hardly knew.

I drove for thirteen hours solid, through the night, through the dawn, through traffic jams and roadworks, through every type of temperamental spring weather England could throw at me. The drive up-country to Scotland, past Inverness and through the Highlands, was surreal. Cities and concrete gave way to jewel-green valleys, long misty lochs, and winding single-lane roads that were heavily potholed. I slammed the van into deep, watery craters in the tarmac more times than I could count, tiredness catching up with me the further I drove, but the van's tyres remained sturdy. They held. Meanwhile, the views became more distracting, more poetic. The sky seemed higher, brighter, cleaner. The land rolled and bucked and dived about me, valleys and hills cradling the roads that grew bendier and narrower the further north I went.

I stopped frequently, getting out of the van to stretch my back and my legs and squat furtively next to the vehicle if no toilet was to hand. I made my last pit-stop just after dawn. I was about twenty miles from my destination, and I pulled into a viewpoint that overlooked a small loch. Behind the loch, a mist-capped hillside rose, green and grey and purple with heather. Marked onto the hillside in a series of striking white lines, was the enormous, crudely rendered image of a man. It had long thin legs, and a strange, rude face. It carried something in its hand, but I couldn't make out what it was. I had seen hill figures like this before, in the South. Usually, the figures were white horses, picked out in chalk, but there was a particularly fine giant on a hill in Cerne Abbas too. I remembered it had a large knobbled club raised high above its head, and proud genitalia pointing skyward.

I looked at the giant above the loch for a while, enjoying the play of light on the hills as the sun rose from behind them and burned away the early morning fog.

Then I got back in the van.

I arrived, eventually, early on the morning of the first day of May. The van pulled into the driveway of the house my Granny had gifted me in her will, crunching over old gravel, the vehicle's belly scraping over tall weeds that sprouted up between the stones. I stopped a few feet from the front door, killed the engine and yanked hard on the hand-brake, deciding to leave the van in gear because of the slope of the drive.

And then, all was quiet.

And I was suddenly home.

At *Taigh-Faire*, the little squat barnacle house above a sandy bay that only a few hours before, I'd contemplated selling.

Drastic, wasn't it? Running off to Scotland. I could have taken myself to a hotel. In hindsight, I could have insisted Tim be the one to leave- we both paid the mortgage on that house, after all. I had just as much right to be there as he did. I could have dug my heels in, demanded that we work through whatever his issues were. I could have worn him down, fought for my marriage. Maybe. Tim was stubborn but logical, a reasonable sort of person, mostly, and I had the perseverance of a terrier shaking a rat by the neck if the occasion called for it. I could have appealed to his logic, given time.

Maybe.

But I hadn't. Instead, I'd run. Perhaps a part of me knew, deep down, there wasn't much point in trying to fix things. Perhaps a part of me knew, deep down, that you can't fix something if the other person doesn't *want* it to be fixed, not really. You can paper over the cracks on the ceiling, but sooner or later, the foundations will shift, and the cracks will reappear, because they never really went away in the first place.

Admitting defeat was not in my nature. I have too much pride for that. But in this instance, I found I didn't have a choice. Something told me that I had lost, that there was no going back now. My home was not my home anymore, and it nearly killed me to admit it, but that was the truth.

So, out of spite, or desperation, or resignation, or all three, I had relocated myself to the wilds of Scotland, where I knew approximately nobody and nothing apart from the looming new reality of my own loneliness.

And, as I sat there in the van, listening to the engine cool down after the long journey, it dawned on me just what I'd done, then, and how far I'd driven.

And a strange, huge feeling came over me.

A feeling of...

What was that? I frowned, and tried to place it.

Was it...?

Yes, that was it.

It was a feeling of return.

2. NOTHING BY HALVES

Of course, I reasoned with myself as I unbuckled my seatbelt. I must have been here before, as a child. Maybe more than once, before my parents left Scotland and headed for the south, chasing their dreams of higher wages and better job prospects. We had lived not too far from here, just along the coast in a small place called Poolewe. I had patchy half-memories of early morning fog and heavy dew, of dark slate and granite, of a fast-flowing river rushing and rumbling beneath a stone bridge, grey skies, purple and green and grey hills. Little sensory scraps of information that never added up to a whole memory. It was the same with Granny. I had vague, shadowy recollections of her, a thin, odd woman who always tried to get me to eat boiled sweets, for some reason. I'd never liked boiled sweets, never liked the way they stuck like glue to the crevices of your teeth for hours after you'd crunched down on them. That never stopped Granny trying to push them down my neck. Persistence, it seemed, was a family trait.

Funny that I should remember that, and not the house, I mused, as I climbed wearily out of the van. Because really, *Taigh-Faire* was located in an incredible spot. The photographs I'd seen did not do it justice, not by a long shot. I did a three-sixty to take it all in, and felt my spirits stirring as I did so.

The house sat on its rock shelf contentedly overlooking an endlessly distracting vista, which lay before me as if someone had painted it upon a giant canvas and hung it out to dry: Gruinard Bay. A wide expanse of deep blue water that spread lazily within rolling, lumpy arms of sandstone and gneiss. *Torridon rocks,* Mother had told me, after we'd left. *Some of the oldest rocks in the world.* I'd heard my Mother talk about the Highlands, about their beauty and how much she missed them, but nothing had prepared me for this. Everything was colour: the rich blue of the sea and the sky above, the pink-yellow sand, the deep grey shingle peppering the beach further along the coast, the green and silver hills, the browns and ochres and reds and purples and yellows of plants and wildflowers. It was almost too much. It hurt the eyes, this unanticipated paradise.

I breathed in the fresh air, tasted salt on my lips. I squinted at the horizon, shading my eyes from the gathering strength of the sun.

From here, I could see a low, long Island in the distance, just beyond the mouth of the bay, not far from the mainland. It held my attention, although I couldn't say why, exactly. My head ached as I looked at it. Just a twinge, but distinct. I blinked. It looked too small to be livable, and I could make out only one detail, from here: that it was covered in tall, slender trees, pine trees. The sort that only sprouted needles from the very tops, while the trunks stretched out long, and thin, beneath them.

How could I have forgotten this view? I thought, heart beating faster than it should, and I took a moment to watch the sun climb higher in the sky over my new territory.

And then suddenly, without warning, I crashed. I realised where I was.

Alone, in the middle of nowhere.

To be precise: five hundred and ninety-eight miles away from the person I had been yesterday.

Five hundred and ninety-eight miles away from the person I had once, in naivety, called my soulmate.

What was I doing here? Really? What did I hope to accomplish by driving to the other end of the country? Tim and I would need to talk. There would be things to sort out, papers to sign. Assets to divide. Practicalities. So why was I here, outside the house that time forgot? Was there even a phone in this house? Electricity? I could see cables running along the outside walls, but had no idea if they were connected to anything.

Mother always said I never did anything by halves, I thought, as I tried to find my footing. I stood in the drive of my new house, fiddling with the heavy door key that sat in my pocket. I thought of my life, then, as a series of chapters in a book. I had finished the previous chapter, and it seemed to me, on reflection, as I stood here with the rest of my life in my hands, as if not much of any note had really happened in that chapter at all, despite the length of it. A marriage, a job, a house, sure. But no children. No travel. A few friends, but an awful lot of time spent grinding through a routine that now felt like something we had done for the sake of it - because that's what people do. Get up, go to work, come home, sleep, repeat. There had been love, at first, I could not deny that. But how long had it been since that love had faded, bleached like the pattern on fabric left too long in the sun? I didn't like to think about it. It was scary, the notion that I had lived so long in the shadow of comfort and routine that I had forgotten how to...

Never mind.

Not now.

I was too tired and fragile to start any in-depth analysis of the whys, and wherefores.

Now was for moving forward, despite my fatigue and shock and bitterness. It was time to turn the next page, sink into a new chapter, and who knew? Maybe, just maybe, this one would be more remarkable.

Ready or not, I thought, fingering the key again, but the thought rang a little hollow in the tired spaces of my mind. I gave the Island one last look, not knowing why I did so. My head twinged again, and I frowned. I needed rest. At the very least, a cup of tea.

The house said nothing.

It just watched, and waited for me.

I unloaded the smallest box from the van, the one that contained my carefully packed word processor, and went to unlock my new front door.

As I did so, I noticed a large old lantern frame bolted to the wall outside. The glass in it had smashed years ago, but I could guess its intended use. I had made comparisons to a light-house when I'd first seen pictures of *Taigh-Faire,* and it seemed I was right. There was no light-house nearby that I knew of, the closest one I remembered being at Rhue, which was forty miles away. So maybe this lantern was designed to warn boats coming into the bay at night that they were close to shore. I had a sudden vision of it lit and glowing brightly, and wondered how I could go about repairing the glass, wiring the lamp up to the mains somehow. It seemed a shame to leave it broken like this, tarnished and unused.

I noticed something else as I stood there with the door key in my hand. Next to the lantern, engraved into a large grey stone lintel set over my front door, was a curious, if worn symbol: a triangle, with a circular dot set dead in the middle. Each of the triangle's points were capped with another round dot, about the size of my index fingertip.

Three sides, three corners, four dots. There was something numerically pleasing about that.

I studied the shape for a moment, feeling a tickle somewhere in the back of my mind. A memory, perhaps. I must have seen this mark as a child, because a nagging feeling of...*something* made itself known. I couldn't place it, but it was there. Something.

I unlocked the front door.

The brief euphoria I'd felt for that single moment outside *Taigh-Faire* vanished when I set foot inside. The house was every bit as depressing as my state of mind. It was damp, smelly and old-fashioned, each room decorated with nicotine-stained, yellowing floral wallpaper or woodchip that had bubbled and peeled as the sea air had crept in underneath. Dead flies lay in heaps on all the windowsills, and the window panes themselves were choked with cobwebs. Bracken, ferns, thistles and nettles crowded around the building, blocking out light from the lower floor. Little smatterings of soot dropped into the hearths of the fireplaces as I walked around, a sign that the chimneys hadn't been swept in years. The kitchen, which was just beyond the hallway, was dirty, and grim, antiquated in all the wrong ways.

And everything was quiet, hushed, as if the walls were clenched somehow. As if the house were holding its breath, balling its fists, wondering what I would do next.

What I did was set my word processor down on the stained old table in the kitchen and then collapse onto a wobbly chair. Then I stared at my new surroundings. An overwhelming sense of sadness descended upon me as I thought about the rest of my belongings, crammed into cardboard boxes in the back of the van. My old life lived in those boxes. The life of a married woman, a successful journalist, an objectively, on-paper, convincingly-in-public happy person. I didn't want to lift the lids of those boxes and peer into her smiling face, not right now. My recent loss was too fresh, too sharp. I couldn't cut myself on the edges of it. Not again. Not right now.

What I wanted to do, suddenly, unreasonably, absurdly, was write. Write it all out. Get everything I was feeling down, somehow, in a manageable, digestible format. Despite the fact that I hadn't slept a wink for over twenty-four hours. Despite the fact that my body was screaming at me, telling me to climb up the stairs and find a bed, lay my head down, get some rest. My body may have been tired, but my brain was crying out for release, and its call felt more urgent. It needed me to write. To make sense of it all. To make it real. Things weren't real until they were written down, not in my world. It had always been that way, as if documented proof of my own undesirability were necessary for me to be able to fully move on: I present to the court Exhibit A, the defendant's dignity, Your Honour. The destruction of which has been meticulously documented, and written down, for your consideration.

I unboxed the word processor, set it up so that I could see the bay through a gap in the ferns outside the kitchen window. The beautiful bay, and the Island beyond. I plugged the machine into an ancient socket mounted too close to the sink to be reasonably thought of as safe, gingerly switched it on, cracked my knuckles, and waited for the small screen to light up, fingers hovering above the keyboard, ready to go.

Nothing happened.

I frowned, and checked the cable, but everything was plugged in as it should be. A faulty socket? I looked around, and found another. I transferred the plug, flicked the switch, and waited.

Nothing.

I jabbed at the keys in frustration.

Still nothing.

Then, it dawned on me. There wasn't anything wrong with the machine.

There was just no electricity.

I groaned, and sank my head into my hands. Of *course* there was no electricity. The house had been empty for years, why would there be? I would need to telephone the company, get an account set up, bills in place.

Fuck.

I felt tears threatening, and swallowed them down angrily. No, I was not going to cry. This was but a small hiccup in the grander scheme of things. *Where there is a will, there is a way.* Another saying from Mother. I had a collection of them, for times like these. And, thinking about it rationally, the power might not be disconnected. Perhaps it was just a blown fuse. Maybe I just needed to find the fuse box, fiddle with that.

Worth a shot.

Having buoyed myself up with my desperate, lonely logic, I started looking for the fuse box. After fifteen minutes of swearing and searching around the house, I found what I needed: a cupboard space under the stairs in the hallway, filled with old boxes and an ancient red vacuum cleaner that, judging by the thick layer of dust coating it, hadn't seen the light of day in years.

Behind that, set into the back wall like a tiny portal that Alice might have encountered in Wonderland, was a small, squat wooden access door. It looked as if it were hiding, like a guilty secret. Beyond it, I suspected, was a cellar, or at the very least a recess where the utility units lived.

I dragged the boxes and vacuum out from under the stairs, sneezing violently as dust crept into my nostrils. Then I lowered myself to the ground and crawled into the cupboard space for a closer look.

The wooden access door at the back of the cupboard was tightly closed, seemingly un-opened for many years. It had the same air of purpose that a prison door might have, contain-ment being the order of the day. It was cold to the touch, and extremely solid, like rock. The latch was made of cast-iron, painted and re-painted many times over with black gloss paint, so that the metal was thick and rippled. The bolt-screws set into the latch were triangular in shape, reminding me of the geometric symbol over my front door. I put an ear to the wood, tried to get a sense of what might be beyond the door, but could hear nothing. I pulled away and felt a cold, clammy patch on my cheek. I shud-dered, held my fingers to the small, dark gap that ran along the bottom of the door, wondering if I would be able to feel a draft at all. Nothing. All was sealed tight, and mysterious.

All in all, the door was a foreboding prospect, but if what I needed lay behind it, I had no choice. I could live for a while without gas and heating, but I couldn't live without power. I couldn't function without my word processor, not in my current state. If I didn't write soon, I would run mad, I was sure of it. Besides that, I didn't fancy spending my first night alone in the strange, dirty old house that my strange, unfriendly old Granny had once lived in without the lights on.

With effort, I unlatched the door.

Taigh-Faire, it turned out, was equipped with a cellar, and as the door reluctantly yawned open, hinges creaky from lack of use, I saw stairs that led down into it. Beyond the stairs, there was only black. It occurred to me that the space down there might be a natural pocket in the bedrock of the stone shelf on which *Taigh-Faire* stood. The original house builders had discovered, then exploited this pocket, and turned it into a cellar. A ready-made natural refrigeration system, the perfect place for keeping food fresh, storing goods and so on. Why the entrance door was hidden inside the bloody cupboard under the stairs was a mystery to me, however. I assumed it was for the same reason that everything else in the house was the way it was, to be as inconvenient and awkward as possible for whomever lived there.

Practicalities and the nuances of building design aside, the cellar gave me the willies. It was audibly a huge space, I could tell that immediately. Huge, maybe even running the entire length of the house. I couldn't see a thing beyond the gloom, but the sound of my own feet shuffling on the top of the stairs echoed back up to me, magnified, like a giant's footsteps. A stiff, cool breeze drove up into my face from down below, which was strange in and of itself, because I had felt no breeze when I'd run my hand along the bottom of the cellar door. I could smell damp and mildew, rock and stone, and I shuddered, grabbing a torch that hung from a nail nearby, hoping against vain hope that the batteries weren't flat. I pressed the switch, and amazingly, it worked. Light flared. I laughed out loud in relief. Small mercies.

Well, then. Here we go, I thought, and climbed down into the cellar.

3. BELOW

For a moment, despite the flashlight, the darkness engulfed me. The cellar was, indeed, enormous, and my torch beam so very little, and weak. I stood at the foot of the stairs, and waited for my eyes to adjust.

Gradually, I got a sense of scale, and height, and I could see that I'd been right. The house was built directly onto bedrock, and beneath the surface level, a large, natural stone cavity sat, far enough below ground that it didn't threaten the structural integrity of the house, but close enough that the cavity had been knocked through and married to the guest house above by a set of rough-hewn stone steps. I could see enormous old whisky barrels stacked up on one side of me, and cardboard boxes, old tins of paint, a ladder, some gardening tools, shelves loaded with bottles half-filled with a strange, amber liquid, and lengths of rope and electrical cables slung over crude hooks that protruded from the stone.

Then, I saw what I needed. There was a

panel off to the left, and on that panel, a long series of boxes. Bingo. I moved away from the stairs and across the cellar, that cold breeze still prickling against my skin, the damp settling on me like a chill hand upon my shoulder. I stopped in front of the panel, and found the fuse box nestled amongst a tangle of ancient wires and cables. I pried open the lid, and checked each switch as best I could in the poor light. There were ancient labels above each switch, but the writing had faded too much to make out. I flipped a few experimentally, with no real idea of what it was that I was doing, but at least I was doing *something*, which was far better than the only viable alternative: sitting on the end of my Granny's bed and staring off dismally into space.

Flick-flick, flick-flick. I made sure all the switches faced the same direction. As far as I could tell, everything seemed in order, but I was no expert. I bit my lip and angrily swallowed the thought that then popped into my mind: that this would be a lot easier if I had a man about the house.

No, I chastised myself, vehemently. *You don't think like that, Megs, never again.*

It was after I replaced the lid that I saw the meter.

A bulky, dust-encrusted, coin-operated electricity meter. I hadn't seen one of these for a long, long time, not since I had been a student in London. Straight out of the seventies, if not earlier, these were. The idea was simple: you fed the meter with coins, and your electricity ran for as long as you had paid for it. Then, it shut off. There was a dial that clicked round once you loaded the meter with pound coins. The unit dial's needle now pointed to '0'.

Relief sunk in.

The meter had run out of money, that was all.

I breathed a sigh of relief, then sneezed again as I inadvertently inhaled more dust. Eyes streaming, I counted my blessings, such as they were. All I needed was money, and then I would be back in business. I could write, I could dump this big tangled mess of feelings onto my word processor and the world would make sense again and then, finally, I could sleep.

And oh, how I needed to sleep.

I rummaged through my pockets, hands cold and uncooperative. Surely I had some change lurking somewhere on my person, a single solitary pound coin at the very least, *surely*. Just one coin, that's all I needed. Enough to get me through until tomorrow, when I could start my life afresh having slept.

Just one coin, was that so much to ask?

My hands found only lint, and an old tissue.

I rummaged some more. Surely.

I found nothing.

Then it dawned on me.

I'd left, in a hurry. Scooped up my belongings, flung them into the van, and driven off, without a care for practical things like maps, or money. I'd remembered my purse, at least, but it was as empty as my heart felt at that wretched moment in time.

And I didn't have a single coin to hand.

I banged the side of the meter box in frustration, half-hoping it would help kick-start something, but of course, it didn't. The meter was out of coins, and so I was out of power.

My fragile confidence evaporated, and my mood sank.

This meant I'd have to go outside, and get money from somewhere. And I was not ready for that. Not by a long shot. I was exhausted, I didn't want to interact with the world, I just wanted to lock the front door and write, and then sleep for a thousand years after I'd done so. I was so unbearably fatigued I could hardly stand, held upright now only by the grace of adrenaline, and that was fast running out.

Shit.

Shit.

The cold breeze I'd felt when I'd first entered the cellar picked up, suddenly. My hair stirred, and I felt air move across my skin, an almost welcome distraction. Frowning, I slid the torch beam around the room. Where was it coming from? I was underground, the cellar walls were solid stone and incredibly thick, so unless there was an air shaft or ventilation brick some-where down here, it didn't make sense.

The breeze stirred again, as if happy it had caught my attention. I fancied I could smell something in the air. Was it salt? Could I smell the sea? Down here, underground, surrounded by rock? Impossible.

And yet something tickled at my nose and triggered a rush of long-buried recollec-tions. Seagulls cried from far back in time. Van-illa ice cream lingered on my tongue, and the memory of cold, wet sand squirting up between my toes made my feet wriggle in their shoes.

Stone or no stone, I *could* smell the sea.

I drifted further into the cellar, as if pulled along by a tight string. The draft intensi-fied. I let the torch light lead the way, watching as decades' worth of dust and grime eddied up into the air, motes and particles swirling around in the dull beam like shoals of fish underwater. Then, the dust parted, as if something unseen cleaved the air in two with a knife, and beyond the clear space, my torch hit an object lying on the ground. The draft was most powerful here. I could hear air mournfully whistling around the edges of the thing, as if it were blocking a shaft, or tunnel of some sort.

The object was round, and about six feet in circumference. Made from stone, it was per-fectly smooth and circular, like a millstone, only larger, thicker, with no hole in the center.

No hole, but a roughly carved symbol instead. One I recognised immediately from the front of the house.

The outline of a triangle, with dots at each corner, and one set dead in the middle.

I crouched down, let my fingers trace the shape in the stone, noticing with curiosity as I did so that no dust seemed to gather there. I felt a slight buzzing in my fingertips as I traced the lines. It was like...electricity. I snatched my hand back. What *was* this? A capstone of sorts, for an old well, perhaps? An ancient drain? A cover for some old power cables that ran underneath the house? There was no way I should be able to feel an electric hum through such a thick slab of stone. Maybe there was an old spring or stream down there, and it was the movement of water I could feel, vibrating the cover.

But then...what about the breeze?

I tried to slip a hand down the side of the capstone, where the draft whistled as it pushed its way through, but the round rock was set tight and flush into the cellar floor, a tiny gap of no more than a millimeter running all around it. I didn't like the buzz that ran through me every time I touched the stone, so I stopped trying to find a space for my fingers, and sat back on my haunches, instead. It was a feat of craftsmanship, this stone. It obviously had a purpose, but what?

And what was the symbol for? What did it mean? A triangle, four dots. I was reminded of star constellations and hieroglyphs as I stared at it. The shape seemed purposeful, the same way that letters in an alphabet seem purposeful. The symbol was clearly tied to the house, somehow. An old Gaelic symbol of some sort? Was it writing? Or something else? Masonic? Geographic? What did it denote, exactly?

A huge yawn brought me crashing back into reality.

Priorities, Megs.

I got to my feet, sighing. It was pointless speculating. The stone wouldn't budge, so I had very little chance of finding out what lay beneath it. It had to weigh half a ton, easily. I was never going to be able to lever it up by myself.

And it hardly mattered at this point in time, did it?

What mattered was finding a way to get the power back on, before nightfall. Which was hours away, but still. I didn't have hours left in me. I had a small reserve of desperate, anxiety-fueled energy. Enough to solve this one last problem. Enough to keep me alive, just a little longer.

I groaned. Why had I left home without money? *Why?*

It was intriguing though, this stone. The symbol. It was a mystery beneath my house, and I would have a hard time relaxing at *Taigh-Faire* now that I knew it was there.

But time was ticking on, and I was tired,

so very tired. I left the stone where it was, went back to the meter and stared mournfully at it for another long moment, then extricated myself out from under the stairs, feeling as if the capstone were watching me leave as I did so. I closed the access door and latched it, then closed the door to the cupboard firmly behind me. Then I leaned back against it, trying to think of what to do next.

Shit, shit, shit.

I caught sight of my own reflection in a dusty, spotted mirror that hung on the wall opposite me. I looked thin, and tired. I was scowling, my brows low, my cheeks pinched. Huge, puffy bags dominated the skin beneath my eyes. My hair stuck out in scruffy peaks around my head, and my clothes hung from me like drapes. I looked ancient, and scrawny, and haggard, and unpleasant to be around.

I looked just like my Granny, I realised in horror.

No wonder Tim doesn't love me anymore, I thought, and tears threatened suddenly.

'Shut up,' I told myself, out loud, this time. The mirror version of me glared back by way of response.

I set out to find coins.

4. A WALK

The closest place to withdraw money nearby that I knew of was the Post Office in the village of Laide, a tiny collection of buildings that lay a few miles up the coastal road from *Taigh-Faire*. I had driven past it on my way to the guest house, not thinking to stop. Not thinking of anything at all, except of getting away. Running from failure.

I had neighbours that were closer than the Post Office. If I'd been feeling brave, I could have knocked on a door or two, explained my predicament, asked to borrow a couple of coins. But a morbid fear of waking complete strangers at such an early hour in order to beg for money while I stood shivering on the doorstep stopped me. As did pride. I didn't need anyone else's money, I had money in my own account. I just needed to access it, and change it into something useful. Food for my ancient meter. A simple thing. A small step. And then I could start anew.

I decided to walk to Laide, rather than drive. I didn't trust myself behind the wheel of my van anymore, and the village was no great distance. The fresh air and exercise might do me some good, I reasoned, as I steeled myself for the task ahead and tried to ignore the call of the beds in the guest rooms upstairs. A walk could be just the thing. It would allow me to prepare myself mentally for dealing with other people. *And perhaps if I walk, I'll stop thinking about Tim,* I hoped, loading a tape into my Walkman and dragging the headphones over my ears. An image flashed into my mind, unbidden: Tim, rolling around in our bed with a woman who wasn't me. Another: Tim, holding hands with someone else. Another: Tim, throwing the things I'd left behind in a large box, and taping the lid shut. This last image was the most difficult to dispel. Tim liked to put things in boxes, particularly emotions. I had no doubt he had already begun to package me away, box me up like an unwanted artefact in a museum. I was a part of his life that he had experienced, and must now move on from. I imagined him writing a single word on top of the box with a dark black marker pen:

Archive.

Thinking about this hurt so much I could barely breathe.

I jammed my thumb onto the Walkman play button. Music filled my ears, orchestral, just enough noise to keep me company and help pass the time as I walked. It acted as a security blanket, the music, wrapping around and insulating me with the familiar rhythm and melody of Mozart's piano concerto number twenty, in D minor. Intricate and upbeat, something for my brain to fix upon that wasn't painful, or challenging. I felt a little better, squared my shoulders, and stood before the front door. Took a deep breath. Could I do this, really? Go out there, mingle with the locals, put my tender roots down here, in the Highlands? Tired. I was so tired. When had it become such a titanic, colossal struggle to simply exist as a normal, functioning human being?

I tentatively laid a hand on the front door handle. Couldn't I manage without power, perhaps just for a day or two?

Get outside, Megs. Just get on with it, you daft bean. I half-heard the last part of this sentence in my Mother's voice, and smiled. She had always called me 'daft bean' when she was exasperated with me. She would have had little time for my nonsense today.

I turned the handle, stepping outside. As I did so, I caught sight of the Island once more, lying directly across the bay from the house. A brisk gust of wind came at me, smelling the same as the air in the cellar. I felt a strange, deep pull in the pit of my belly. I stopped, held there by something I didn't fully understand, but it felt like a connection, like another piece of string, stretched taut from that place to this, binding me. My eyes fixed in place, until it felt that I could look at nothing else. The Island seemed to grow in size, filling my vision. I felt a sudden desire, a fierce compulsion to get out there, somehow, and explore. The Island...it called for me, and I yearned for it. But how to get to it? By boat? I would need to find one. Could I swim? It looked achievable.

Then, I realised what I was doing, and shook myself hard. The string snapped. It left me feeling oddly lost, directionless. Confused.

What is happening to me? I thought, reaching up above my head with my right hand and absent-mindedly stroking the symbol carved above my front door, my four fingers working their way into the dots at the tip of each point on the triangle, and the dot in the centre. When I realised what I was doing, I yanked the hand back, staring at it. The skin on my fingertips felt alive, like it had in the cellar. A buzzing sensation, almost like pins and needles, as if I had touched pure energy and come away with the residue beneath my nails. The small stump that was all that remained of my little finger felt peculiar. As if, for just a second, it wasn't a stump at all, but a whole digit, and it buzzed and tingled just like the other four.

I flexed my hand.

A magnetic force of some sort? I peered at the lintel over the door. It looked as if it were carved from the same dense, grey stone that the capstone in the cellar was carved from. Perhaps there was iron in the stone, or something magnetic, an ore of some sort.

I let out a shaky breath, smacking my hands together to get rid of the buzzing sensation. I was overtired, that was all. The house had me on edge.

Get going, Megs, I told myself. *You can do this. Even if you can't, you have to try. Otherwise all those things you thought about yourself since Tim did what he did will be true.*

I started to walk.

White fluffy clouds scudded across a patchy blue sky. Bracken and heather lay thick on either side of the road I marched along, framing my world. Beyond, the bay's waters sprawled out placid to the horizon, broken only by the uneven hump of the Island whose name I still did not know. It seemed to be following me around, that Island, following me as I walked. No matter where I was, I could see it. Even with my eyes closed. If I blinked, it was still there in my mind's eye. It was almost as if it *wanted* to be seen, which I knew was nonsense, but felt like the only way to describe what was happening. If I tried to look away, the back of my neck prickled uncomfortably, and an odd, jittery feeling made itself known in the pit of my belly. If I looked at it, or thought about it, my fingertips buzzed and burned until it was almost unbearable. And yet the further I walked, and the more distance I put between myself and that hunk of land sitting in the ocean, the more uncomfortable I felt.

I ended up walking with my neck craned awkwardly so that I could still keep the Island in sight as I moved. Eventually, I grew a stiff crick in the neck from staring at the place for so long whilst moving in a different direction. I wrenched my eyes back to the road ahead, wincing, but the Island still hovered in my peripheral, like the tip of my nose: always there, but just out of focus.

I wondered why it insisted upon me so. Had I been there once, as a child? Maybe that was it. Maybe there was another repressed early childhood memory hiding in me somewhere, trying to work its way to the surface, like a bubble of gas drifting up from the bottom of a brackish pond. I had only lived in Scotland for a few short years, though. Visits to Granny had been few and far between. Wouldn't I have remembered a trip out to an Island with her? Maybe not. The brain is a mysterious organ, fickle about what it chooses to remember, or forget.

And speaking of fickle, my own traitorous mind had turned on me in the time it had taken to walk barely a mile up the road, and now that the dust had settled on my departure, I could tell it was angry with me.

Angry that I had left my house.

Angry about Matthew, and the Christmas

party.

Angry about my stupid, selfish lapse in judgement, and my behaviour.

Angry at the heavy breathing, the taste of whisky, the smell of sweat and aftershave, the feeling of my legs being held apart, the sensation of being full, the orgasm, the breathless excitement of a shared secret as another man pulled my dress back into place.

Angry about my situation, my newfound state of loneliness.

And angry at Tim.

Tim, who had brutally guillotined our marriage and taken me completely by surprise. I hadn't seen it coming, not for one second. That infuriated me.

Especially because I didn't know *why*.

If it wasn't infidelity, what was it, exactly?

The further I walked, the more this question maddened me.

He said he didn't love me anymore. *Why?* Was it my personality? Was I too boring? Too straight? Too messy? Too married to my job? No doubt my personal idiosyncrasies had exaggerated themselves over time, including my strident need for privacy. If I thought about it, I would have to admit that yes, increasingly, I found intimacy difficult.

Had I, in fact, pushed *him* away?

Or maybe, just maybe, I was too old

for him now. Maybe Tim had met someone else. Someone younger than me. Someone with firmer tits, flawless thighs, an arse like a pair of tennis balls. Did she like to screw all night, and all day too, with wild abandon, like young people do in the movies?

The irony was that he would have hated this train of thought, and had I been voicing these concerns to him in person, he would have rolled his eyes at me.

'Why do you do this to yourself?' He would have said. 'Why do you let your thoughts spiral out of control in this way? What good does it do, to obsess over things like that, again and again? You're just hurting yourself. What good does that do?'

No good. No good at all.

But I didn't know any other way to be. I didn't know any other way of dealing with it. I had always felt things deeply, that was my nature. It was why I was a writer. Sometimes, the feelings were so huge, they needed a place to go. And that place, more often than not, was my word processor.

I thought of the word processor sitting on the kitchen table at *Taigh-Faire.* I felt the weight of the words that I couldn't set down pressing on me. All I needed was a handful of coins, and I could put down the burden. Such a stupid, small barrier between my brain and acceptance. A handful of coins, a tax for my own peace of mind.

And then, I felt a different weight crush my shoulders as I walked. The weight of responsibility.

All of this was my fault.

Because I had failed.

As a wife, a friend, an adult, a woman. Failed. On all counts.

A sadness so deep and so profound settled upon me that I gasped out loud, and almost forgot, in that moment, how to walk. I had to consciously command my left foot to step out in front of my right foot, and so on.

I. Had. Failed.

And as soon as that miserable thought crossed my mind, I came upon a man standing on the side of the road, and dashed the gathering tears from my eyes with relief. Here was a temporary reprieve. A welcome distraction.

Or so I thought at the time.

He stood with his back to me, and carried a thin, light rifle across one shoulder, the type used for shooting rabbits and small game. A dog sat on its haunches next to him, a black and white collie. Both of them stared silently out across the bay.

At the Island.

Him too? I thought. *Do his fingers itch too?*

The pair looked as if they were waiting for something. Yes, that was it. They looked expectantly off to the distance, as if they knew something were about to happen, and were standing in that exact spot on the roadside for the sole purpose of watching it. Spectators at a private event, the details of which I was not privy to. Guests, welcomed, while I was merely trespassing through.

What, though? What are they waiting for?

Pungent smoke clouded around the man's head as I approached. Neither man nor dog heard me coming up behind them. I pulled off my headphones, cleared my throat by way of introduction.

'Excuse me,' I called out, uncertain. 'Can you tell me if the Post Office in Laide is open yet?'

The man turned, slowly, to look at me. He was dressed in a long waterproof wax jacket, a flat cap, and ancient, worn-out boots with great cracks running under the toes. A tired looking cigarette dangled on his lower lip, dark smoke drifting skyward. Something glinted on his hand: a ring, gold, or brass, I couldn't tell.

He didn't answer the question.

I waited for a moment or two, and then repeated myself, louder this time, in case he hadn't heard. His demeanour didn't change. He just kept looking at me.

His dog caught my scent and also turned its head, moving from two legs to four as it did so. It had a distinctive black patch over its eye.

Before I could repeat myself for a third time, the dog's hackles rose. Its lips curled, showing white teeth and mottled gums. I stepped back, afraid. The dog began to bark furiously.

I backed up another few steps, held my hands up to show I meant no harm. The dog's master did nothing. He just stood, watching me, and the collie lowered its head, began to stalk towards me, canines bared, tail held out rigidly behind it.

My mouth went dry with fear.

'Hey!' I shouted, and pointed to the animal. 'Aren't you going to control your dog?'

The man did nothing. The dog began snapping at my heels. I reared back hastily, nearly tripping and falling, only just managing to stay upright. The collie's bark was loud, angry, and incessant. Convinced I was about to be bitten, I flailed about, trying to scare the animal away, but it was no good. It could sense my fear, and that seemed to spur it on as I tried to defend myself.

'Hey!' I shouted again, terrified, as the dog went for my right leg and latched on. I felt teeth scrape past my skin, but the animal thankfully got a mouthful of jean fabric in its jaws instead of flesh. It started whipping its head from side to side, like a terrier with a rat, trying to throw me off balance, and almost succeeding.

I screamed.

And finally, the man relented.

He spat out his cigarette, crushed it under his boot, and clapped his hands together sharply. The dog froze, mid-shake, although it didn't let go of my leg. The man clapped again. I waited, heart in my mouth, horribly aware of how close to the skin of my calf the dog's jaws were.

There was a moment of stasis, during which the dog stared up at me, frost-blue eyes brimming with a type of violence I had never seen in an animal before. Then, it gave my trouser leg one final, reluctant, vicious shake, and let go. Rigid, I did not dare move a single muscle for fear of another attack. The dog didn't back away. It just stood there, as if waiting for further command.

And the command came.

The man clapped his hands together one last time, smiling as he did so. The dog cocked an ear, listened, wheeled about, lifted a leg, and pissed on my shoes.

I stood there aghast as the hot urine streamed onto my boots. Then the animal shook itself, as if pleased, and trotted back to its master. It sat down obediently at the man's feet once more, tongue lolling in satisfaction, ears pricked.

And they both watched me like that, side by side, watched while I tried to recover my composure, my boots shining wet with dog piss, my heart thundering in my chest. I wanted to shout and scream at them both, to ask the man what the hell his problem was, rail at him, but I was too frightened. Too shocked. Too exhausted.

Instead, I turned on my heel, and moved quickly on up the road, trying to put as much distance between myself and the disgusting pair as possible.

I could feel their eyes on me as I went.

And behind them, the Island.

5. LAIDE

Jesus Christ, I thought, over and over as I walked. I shook as I tried to process what had just happened. Fear quickly turned to outrage.

Jesus. Christ.

That dog had attacked me! *Pissed* on me! What's more, it looked as if his master had *told* it to. My mind reeled from the encounter. I knew I ought to report him to the Police, a dog like that shouldn't have been roaming around freely. What if I had been a child? Or someone elderly? What if I had fallen? Would I be lying back there on the road now with my throat torn out? A crimson scarf about my neck, eyes fixed on the sky?

Why, *why* had the insane man set his dog on me? All I had done was ask a simple question!

The miserable sting of indignity and embarrassment whipped my cheeks, and as I stumbled along, I felt the dog's piss soak through the leather of my worn boots and into my socks. I had no choice but to continue, because turning around and going back up the road meant going back past those two, and I wasn't brave enough for that.

I should never have left the house, I thought, wretchedly. And then:

I should never have left my home.

Damn you, Tim. This is all your fault! Not my fault, yours!

I looked back over my shoulder with every few steps I took, worried that I was being followed. But the odd couple were done with me. I saw only two statues, growing smaller with every step I took. Backs turned, faces pointed out to the bay.

Staring at the Island.

Crazy bastards, I thought, my lips trembling, my mood verging on hysteria. And yet still, I walked on.

The dog's urine saturated the thin fabric of my socks, which then started to rub against my skin uncomfortably. After another mile, blisters sprouted on my heels. I ignored them the best I could, but soon found myself limping.

Eventually, the morning sun disappeared behind a large bank of cloud. It grew colder, and I was glad to keep moving, past the hamlet of Second Coast, past the hamlet of First Coast. The road here undulated across the coastline, weaving up and down and around the contours of the land. I passed a small waterfall, which pooled and then ran across the road as a cold, clear stream, rushing on its way out to sea. Ferns nodded on the verge as the water passed beneath. A skylark erupted from the undergrowth and rose almost vertically, high into the air above me, screaming its flight-song as a warning. There was probably a nest nearby on the ground somewhere. The bay stretched out to the right of me, calm, its waters placid. There was such beauty, all around. It didn't feel right, after the dog. It felt...deceitful. Like a distraction.

I passed a collection of farm outbuildings, and a Bed & Breakfast that looked long-closed, despite the sign that said 'VACANCIES' hanging out front. I passed a solitary phone box, so overgrown that it was essentially a glass and metal box full to bursting with nettles and brambles, the phone all but smothered within. I passed a derelict caravan, and began to get an appreciation for just how remote and sparsely populated this stretch of coastline was in comparison to my home in the south. It must have been a lonely childhood, what little of it I had spent here. More memories came back to me in fits and starts: cycling down a road like this on a yellow bike with streamers attached to the handles. Snow on the hills. Sun on blue water. Sky, so much sky. Boiled sweets, with a curious, bitter flavour.

And against the sky, a wooden frame.

This was both memory and present, for

just beyond the caravan, set into a patch of heath not far from the phone box, I came across an odd thing.

A tall, upside-down, u-shaped frame, made of wood, stopping short of ten feet high.

There was no platform beneath, but well-trodden, worn soil all around it. There were markings on the wood of the frame, letters carved in a language I didn't understand. Gaelic, I supposed.

I paused, trying to figure out if the wooden structure was old, or new. The wood had aged, greened a little, but the frame was solid, well-constructed, treated against the weather. There was no rot, no flaking of the wood. The structure looked functional. Whatever that function was.

As I stood staring at it, I realised something else. I realised that if I stood on this side of it, with the road behind and the bay before me, it framed the Island beyond perfectly.

I pursed my lips. Of course it did.

Memories flared and died like sparks above a bonfire as I stood and stared at the thing. Whatever it was, I'd seen it before, I knew that now. I struggled with my memory, and then gave up, too tired to try and recall how, or when. There was no use dithering here with wet, sore feet while I tried to recover buried memories from decades ago. It was like digging for treasure buried ten feet deep with a rusty teaspoon:

a thankless, pointless task. So, I'd seen the structure before. So what? What did it matter, really? I had bigger problems.

I moved on, and finally passed the sign for Laide, turning off the main road to a smaller by-road inland on which the Post Office sat at the junction of a hairpin bend. I breathed a huge sigh of relief as it came into view. It was a small, squat and ugly building that crouched in the middle of a tiny tarmac forecourt. It was also a general store and a petrol station. The original Post Office building, a tiny stone cottage with an old slot set in the garden wall for mail, nestled into the verge opposite. Old and new, unsympathetically juxtaposed.

There was a cashpoint set into the side of the modern building. Next to it, a plastic advertising board with a faded, rippled poster of *The Last of the Mohicans* clinging on for dear life inside. I could not remember the last time I'd taken a trip to the cinema. Did they even have one around here?

I used the cashpoint to withdraw a wad of money, then went inside.

Laide Post Office was run by a mousy-haired woman who sat behind a high counter at the back of the building. She looked me up and down as I pushed my way in, a small bell hung over the door tinkling and giving away my presence as I did so.

'Hi,' I mumbled. The woman pulled up a smile that I could tell was reserved only for tourists and strangers. Warm, but false.

'Welcome,' the woman replied, as friendly as you like, but the word sounded strangely formal, ceremonial almost, like an incantation.

'How can I help you?'

I stumbled and fumbled my way through my predicament, pulling out my wad of ten pound notes and proffering them hopefully at the end of my messy tirade. My hand trembled, and the woman looked at it. It was my right hand, the one with the missing little finger. I usually wore a leather strap to cover the stump, held in place by a bespoke halter that came down over the back of my hand and fastened around my wrist, but I had taken it off during the long drive to Scotland, and forgotten to put it back on before leaving the house. I blushed. I didn't like people looking at what I considered my deformity. It made me memorable, made me stand out, and I hated that.

The woman narrowed her eyes when she saw my hand, as if recognising me. She cast her eyes over me again with renewed interest, taking in my wild hair, my exhausted face, my rumpled clothes and the bottoms of my jeans, which were still damp. I could smell the dog's urine now I was inside, potent and unpleasant as it dried into the fabric of my shoes. I was mortified. I thought about explaining, then gave up on the idea. What was the use? What was the use in going over something that had already happened? That's what Tim would have said, and I was in agreement. I no longer had the energy for anything other than the task at hand.

The woman stared pointedly at my wet boots once more, then sighed, her smile slipping.

'Black and white collie dog, big black patch over its left eye?'

'What?' For a moment I couldn't make sense of what she was asking me.

The woman nodded at my feet. 'Your shoes are wet. Was it the dog?' Her eyes glinted with something steely, but only for a second. A flash, but I could tell she was angry, beneath the pleasantries.

Startled, I nodded, and my indignation bubbled out of me, despite my earlier resolve.

'Yes! It...It attacked me, on the road, in broad daylight! And its owner...well, he just sort of *stood* there, and did nothing!' I still couldn't believe it had happened, and saying it out loud made it sound even more absurd.

The woman examined me again, mulling something over in her mind. Then, she seemed to flip a switch internally, and the smile came back, brighter and more forceful than before. She flapped a hand airily, shaking her head.

'Oh, that's Murdo, and his boy Patch. If it makes you feel better, you're not the only one that dog has gone after. A few of us around here have gotten scars from Patch. And damp socks.' She sighed ruefully.

I was taken aback. 'Really?' I cleared my throat. 'Shouldn't...ah, shouldn't the Police know about him, or...or animal control?' I was amazed and more than a little peeved to learn that I was not the first victim of the dog's attention.

The woman levelled me with a steady gaze. 'Oh, no need for anything like that,' she said, and I suddenly felt like a child about to be dismissed. 'I'll have a word with Murdo for you, if you like,' she continued. 'It's about time something was done about that dog, but there's no need to make it official. We like to sort our own business out around here. Keep it local, you know.'

She winked at me, then deftly changed the subject.

'Walk across from Second Coast, then, did you?'

I nodded, feeling uneasy. How had she known that? I could have come from anywhere. 'Just beyond, actually,' is what I said out loud.

'Are you over at *Taigh-Faire*, then?' She gave me another comprehensive once-over from behind her spectacles. She pronounced the words differently to how I had imagined them in my head, the 'r' of 'faire' coming out almost like a 'th' sound, or a toothy 'd'. The Highlands accent in these parts was lighter and more sing-song than I thought it would be, a lilting speech, and I found I had to concentrate sometimes to make sure I heard things properly. I hated myself for this, it reminded me of how much of a stranger I was despite having been born not far from here, but I tried to remain polite. All I had to do was get through this encounter, then I could go back to the house, stick some coins in the infernal meter, close all the curtains, and lose myself in the words.

'Yes. How did you know?'

The woman said nothing, finally taking my money and opening a cash drawer under her counter. I caught sight of something as she pulled her hand back: a small blue tattoo on the inside of her right-hand wrist.

A triangle. Four dots.

One in the middle, one at each point.

She began counting out pound coins, slowly and deliberately, eyeing me over the rims of her thick glasses as she did so.

'Staying for long? I thought the guesthouse was closed.'

I cleared my throat. 'I, um...I live there now, actually. The house was my Granny's. She left it to me in her will.'

The woman stopped counting, but only for a moment.

'Patricia's granddaughter?' She asked, and I nodded.

'Yes. My name is Megan. People call me Megs.' I stuck out my hand, my left hand this time, and the older woman shook it.

'Fiona,' she said, and went back to counting, stacking the coins into little columns on the counter top. 'I thought you looked familiar. I have a good memory for faces. And names.'

I tried not to let that unsettle me. 'Yes, I lived not far from here when I was a little girl. We moved south when I was eight years old. I imagine I look very different now.'

'Not so different,' Fiona said. 'We remember you. You were the one that got away.'

We? I thought she might wink again, having made a joke, but her eyes remained downcast, focussed on counting out coins. I began to feel as if I were losing grip on the conversation, and decided to wait, rather than venture any more information.

'That old house has been empty for so long, we were sure it had been sold off for development,' Fiona remarked eventually, a little too casual, her eyes still on the money. I wondered for the second time who 'we' was, but let it pass.

I shrugged. 'I was thinking about it. But...' I stopped short, feeling a sudden, intense prickle on the back of my neck, and a headache that had been building since I left the house peaked sharply, making me wince. I clapped a hand to my forehead, and whatever I had been about to say flew out of my mind. It took me a second or two to recover, to remember what I had been talking about. I blushed as I tried to regain equilibrium.

None of this seemed to phase Fiona, who kept her eyes on the stack of coins.

'It's been in the family so long I couldn't quite bring myself to sell it,' I managed after a few moments more, massaging my tender temples. It was half-way to the truth.

Fiona chuckled. 'And now you have to put up with electricity from a coin operated meter. Must be quite a shock for you.'

I ignored this, and waited for my change. 'I'm sure I'll get used to it,' I said, noncommittally. The triangle taunted me from the woman's wrist.

'Aye, I'm sure you will.'

'Can I ask you something?' I decided to bite the bullet, as the opportunity was too good to pass up. Fiona waited, tight-lipped, so I continued, pointing at the woman's tattoo.

'What does that symbol mean? I keep seeing it everywhere around my house.'

Fiona didn't answer. She held my gaze with her own, and her eyes were different colours, I realised, behind the lenses of her spectacles. One brown, one blue. The blue eye reminded me of the collie dog's eyes. It was pale, and cold.

I shuffled uncomfortably, and she eventually went back to the money, lowering her head. I realised I had been holding my breath, although I couldn't say why.

'So,' she said, after a beat or two. 'You've been down in the cellar, then.'

Clearly, everyone knew everything about everything around here.

'Oh yes. Quite a space.'

'And you've seen the capstone.' It wasn't a question.

I nodded. 'Oh yes. Do you know anything about it? What's underneath?

Fiona's smile turned a little brittle.

'You look like Patricia, by the way,' she said, avoiding the question.

I frowned, confused, then realised Fiona was once again changing the subject. I stifled an internal scream. My headache beat at my temples, and I fought off another wave of complete and utter exhaustion.

'You might not have grown up around here, but you've got Highlands in you, I can tell,' the woman continued.

Fine. If she didn't want to answer my question, then maybe I didn't want to know, anyway.

Except I did.

'I just wish I knew more about her,' is what I said out loud.

'Oh, it won't be long before you hear the

stories,' Fiona went on. 'Patricia was a character. Eccentric, you could say. She used to swim
in the bay every morning, come rain or shine,
no matter what the season. I've seen her out
there in midwinter, wee bathing costume on and
nothing else. Never seemed to do her any harm,
though. She lived to a grand old age, didn't she?'

Something dawned on me then, and I felt
ashamed that I hadn't thought of it before.

'I don't suppose...' I cleared my throat. 'I
don't suppose you know where she is buried?' I
asked. 'It's just...well, I never went to the funeral,
and I ought to pay my respects, now that I'm
here.'

Fiona bagged the coins for me in little
plastic envelopes, and handed them over, her
eyes full of something like thinly veiled amusement. Whatever it was that she found funny,
however, she kept a secret.

'Of course, dear. She's over at the beach
cemetery. Laide Burial Ground. Take the road
that runs behind this building, follow it around,
there's a small access gate on your right hand
side. You can't miss it, it's right next to the caravan park on the beach.'

'Thank you,' I said, realising with a sinking feeling that I had just given myself one more
task to complete before I could get back to my
word processor. I turned to go, cursing the sudden onset of familial duty that had added to my
already hefty mental load.

'One more thing,' Fiona said, and something in her tone made me pause.

'Yes?'

'If you find yourself tempted to go out to the Island, don't. The Island deceives. Always remember that.'

There was a dead silence in the Post Office as I took this in.

'What?' was all I could say, after. That damned Island was following me everywhere, even into this woman's mouth!

'Good day to you,' Fiona replied, and then she pulled a shutter down over the counter, effectively ending our conversation and concealing herself from view.

I blinked. Was she watching me through the gaps in the shutter?

I smoothed a hand over my hot, sore forehead once again.

Everyone in this town is mad, I thought to myself.

And there was nothing else to say after that, except:

'Thanks for the advice.'

I delivered this parting shot with sarcasm to the metal shutter-screen. Was it my imagination, or did I hear a laugh from behind the shutter as I turned to go?

Mad, I thought again.

Something caught and held my attention as I went to leave. There was a series of photographs pinned to the far wall with thumbtacks, some black and white, some in faded colour, the edges of each picture curled from the heat of an ancient radiator mounted directly below.

They showed mundane scenes of local life, mostly. A harvest festival, a man dressed as Father Christmas handing out toys to wide-eyed children, an Easter egg hunt presided over by a person- perhaps the same unfortunate who had to be Santa each year- in a hideous, worn, saggy rabbit costume, and then a photo which made me pause.

It showed the strange wooden frame I'd passed on the way in. A congregation of white-clad people were gathered around it, but their faces were blurred, and the light was poor, the camera's exposure settings not set correctly. This is not what bothered me. What bothered me was that the people gathered around the frame were facing out to sea, facing the Island, and they all had their right hands raised, to the level of their faces. Every single one of them, as if saluting, but not quite. Index fingers all extended, pointing skyward. It was odd, but the thing that caught my attention the most, beyond the strange mass gesturing of those assembled, was the woman I could see standing at the front of the crowd, off to the left hand side of the photo. She was wearing a long, striped, full skirt that came down to the ground, and above that I could see she was thin, stick-thin, and although I could only see the back of her head, I knew who it was. I could tell by the hair-clasp fastening her white, stringy hair to the back of her head. I could tell, because this hair clasp was sitting in a shoe-box on the dressing table in the master bedroom at *Taigh-Faire.* I had a vivid memory, then, so vivid it took my breath away, of that clasp being jammed into place with deadly precision by a pair of gnarled, old hands, one of which was missing a little finger.

It was my Granny. Staring out to sea, at the Island, just like everyone else.

Waiting for something.

6. CHAPEL
OF SAND

All I had left to do after that was to go home, and I wanted to, so badly, but there were obstacles. Obstacles like the man Murdo, and his dog. Were they still there, standing by the side of the road, waiting for my return? The thought made me hot, and anxious. I couldn't bear the idea of another confrontation. I thought about walking a different route back, but I was in no mood to get lost, and the coastal road was the quickest, easiest path to *Taigh-Faire*.

And, on thinking of Granny's house, I became aware of a new obstacle, an obstacle that took the form of duty, and obligation. Because, as I'd said to Fiona, I had not yet paid my respects to my Granny, despite readily moving into her old house. It felt ungrateful and churlish not to do so now I was here, especially if the cemetery she was buried in was just down the road.

Or perhaps that was just another excuse, another reason to avoid Murdo. As if an angry, incontinent dog and a rifle weren't enough of an excuse by itself. I shuddered, recalling the dog's frosty blue eyes, and realised something about myself, then.

I was cowardly.

It was not a nice feeling.

I left the Post Office and dithered on the forecourt, trying to make a decision. From here, I could just see the edge of the bay, and the rolling hills beyond. The Island was mercifully hidden from view behind a crop of houses, out of sight for the first time since I'd left the house. And perhaps it was a coincidence, but my headache eased, just a little. The feeling of being watched lessened, ever so slightly.

I turned my feet towards the cemetery. *One last thing, and then you can rest,* I told myself.

Naively, as it turned out.

Laide Burial Ground was a tiny pocket graveyard resting peacefully on a low bank that directly overlooked Gruinard bay. One side of the cemetery was lined with a hedgerow of rowan trees, thistles, shrubs, baby oaks and long, thick stalks of grass, where crickets chirruped and tiny birds hopped from branch to branch, singing and plucking brilliant green bugs off of leaf buds. The other side of the burial ground was edged by a squat stone wall that held back the shore of the bay. Inside the boundary of the hedge and the wall, the graveyard itself: a neat emerald patch peppered with headstones of all shapes and sizes. It was a romantic location, to be sure, and one I might have been happy with myself as a final resting place.

Had it not been for the locals.

Don't judge, I thought as I unlatched a small wrought-iron gate and made my way in. *You've met two people so far. Mother always used to tell you how friendly people were up here. Don't tar everyone with the same brush. Two bad eggs does not a dozen make.*

And yet my blistered, damp feet said otherwise.

In the middle of the cemetery, which was tidy and well-kept, the slumped remains of a tiny chapel stood watching over the headstones with a quiet, ruined grace. Time had not been kind to it. The sea air had weathered the stone, and the walls had crumbled so that only the gables at either end were left standing. Those leaned inwards precariously, seemingly on the verge of collapse. A wind-worn mullioned sandstone window frame in the east gable yawned into the bay, held in place by an iron bar.

And through that window, I could once again see the Island.

Of course.

It appeared larger, now, closer, as if it had used the time it was out of sight to creep nearer to me. It hunched there on the horizon, low and long, and my head almost exploded by way of response. I gritted my teeth, bit back a groan.

It had to be a psychosomatic response of some sort. It had to be. I was no psychologist, but I was willing to theorise, for the sake of my sanity. The headaches had to be a physical manifestation of my current state of mind. My brain had fixated upon the Island subconsciously, used it as a focal point for my pain and exhaustion. There was no other explanation for the agonising pangs that flared on and off as the Island passed in and out of view. No other logical, reasonable explanation that I was willing to countenance, at any rate.

Granny, I thought, looking to distract myself from the headache by any means possible. *Find Granny.*

I spotted a small sign on weathered posts propped up against the end of the chapel. I went to it. 'CHAPEL OF SAND OF UDRIGAL', it read. I skimmed the text beneath...*One of the earliest churches on the west coast...medieval...east gable...abandoned...*and then stopped when I saw the surname Mackenzie. My Granny's surname had been Mackenzie. I re-read the sentence. *Rebuilt by Robert Mackenzie in 1712.*

Once again my heritage made itself known. This cemetery, and the chapel too, were a family concern. Fancy that. How many of my ancestors were buried here?

I drifted between the headstones, steadying my head with one hand and reading names out loud where I could. Some of the stones had lost their inscriptions, the writing polished away by the weather. Others, those that looked Victorian in shape and design, had the text inlaid with brass or ivory. These had stood the test of time better, were easier to read. I saw lots of good, solid Scottish names therein: McGregors, Macivers, McLeans, McRaes, and so on.

And then there were the stones that had no names, no writing on them at all, but instead had rudimentary carvings, symbols, or maybe they were runes- I couldn't really tell the difference. There was one row in particular of these odd stones, marching out in a little line across the cemetery and down towards the sea. The markers were slender, like thin stone tablets, rounded at the edges, and placed close together in the ground, so close that they looked like teeth sticking out of green, loose gums. On each one, the same symbol was carved. A rudimentary stick man, with an odd device coming out of the top of its head, and off to one side. It was a familiar shape, and niggled at me as I stood there. Where had I seen that image before?

I puzzled over the stones, and then it hit me. Of course! It was the symbol for Hangman, the word game you played on paper. The shape was that of a stickman, hanging from a noose. I'd drawn that shape myself, many times, as a child bored in lessons, and later, as an adult in meetings.

Curious. Why was that symbol marked on

all these stones?

I chewed on it, letting my eyes travel up, taking in the view of the bay beyond, but not enjoying it. Mysteries upon mysteries. I thought about the woman in the Post Office, Fiona, and the man with the angry dog. Murdo. My boots were still damp, and reeked of piss. What was the dog's name again? Patch. My boots reeked of Patch's piss. It felt as if I'd left my house years ago, instead of mere hours. I was beyond exhausted, both physically and mentally. I felt strange, disconnected. A little feverish. My headache was so bad now that it was bordering on a migraine. I squinted out to sea, a miserable creature with a sore head and a sore heart, and glared at the Island that sat proud in the bay, mocking me.

The Island deceives, Fiona had said, unprompted. As if she'd known that it had taken to haunting me. But how could she have known? Did she feel the effect of it, too? The pull? The pain?

An idea slid into my tired mind. I worried at my lip, staring at the Island. The spot where I stood in the burial ground represented the furthest distance from *Taigh-Faire* that I'd travelled since I left the house. The furthest distance from the Island, too, not counting everything from before my arrival in Scotland.

I thought about that feeling of a string, tying us together, and the idea went further: at the end of the string, a sharp hook, sunk into my tender flesh.

Could it..?

No. Don't be a daft bean, Megs, I heard, again in my Mother's voice.

But could it?

Only one way to find out.

I turned my back to the bay, walked a few long, deliberate steps in the opposite direction. Pain clamped down upon my skull with renewed intensity.

I stopped dead in my tracks, sucking in fresh, salty air in an effort to avoid being sick, wheeled about, and walked back the way I'd come, so that I was closer to the Island once again. A few steps closer, but it made all the difference.

The pain receded, if only a little.

I repeated the experiment several times, to be sure, but I needn't have bothered. I wasn't imagining it. It was clear what was happening.

My headache grew worse the more distance I put between myself and the Island.

Reality began to slip sideways.

How was that even possible?! What did it *mean?* My earlier theories about my subconscious mind evaporated. I felt the Island tugging at me, constantly tugging at me. Its pull was palpable, a tangible thing. The longer I kept from looking at it, the worse it got. The whole thing was incredibly unnerving, like a storm threatening in the distance. I felt heavy, and slow. Things took on a nightmarish quality around me. The little teeth-like headstones loomed, far taller in my mind than they were in real life, where they barely came to my knee. The sound of the sea, gentle and muted until that point, crescendoed suddenly. The sky brightened until my eyes watered. Trees and flowers took on a burning outline of silver. I tasted something metallic in my mouth.

I put my hands over my ears, completely overcome. My head became a raw, pulsing wound, so painful and agonising an object that I could hardly bear to be attached to it.

And then, it stopped.

The noise, the headache, the brightness.

Stopped.

A pin burst the taut bubble of suffering that was my skull. I sagged with relief. The absence of pain in my head felt incredible, like being reborn.

I stood and waited for it to return. It didn't.

I cautiously lifted my eyes to the Island. It seemed further away, now. Diminished.

What the fuck is happening to me? I thought, not for the first, or last time.

I started searching the enclosure again for Granny's headstone. Maybe if I kept busy, the headache wouldn't return, I reasoned. Maybe.

I eventually found her grave right at the

edge of the cemetery, next to the low stone wall that bowed down to the shallow beach below. I knelt, and contemplated the grey, smooth stone bejewelled with a light crust of sea-salt. It read, simply, PATRICIA MACKENZIE, and underneath there were no further words, no birth date and death date, no poetry or odes or bible scripture.

There was, instead, a symbol, embossed into the stone with a golden, metallic inlay.

I sighed.

It was a symbol I knew well, now. Not a hanged man, this time. Rather, a triangle, with a round, deep dot at the end of each point, and a fourth dot set into the very centre. It was the same symbol as the one carved above my door, at *Taigh-Faire*, and on the capstone in my cellar beneath my house, and tattooed onto the wrist of the mousy-haired, peculiar woman who ran Laide Post Office.

I traced the line of the triangle with my index finger, and felt that now familiar tingle spread up my arm.

I pulled back, and realized something.

The top point of the triangle wasn't facing due North, like its twin on the lintel of my house. The tip of this triangle was angled slightly, pointing North-East, to one thing, and one thing alone.

To the low, dark object in the background, perfectly aligned to Granny's headstone, as if someone had drawn a straight connection across the sea from that point to this, the tip of the triangle.

The Island.

I swore and stood up quickly, feeling the blood rush to my head as I did so. My skin crawled, as if eyes were upon me. I turned, and found to my surprise that there were. Three sets of eyes, in fact. From higher up the road, peering through a small gap in the hedgerow that over-looked the cemetery.

It was Fiona, and the man Murdo, with his rifle slung across his shoulder, and his dog. Patch.

Standing there, in a neat little line, and all of them watching me.

Dry-mouthed, I waved, hesitantly. Fiona didn't respond.

The dog started to bark.

Not again, I thought, fear trickling down my back like cold water.

Murdo cuffed the animal behind the ears, a sharp warning, but the dog kept its racket up. I swallowed, hoping against hope it wasn't about to charge down the road and attack me again. What would I do then? I was far enough away that I could probably vault the wall, run across the beach, but at the most, I'd only get a small head start, because dogs were fast, and-

And Fiona leaned into Murdo. She said something in his ear, patted his shoulder sympa-thetically, took his rifle from him, stepped a few paces back, aimed at the dog, and pulled the trigger.

There was a pop of gunfire, a small burst of red, and the dog fell silent, disappearing from view.

I covered my mouth in shock, falling back against my Granny's headstone.

And then both man and woman, stony-faced, deliberate, looked at me, and raised their right hands.

The photo, I thought, as they did this. *They look like the photo! All those people, and my Granny, with their hands raised. And now, these two. What does it mean?!*

At the exact same time, the pair extended their index fingers. They waited a beat, then in perfect unison, they traced a shape into the air by their heads.

A triangle.

I had seen enough. I scrambled over the wall away from them, stumbling across the beach so that I didn't have to use the road and get anywhere near the town, anywhere near the crazy fucking locals ever again. I ran as fast as I could, sweat pouring down my back, the pound coins jingling, heavy and loud and burdensome, in my pockets, and when I couldn't run any more, I walked, so fast I thought my hips would catch fire. The beach ran out, became a boulder-strewn shoreline, but by then I had put enough distance behind me that I felt safe enough to rejoin the road. I veered inland, scrambling through scrub and bracken and heather to get back to tarmac. When I had recovered my breath, I ran once again, the road hard beneath my feet, the sound of that single gunshot repeating through my brain, nipping at my heels, hounding me as I ran.

It's about time something was done about that dog, Fiona had said.

And I kept seeing triangles in the air.

At last, after what felt like an agonisingly long time, *Taigh-Faire* came into view, shabby, yet proud upon its ledge. I had never been so happy to see a place in my entire life as I was at that moment. Exhausted, I climbed the steep driveway, frantically feeling for my keys about my person as I did so.

And found Matthew waiting for me on my doorstep.

7. MATTHEW

A part of me had known it wouldn't take Matthew long to track me down after Tim and I split. Because Matthew was like that. He cared for me, and I for him, and I knew he would be worried about me. But also, when I thought about it later, I couldn't help but feel as if he had been biding his time, waiting for this. Waiting for his moment. And now, he was here. His timing couldn't have been worse. Matthew and I used to work for a large daily national newspaper, back when I was younger and considered myself a journalist. We'd been friends long before we'd fucked at the office Christmas party. That uncharacteristic 'slip' on my behalf, or so I told myself at the time, to try and assuage some of the guilt that came in the wake of the deed.

After we fucked, I warned Matthew that I didn't want anything else from him but his continued friendship. This wasn't strictly true. I was confused. I *did* want more, but I was frightened of what that meant for my life. Terrified of upsetting the apple cart, of breaking up not just one marriage, but two, of becoming the person everyone hated. So, instead of taking the plunge and running off into the sunset with him, I lied. I hurt him. I used words like 'friendship' and 'special relationship', whilst all the time being aware that our marriages were glass walls between our individual needs and desires. We could see each other through the walls, but couldn't quite breach the glass.

'Can we remain friends, after this?' Matthew asked me, sadly, when we took a walk one evening to discuss the situation. 'Really?'

'I think so, if we work hard at it.'

'But I am always going to want more than that, Megs. And I don't know how long I can bear not being with you. I can't stay in limbo forever.'

'It isn't limbo,' I said, selfishly. 'I just need you in my life. I need you.'

'But not enough to leave your husband for me.'

'It isn't as easy as that.'

'I am willing to do whatever it takes, Megs. I'm not saying it would be easy, but I'm willing.'

'I know,' I said.

Later, when he was stolen away from me, those words would haunt me for years to come. Because I realised, too late, as is the way with profundity, that I had wasted years of my life not loving as one should love. Years, because I was afraid. He had not been afraid. He had been nothing but honest about what he wanted, willing to disrupt everything, just to be with me.

Until the Otherworld took him.

But I am getting ahead of myself.

So, yes. I was very clear afterwards that sleeping with Matthew had been a mistake, a one-time occurrence. Matthew was very good about it, considering. He took it on the chin, but I always knew that he wanted to take it further. I think he thought he was really in love with me. I think perhaps I was really in love with him too, but we were both married, so we let it lie. And, amazingly, somehow, we did remain friends. And I did not make friends easily.

I hadn't told anyone where I was going when I had left Tim, but that never stopped Matthew before. As journalists go, he was one of the best connected in the industry. And tenacious with it. In hindsight, I should have realised how far he was willing to go for me.

In hindsight, I should have realised a lot of things.

At first, I didn't see him. I dragged myself slowly up the driveway of *Taigh-Faire*, head bowed, panting. I couldn't forget the image of those three silhouettes watching me in the cemetery: man, woman, dog. The gun. The small cloud of red mist. The yapping, cut off mid-bark.

Hands, tracing triangles in the air.

Did they shoot the dog because of me?

And that symbol...I *had* to know what it meant. It was driving me mad. Was it a local superstition, like a sign against the devil? My fingers itched with the memory of touching Granny's headstone, touching the outline embossed in the stone. It had been pointing to the Island, because everything since I had climbed out of bed that day seemed to be pointing to the Island.

Triangles, secrets, symbols, an Island, an angry dog, headaches, death...

I couldn't make head nor tail of any of it.

I folded into self-pity. I just wanted to write. That was all. Sit down, turn on my machine, and write. Then sleep. I had now been awake for so long now I was half-delirious, yet I still needed to write. Purge, then rest.

The Island deceives, Fiona had said.

Deceives how?

The adrenaline that had carried me home dispersed, and I sagged. I was so emotionally and physically fatigued I could feel my spine bending under the weight of it all, like an old tree limb carrying too much weight.

It was then that I realised I was not alone.

I looked up at the house, and saw him, leaning casually against my front door frame with a white plastic bag of groceries dangling from one hand. He was tall and slim, with salt and pepper hair and a ready smile. He had been there all along, and was now laughing at me, shaking his head at the spectacle I presented as I puffed up the incline.

I stared, disoriented, not recognising him at first. When I finally realised who it was, I did the only thing that I could think of. I burst into tears. And once I started crying, it felt like I would never stop again. I let out everything I had been feeling since I'd left home the day before. The confusion, the loss, and fear, and frustration. The shame, the embarrassment, the bloody, stupid dead dog. I cried, and cried, and cried, and then I felt strong hands slide around my shoulders, and Matthew circled me in an embrace, and squeezed me gently, and spoke into my hair.

'Megan Douglas,' he said, and he was no longer laughing.

'Oh, sweetheart. What the hell happened to you?'

The storm of tears passed after a while, and Matthew ushered me inside, unlocking the front door with the key I meekly gave him, and steering me to the kitchen table. I collapsed like a sack of rocks into the chair he pulled out for me, and rested my head on the table top, too tired to sit upright. Within moments, I realised that my headache was back. That it had started as soon as I'd crossed the threshold to *Taigh-Faire*.

But why? Like everything else, it made so little sense. I was closer to the Island now than I had been in Laide. My back wasn't turned to it either- I could still see the damn thing through the kitchen window.

So *why?*

A burning, irrational hatred for it bloomed. Fuck it. I didn't care anymore. Curtains. If I was to stay here, I would need curtains. Block the damn thing out of sight for good. I didn't care if my head popped like a balloon, clean off my shoulders. I just didn't want to look at it anymore.

Meanwhile, Matthew confidently made himself at home, hanging his coat up in the hallway, unloading the groceries that he'd bought from the plastic bag, banging cupboard doors and drawers as he found his way around the kitchen. Every bang and slam made my headache worse, and I gritted my teeth, trying to think of a polite way to rid myself of him. I appreciated that he'd come all this way, I understood his concern and what he was trying to do, but it was too much. Too much to deal with right now.

'I would have called,' he said, as if reading my mind, 'But your phone is disconnected.'

Was there even a phone line? I hadn't had time to check.

'Where are your cups?' Matthew slammed another door shut with gusto. Too loud. He was being too damned loud.

'Cupboard over the kettle, I assume.' I hadn't had time to check for those, either.

'Ah.' He retrieved two ancient tea-stained mugs that must have belonged to Granny, and set them on the counter. Then, he caught sight of my word processor, sitting on the kitchen table.

'What the hell is that?' He asked, incredulous.

'It's my word processor,' I said, feeling my eyelids droop, even as I longingly stroked the dead keys. My head hurt so badly I was fighting back vomit once again, taking slow, steady breaths to help keep it down. Matthew didn't seem to notice.

'Christ, Megs, what decade are you living in? Get yourself a computer like everyone else.'

'Matthew, why are you here?' I whispered.

He ignored me, opened my fridge, saw that it was completely empty, and winced.

'Honestly, Megs, what is this nonsense?' He began to put away the supplies he'd bought: milk, tea, biscuits, coffee, bread, eggs, ham, cheese, and fruit. Almost as if he'd known what sort of state he would find me in. Almost as if he understood how completely my world had fallen apart, and decided to come anyway, the very day after it happened. Almost as if these things were a bribe, calculated to make me more amenable to his being here.

Or maybe I was being unfair.

'Matthew.' I tried again, but speech had

GEMMA AMOR

become difficult. If I held myself very still, and pressed my hands into my eye sockets gently, and thought of dark, cool spaces instead of blue skies and blue seas and gravestones with hanged men on them and wooden frames that stood proud and mysterious, my headache quieted a touch. Just enough for me to speak. Just enough.

'How did you find me?' I croaked.

Matthew thought about it, carefully, before answering.

'I went to your house last night,' he said, eventually. 'I called by on my way to the pub, in case you fancied a drink. Just on the off-chance.'

Just on the off-chance. I didn't believe that for a moment.

'And?' I replied, not wanting to know, but being unable to help myself.

'Someone that wasn't you opened the door.'

I took my hands away from my face, slowly, and looked at him. He was trying not to show how sorry he felt for me.

Someone that wasn't me. In other words: another woman.

'Was she pretty?' I said, slumping further down across the table. 'Young?'

Matthew came over to me. He gently cupped my hot face in his hands, his eyes searching mine.

'She wasn't a fucking patch on you, Megs,' he said, and I rested in his hands for a moment,

98

unable to do anything else. He stared at me a little longer, then went back to trying to make tea. I didn't have the energy to tell him it was a wasted endeavour: there was still no money in the electricity meter.

'After Tim told me you'd left, I remembered a conversation we had once about your Granny's cottage, out in the arse end of Scotland. And I knew you'd want to get as far away from him as possible. I refrained from punching him in the face, by the way. You can thank me later for that.'

I thought about a woman who wasn't me, already living in my marital home, sleeping on my old side of the bed, cleaning her teeth in my bathroom sink, warming her toes in front of my fire. Fucking my husband on my cotton sheets.

I hadn't been gone longer than a few hours before she'd moved in.

At least it explained why everything had ended so abruptly. I thought of my own behaviour towards Matthew. Tim, like the man standing in my kitchen, had been braver than I. He had seen the writing on the wall, and had the guts to act upon it. I couldn't be angry with him for that. Not when I'd done what I'd done.

Still. It hurt.

Christ, Tim. Couldn't you have waited even an hour or two longer to replace me?

'Matthew,' I said, my voice thick with emotion. 'Thank you for coming, thank you for caring about me, but I wished you hadn't. I need...I need some time. I saw some things today, and...and...'

My lip started to wobble.

He stopped clattering around, and for the first time since his untimely arrival, he allowed himself to see how distraught I was. He saw how I held my head, in pain. He saw my red eyes, my exhausted, pale face, my slumped posture, and finally, finally, it sank in.

That I wasn't ready for him, not yet.

The wonderful thing about Matthew was that he was, unlike me, magnanimous in defeat. He was also one of the kindest, most loving people I'd ever met. And he was looking for an outlet to pour that love into, even if it meant simply caring for me until I had the mental capacity to recognise that love.

And I could see him, then, swallowing the grand proclamations he'd driven so far to announce. I could see him shutting it all down, putting it away for another day. He'd waited long enough, what was a little more time, to him?

'You need to sleep, Megs,' he said softly, and helped me to my feet.

I protested feebly. 'I need to write,' I mumbled, but writing was out of the question now, with my head pounding as hard as it was.

He half-carried me upstairs to the master bedroom, which was Granny's old room. I went with him, limp and compliant as a rag doll, my will and energy completely spent. Once in the room, he set me gently down on the bed, removed my still-damp boots, his nose wrinkling from the horrible smell they gave off. He didn't ask questions, he simply stripped me of my socks, jeans and pullover, and lay me down across the bed, as if I were a precious thing, to be handled with the utmost care, in case I broke.

I thought then that he might try to make love to me, and I thought about how I would have to say no, not right now, but I should have had more faith in him. I should have trusted him. I thought that so many times, after. How I should have trusted him enough to let him in.

Because he didn't try to make love to me. Instead, he settled a pillow under my head tenderly, stroked my hair, and closed the curtains, transforming the room into a muted, brown cave. Then he left me to lie in the dark, alone at last.

I thought I would not sleep. I thought I was in too much pain, I thought my brain was too noisy, too burdened with information, but the darkness of the room, and the distance I had driven, and the things I had seen, dragged me down. And sleep came quickly.

And it brought me a gift.

A dream.

It brought me to the beach.

8. THE BEACH

The beach was wide, the sand a dark ochre shot through with shiny, jet-black streaks that looked like oil deposits at first glance. Tall, silvery grass sprouted from a steep embankment next to the beach, and stretched up towards a dull sky. Behind that, great cliffs climbed, striated with different coloured layers of rock, some red, some white, some yellow. The cliffs stretched out in each direction as far as the eye could see. What lay on top, or beyond, I couldn't tell.

On closer inspection, the oil streaks were actually glossy patches of molten sand, something I had never seen before. The beach had melted in places, the individual grains having coalesced into random, sprawling puddles of glass, presumably under the effect of an intense and highly localised heat. Glimmering patches of this glass lay all around me. I pivoted upon my heel, swivelling about to take in the entirety of the scene. A hard, slick outline of the peculiar glazed sand surrounded the point at which I stood.

The outline had straight edges, three of them.

Forming a triangle.

Within which, I stood, like an anchor point. Or a dot, set dead in the centre.

Outside of the triangle, all was chaos.

Like a reluctant tourist I left the safety of the shape and picked my way cautiously across the blasted landscape.

And the further I walked, the more I saw.

There were things jumbled up in the sand, half-submerged under it and fused with it and trapped, like bugs in sap, in the strange beach-glass: books, debris, a horseshoe, a suitcase, a bicycle, a child's buggy, upended, wheels pointing at the grey sky. A white marble headstone. Was that an Arabic script carved upon it? A cast iron water pump, old-fashioned handle bent awkwardly in invitation. A rusted plane wing, jutting out of the beach like a huge rotted fin, metal exoskeleton visible beneath the warped outer paneling. A drooping lamp post, again misshapen from exposure to some force, or energy, or incredible heat. A computer monitor, screen smashed. A fully decorated plastic Christmas tree, angel perched absurdly on top, tinsel glittering in a faint breeze that danced along the beach. A violin, strings curled and wavering loose in the air. Partial train tracks erupting skyward from the sand. All these things littered the land around me as if they'd been scooped up from the ordinary, everyday human life I inhabited whilst awake, and then dumped without ceremony onto the shore, where the dark sand had hungrily swallowed it.

But that was not the worst thing about the beach. Not by a long shot.

Worse, far, far worse than the wanton, widespread chaos, were the bodies.

Human bodies, or parts of them, lying everywhere, like gruesome driftwood washed ashore by an angry tide. Sometimes an arm, sometimes a foot, sometimes a portion of a face, like an eye, staring fixedly but seeing nothing, the rest of the visage mercifully covered with sand. I saw a mouth, or rather, I almost trod upon it before I realised what it was. A small, pink mouth poking out of a smooth, exposed patch of beach. The lips were peeled back to reveal two rows of white, straight teeth. I peered at this in horror, trying to make sense of what I was seeing, and the teeth snapped together, hard. I cried out in disgust and fear. The mouth yawned opened again, slowly, stretching wide as if it were screaming. Sand poured in between the lips, quickly filling the space behind the teeth. I saw a squirming tongue. I saw the mouth gag, and spit, and then it dawned on me. There was someone down there, a whole person buried beneath the surface of the beach. I saw sand and phlegm spray from between the lips as the person struggled to rid themselves of the invading grains of sand, and understood with an abject, complete terror that whoever was stuck down there underneath the sand was still *alive*.

Suffocating.

I dropped to my knees, and tried to dig my fingers into the beach, excavate the rest of the face, clear the nose, the mouth, find something to get a hold of, something to pull. The sand was dense and heavy, and every pocket of space I cleared simply filled straight up with more of the horrible, silky stuff. I managed, through sheer force of will, to eventually push one of my hands down past what felt like an ear, work my fingers deep behind the person's hair, which felt short and scrubby, get a frantic purchase on the twitching head. Then I began to pull.

The person vanished.

My hand was sucked down, as if by a hungry maw.

I fell back, wrenching my arm free of the sand.

And at that point I realised, with a lucid type of panic, that I was dreaming. Dreaming, but unable to jerk myself awake. This was a nightmare, and, as with all nightmares, the rules of reality did not apply. But, unlike most nightmares, I found I could not escape from it.

Could not escape from the horrible, hellish beach.

I began to cry, and stumbled to my feet, looking out to the ocean, hoping for some visual solace. Instead, I saw buildings, drowned by the sea. A slate spire rose from the tideline. There was a small iron cross fixed on top. Waves lapped against richly coloured, stained-glass windows. A wooden saint with a stern expression carved upon his face kept his head held just above the waterline. Further out in the ocean, away from the beach, there were more roofs, a smattering of them, barely visible above the water. They looked like odd, boxy turtles swimming alongside each other, lurking on the surface. This illusion was broken only by the chimney stacks that jutted incongruously out of the surf atop the slate. A seagull perched on one, threw its head forward, and bawled at me, wings outstretched.

I walked on, trying not to think of whether there were bodies trapped inside the houses, drowned instead of buried beneath the sand, floating, face down, eye sockets filled with crabs and barnacles. The chapel was close enough to the shoreline that the majority of it must be beneath ground level. Was there a priest interred within, kneeling beneath my feet, knees and head bent in prayer? I kept my eyes averted from the things in the sand. I felt overwhelmed by the thought of so many bodies, so many people suffering and dying agonising, painful deaths. Tears dripped from my chin. *Too late*, I thought, but I had no idea where the thought had come from, or what it referred to. *Too late for so many.*

What was I thinking?

A flake of something white drifted past my nose. I put my hand out to catch it. Snow? No. The flake crumbled to a fine dust as it hit my hand. Ash. I looked for the source. Further along the beach, I saw a great fire burning, where seconds before, there had been nothing. Was that a car on fire? I couldn't be sure, but I thought I glimpsed blistering cherry-red paintwork amongst the flames. And behind the paintwork, there sat a blackened, humanoid outline. Curled and stiff, charred beyond recognition. The driver.

The blaze sent a towering column of black smoke into the sky. Ash drifted out of it and across the beach, over the waves. Human ash.

I was surrounded by death.

I waited in vain for the dream to end. It didn't. Instead, I stubbed my toe on something: a large lump of concrete, smoothed by seawater. I looked down, hissing in pain. Jutting out from the centre of the lump was a sign, or half of one. The rest had been eaten by the sand. It was metal, and rusty, only one word visible, printed in stern red block lettering:

PROHIBITED.

Half a sign, half a missive. Even in my dreams, the bigger picture eluded me.

The waves lapped incessantly upon the beach, drawing me further along. I saw a shimmering cloud of something brown and amorphous flit across the surface of the sea, and then disperse. A gas cloud of some sort? A swarm of insects? It was gone before I could really tell.

And then, I came to the cherry tree.

Like the burning car, it had not been there moments before, but then, without warning, it was. It blinked into existence so abruptly that I almost walked into it.

It was in full bloom, encased perfectly and completely within a large sphere of blackened, light-flecked glass. It was impossibly beautiful. I stopped dead in my tracks. After so much horror, I did not know how to accept the thing before me. The effect was one of a giant crystal paperweight, the tree meticulously arranged inside. Every petal, every twig, was perfectly, brutally static within the glass. The sun, with a timely fanfare, broke through the dense bank of cloud overhead and shone down, harsh and bright, throwing the white petals and dark sand into chiaroscuro competition with each other.

The cherry tree, locked forever in place in full, blooming glory, was incredible.

Poignant, heart-breakingly so. Like a memory of death corked in a bottle.

I peered through the glass bubble and saw birds, tiny finches, feathers puffed out, beaks stuffed with insects, sitting on branches, encased in the glass. Motionless. Eternal.

I wanted so badly to wake up, then, but found to my distress that I still couldn't. I knew I was dreaming. I knew there was another place I should be. I knew there was another body to inhabit than the one that stood before this tree, another body that was wrapped up safe and warm in an old, musty bed, whilst downstairs, a man who was not quite a friend, and not quite a lover, watched over and waited for me.

I knew this, but could not convince my mind to let go of the dream. I was trapped, as surely and completely as the cherry tree was trapped in the glass before me.

And so instead of waking, I stayed. I stared, hypnotised, until my eyes dried of tears and grew sore. I exulted in the presence of the tree whilst simultaneously screaming at myself internally to wake up. Then I dropped my gaze, overcome. And saw fistfuls of small, dark crystals encircling the tree-bubble, radiating out across the sand in an organised series of lines, a geometric pattern that was part triangle, part spiral. I knew these shapes to be no accident of nature. They were deliberate. They were boundaries. Like lines drawn in the sand, only more powerful. Whatever was within was sacred. Protected.

Or imprisoned.

I bent down, broke a crystal off at the root, and examined it. It was smoky, like quartz.

I squeezed it. Smoky and solid. *Treasure from another reality. Nightmare diamonds,* I thought. I put it inside my pocket.

Something shifted inside the glass.

A tiny movement, but I caught it. I edged closer to the tree-bubble, leaned forward to get a better look, overbalanced...

...and fell headlong through the glass.

And I was somehow inside. Somehow part of the beauty, but instead of suffocating, instead of hanging suspended within the crystalline globule like a mosquito in amber, I was able to move and breathe within the glass, because this was just a dream, after all.

Wasn't it?

The cherry tree held its arms out above me. It was even more beguiling, close up. The finches gripped the branches with their tiny clawed feet. As I stepped closer, there was a clear, distinct noise, like that of a thin crack appearing in a glass windowpane. Something small tumbled from a branch overhead, and fell at my feet. When I located it, I realised it was a single cherry blossom. I felt a surge of sadness, for the perfect thing was now a little less perfect, and I was to blame.

And then I saw what lay at the base of the tree.

Waiting for me.

It was smothered by the snarled tangle of tree roots that snaked and crisscrossed around my feet and then plunged down into the beach, anchoring the tree firmly in place. For this reason, it was hard to make out at first, but I eventually determined that it was an old, mossy rock, about the size of a large football, assimilated into the root mass like the head of a Buddha statue I had seen once in Thailand.

And carved into that rock, was a crude face.

A deity of some sort? A god? A former king, lord, pharaoh, leader...prophet? I knew, without knowing *how* I knew, that this was an ancient thing. The face was aged beyond my comprehension of time, and origin. It had squat, basic features. A wide mouth, like a frog's. A flat, worn nose. The barest impression of eyes, depicted as two round, expressionless orbs.

The orbs were staring at me.

I felt something deep within my body wake up. There was no other way to describe it. It was a sensation of arousal, of something long dormant rising to greet the world.

The blank, primitive face glared at me from its throne of roots, and I couldn't help myself. My hand itched and burned, and I couldn't help myself.

I did something I shouldn't have done.

I went to it, and reached out, and touched the face with my bare hands.

I knew as soon as I touched it that I shouldn't have. An all-consuming wave of panic and dread swept me up the moment my fingers made contact with the soft, green stone.

There was a terrific rumbling, a movement from the bowels of whichever earth I was above. The tree juddered overhead. A small shower of petals drifted down around me like the ash that had drifted across the beach earlier.

I gasped, and fell back, and the face in the stone opened its eyes.

The crude orbs had been eyelids, closed eyelids. These slid backwards, mimicking the movement of the scale that cover's a snake's eyes. Beneath lay two dark, hungry spheres.

The god beneath the tree opened its mouth, and I saw my mistake for what it was: the rock was not a rock at all, nor was it a carving. Rather, it was something that had been sleeping, sleeping for many, many years beneath this cherry tree, safe, cradled, undisturbed.

And I had just woken it up.

The eyes, hideous and vacant and black, rolled. The creature spoke with a voice so loud my ears and nose erupted, blood fountaining down my chest and the sides of my face. The words were delivered in a language I didn't recognise, but that hardly mattered.

I knew anger when I heard it.

I scrambled back like a crab, out of the tree-bubble, sobbing. But the damage was done. The beach trembled and quaked. Huge waves smashed against the shore with a sudden brute force. A lump of rock detached from the cliff nearby with a sharp *crack,* and smashed to the ground. Ash swirled around me, driven by a fierce, whipping wind.

What have I done? I thought, frantically slapping my own face, over and over, in one final, desperate attempt to wake myself up. Blood from my nose spattered to the sand, and a small grasping hand that poked out of the beach near my left foot trembled, then grew still.

What have I done?!

I didn't wake up.

This isn't a dream, I realised.

This is something else!

I screamed. There was no way off this beach. There was no way to wake up from this hellish dreamscape. I would be trapped here forever, stuck as fast as the bodies in the sand, an angry god's eyes upon me, its voice ravaging my fragile mind, and...

And...

And then something monstrous bellowed in the distance.

'No more, please no more,' I whispered, squeezing my eyes shut in denial and clapping my hands, my treacherous, meddling hands, to my face.

There was a flash of movement from behind the closed lids. A shadow moved across them.

A big shadow.

GEMMA AMOR

An impact tremor ran beneath my feet, and then another. Huge and heavy footsteps approached.

Something was coming.

I took my hands away, shaking in fear, and saw, for a split second too long, something vast.

Something black.

Something hideous.

It stalked on two legs across the sand towards me. It was massive, and fast, and moved in a dangerous, fluid, predatory way.

It looked like a giant man.

I screamed again.

Then, the creature was gone. It vanished, mid-stride.

The seagull that had been perched on the roof of the drowned house took flight, fighting the fierce wind that now blew. It circled above my head and screeched at me in derision. The bird's taunting cries took on form, like human words, and I thought that I heard it squeal out my name, over and over, 'Megs!' 'Megs!' 'Megs!'

I cowered beneath it, and as I did so, without warning, I felt the sand under my feet soften, I felt myself sinking down, down, down, the beach rising up past my ankles, past my knees, past my waist, up to my chest, closing in around my neck, and I found I was not ready to die, I found I could think of no worse fate than to let the beach swallow me whole, I found I was stuck, helpless, as my death came at me, a smooth avalanche of oblivion, and then finally, finally, I awoke to a gathering darkness, and my house, and the sound of Matthew calling my name.

9. CALLING

'Megs? Megs, wake up!'

Matthew stood behind me, gripping my shoulders, shaking me.

'*Megs!*' He hissed again, and this time, I roused, gasping and shaking as if surfacing from deep beneath the waters of a pool. Then, instinct took over, and I flailed, struggling against Matthew's hold, useless gibberish words spilling from my lips. I was stuck, I was stuck in the sand, and there had been things on the beach, such terrible, terrible things, and there had been a tree with an angry god beneath it, and there were corpses scattered across the sand like driftwood, and I was stuck, I was stuck...I was...

Only I wasn't. I was standing in the hallway of *Taigh-Faire*, half-naked. My right hand was tugging on the door of the cupboard under the stairs, my fingers stinging as if I'd been slapping the wood, trying to get in.

My breathing slowed. Matthew kept a firm but gentle grip on my shoulders. I stopped fighting him when I felt something cold in the palm of my left hand. I opened it.

My hand had been curled tight around something small, and angular, and hard. I blinked, and saw a crystal lying upon my palm, flecked with smoky grey lines and ash-coloured flaws.

I dropped it.

Dream-crystal.

I shook my head, over and over, as if trying to shake water out of my ears. *It can't be. It can't be!*

Was I actually awake? Or was this just another part of the nightmare?

The crystal hit the floor and broke into two pieces. As I stared at them, terrified, they vanished.

Into thin air.

Permanence had become a thing of the past.

Two dark, wet spots took the place of the crystal shards on the floor. I sniffed. There was blood dripping from my nose. It splatted by my feet. I touched my ears. Those were bleeding, too.

I remembered a great, thundering voice speaking alien words of displeasure.

What the fuck was *happening* to me?

Cold, disoriented and bloody, I finally reached out for the warmth of another human being. I reached out for Matthew.

'M- Matthew?'

He took my hands in his, and spoke softly, reassuringly. He was always so kind. So kind.

'It's okay, Megs. It's okay. You're awake now. You were sleepwalking. I didn't hear you at first, you were so quiet, but then you started hammering on that door as if your life depended on it. Scared the living Jesus out of me.'

'I'm sorry,' I said quietly, but I couldn't concentrate on him. Something nagged at me, something beyond the mental struggle I was having to reconcile what I'd seen with what I knew to be possible. I was awake, I had to be, but what about the crystal in my hand? The nosebleed? How could someone...

How could a person bring those back from a dream?

'You're bleeding, come here.' Matthew tutted and pressed a handkerchief he drew from his pocket onto my nose, tilting my head back. I let him do this, my mind otherwise occupied. I let him cluck and fuss over me as he stemmed the flow of blood.

'Honestly, I don't know how you've managed this long without me, Megs,' he scolded, gently.

Was it a dream, or not? This question consumed me. If so, it was unlike any other dream I'd ever experienced. So vivid. So awful. And I had this unpleasant, lurching, gut-wrenching feeling inside of me. As if I'd done something wrong. The feeling you get when you know you've made a mistake, a huge mistake.

The more I came to, the more aware of my body I was. I found that my headache was back. In its wake followed the aching skin, the feverish chills. My mind wheeled round and around. I thought of a green, mossy stone, a crude face carved into it. I thought of a woman reaching out, touching what should not be touched. I shuddered, violently. Matthew soothed me and held me close, to warm me up.

So kind.

'Megs?' Matthew tried to get me to look at him, but I froze suddenly, and shrugged him off. The nagging thing that had been bothering me took on form, substance. I felt a sharp, cool breeze whistling out from under the cupboard door, past my legs. I frowned. There had been no draft there before. I remembered. There had been a draft in the cellar, around the capstone, but I hadn't felt it beyond the door.

'Can you feel that?' I asked, pushing Matthew away and moving to unlatch the door. 'That draft. It shouldn't be...there shouldn't be...'

A strange feeling came over me. What was that noise I could hear? High-pitched, it set my teeth on edge. It was like a moan, or a single, long note played off-key.

'Megs?' Matthew's eyes were full of concern. 'What's going on?'

'I'm not sure,' I replied, feeling suddenly

very far away from everything.

'Come away, Megs,' he said, and I felt a flash of annoyance. The noise grew a little louder.

'I need to check something out,' I argued, with some force this time, unlatching the cupboard door with cold, fumbling fingers. Matthew stared at me, perplexed.

'At this hour? What on earth for? There's nothing in there, Megs. You just had a bad dream. Come on, come away, we need to clean your face.'

I ignored him, and opened the cupboard door.

'Megs, you're being silly. Besides, there's no power, you'll never find what you need under there in the dark!'

'Help me with this,' I replied, grabbing hold of the vacuum cleaner that I'd put back after my last visit to the cellar.

'Megs.' Matthew's voice took on some urgency. 'The gas hob still works, I made tea,' he continued, and there was an odd, heavy look on his face. 'Come away from there, would you, and have a cuppa with me first? I have things...' He took a deep, shaking breath. 'Things I want to say.'

Poor Matthew. He had come such a long way.

'I don't like tea,' I murmured, perhaps cruelly.

'Please?' He asked, the question almost a plea.

'No,' I shook my head. 'No. There is something...something I need to do.' I didn't know what it was, exactly, but I knew it to be true. There was something down there beneath the house that needed my attention, and needed it urgently. I could hear it singing to me, high and steady.

I started dragging things out of the cupboard. Matthew tugged on the back of my shirt, and I felt another flash of annoyance.

'Megs? Are you still asleep, Megs? Megs!'

'Leave me alone, Matthew!' I spun around, and gave him a savage look. I sounded cold, and hollow, even to my own ears. 'Don't you understand? I have something I have to *do*.'

But Matthew didn't leave me alone. He blinked, and smoothed the hurt look on his face away with an expert haste that would have made me regret my actions had I been in my right mind. Then he muttered something under his breath, and began to help me clear out the cupboard, revealing the small, hidden cellar door on the far wall once again.

It waited for us, so dark and black in the gloom that it burned a rectangular mark into my vision, and when I blinked, I still saw it, like a white shadow on a photograph negative.

'What the hell is that?' Matthew breathed.

'The way down,' I replied, and I could feel a strong, whistling draft, bursting out from the small gap beneath the wooden door. It brought with it the smell of the cellar, and that salty tang to which I was quickly becoming accustomed.

I lifted the latch. A fresh blast of freezing cold air pummeled our faces. Matthew rubbed his eyes. 'Christ!' He said, blinking dust and grit away. 'What the hell have you got down there, a portal to another world?'

And I remembered a beach in my dream, where the sand was glass and a tree bloomed eternal inside a crystal cage, and I knew it was all connected, my dream, the stone face in the tree roots, the beach, the giant that stalked the sands there, the cemetery in Laide, the wooden structure by the side of the road, the strange folk I had met, the peculiar symbols all around me, my Granny, this house, the cellar carved from bedrock, the chalk giant by the loch on the way into Laide, the circular capstone that lay beneath us...

And the Island.

I made a move towards the now yawning black mouth in front of us, and Matthew grabbed for me again, pulling me up short. I bit back an angry retort. I was growing tired of being manhandled.

'Wait,' he said.

I glared at him.

'What do you think is down there, Megs?'

He asked, and it was a fair question, I supposed. 'Why the urgency? What's going on?'

I didn't have answers for him. I just knew I had to. I had to go down, I had business to attend to. I didn't know what it was, I didn't know anything beyond the driving sense of urgency that pushed me through the squat little door and down the rough-hewn steps. It was impossible to explain this to him, impossible to explain how I knew that ignoring whatever it was that called to me would have disastrous, catastrophic consequences. I had no choice. This was now the only course of action open to me.

'Can you just...' I searched for the words, removing his hand from my arm as calmly as I could.

'What? Leave you alone? I'm not feeling very welcome, Megs, I have to say.'

I sighed. An older version of me may have pointed out that I hadn't invited him to Scotland, rather he had just shown up on my doorstep, groceries and assumptions in hand. I might have pointed out that, although it came from a place of concern and love, driving all the way upcountry to see me the day after my husband broke from me was also a rather selfish act, and it may have been better to have thought about my need for space, and distance, and time, before entertaining any new relationship, for that was undoubtedly why he was here: to declare his love, unchanged and constant.

I might have also pointed out that I wasn't sure how I felt about him in return. Not yet. I knew there was love, I knew my stomach still flipped when I thought about us together, but that was as far as I had gone with that particular thought process. Just because Tim had moved on at lightning pace, didn't mean I was ready to do the same.

I might have said these things, but I didn't. I did not have the energy for anything other than what lay below my feet. Whatever that was.

'Can you just trust me?' I finished, eventually, and there wasn't much Matthew could say to that. He nodded, and I handed him the torch that hung on its nail by the cellar door.

Then, we went down.

10. OPEN

As soon as we got to the bottom of the steps, it made itself known. The high-pitched, keening, whistling noise, coming from the far end of the cellar. My headache spiked in response to it.

The capstone waited for us there, cold, smooth, and patient. The draft I had felt before had intensified, and the air was all but screaming as it blasted through the thin space around the edge of the stone.

'What the hell is that?' Matthew breathed, but I didn't answer. He was not real to me at that moment in time. The only thing real to me was the stone. The sound of the wind leaking out from behind it. The growing pressure behind my eyes and across the back of my skull.

I knelt, almost reverently.

And then I placed a hand on the capstone, and felt the peculiar vibration I had come to expect surge through my skin. It travelled along my arm, and around my body. I wondered distantly at the damage these hands were doing to all the things they came into contact with:

people, places, traditions, ancient things I didn't understand. What power there was in a single, unschooled touch. This time, however, I didn't pull my hand away. This time, I gritted my teeth and told Matthew to hold his light closer to the stone, revealing the symbol.

I studied it, thinking that the triangle wasn't the important part, not really. It was the dots that mattered, the circular dots at the end of each point, and the one in the middle. Four dots. I looked at my right hand. Four fingers, if you counted the thumb. The stump of my little finger seemed to not look so ugly, all of a sudden. I'd been ashamed of it my whole life, but now, it seemed fortuitous, this missing finger.

Intentional. My mind played with the word.

And I wondered something, then. I wondered about the dots, and how there were four of them, and how I had only four fingers on my right hand, and how those two facts seemed to be so intertwined.

I gently placed the tip of each finger on my right hand into the holes around the triangle. It felt awkward at first, I had to drop my index finger down so that it would fit into the central dot, and my thumb wasn't as long as my other digits so I had to try and push it out further to compensate for this, but once I figured out how to arrange my hand, I found that some of the dots were deeper than others, so everything slotted into place neatly and felt right, *really* right, and natural, as if I had remembered how to do this from a long, long time ago. As if I were slipping on an old glove, one moulded to my shape.

And was it me, or did the symbol start to glow faintly? Matthew swore, and a light green shimmer gathered around the edges of my hand. And, as we stared at it, the capstone moved.

Ever so slightly, at first, with a shifting, grinding, grating noise. The wind that whistled around the stone's edge shrieked louder. The capstone sank, depressed inwards by an inch. Matthew hissed in surprise.

The stone shifted again.

Impatient, I pushed. Gently at first, and then harder, and harder, putting my shoulder into it, bearing down, as if pushing open an old, stubborn door.

Which, it turned out, was exactly what I *was* doing.

'Megs, be careful!' Matthew warned, and I redoubled my efforts.

The stone gave way.

PART TWO: TRUNK

11. THE TUNNEL

It rolled inwards and then sideways out of view as if on a mechanism, revealing a large, long dark passage beneath.

And the wind stopped. As suddenly as if it had been choked off at the source.

An eerie silence filled up the cellar.

'Christ,' said Matthew, agog. 'Did you know that was there?'

'No,' I said, shaking my head, which was still throbbed, but I wasn't sure I was telling the truth. A part of me must have known, all along, or why else would I have slotted my fingers into what was obviously a hand-operated lock, or seal? How else would I have known how to do that?

'Where does it go?' Matthew went on, peering in, letting the torch beam slide ahead of him. I saw rock, shadows, and nothing else. The space beyond the reach of his light was deep, impenetrable black.

Where *did* it go?

I had a good idea.

I took the torch from him, and guided the beam around the passageway. It wasn't a man-made tunnel, that much was quickly obvious. It seemed like a large natural crevice in the stone, with a sandy path worn along the bottom. It was wider at the top than it was at the base, and had it been light enough, it would have been more than obvious that the aperture in the bedrock made a 'V' shaped cross-section.

Or, if you were looking at it from the perspective of a woman who had been living at *Taigh-Faire* for too long already, a triangle.

I crouched, threaded one leg through the entrance to the tunnel, preparing to lower myself down. Matthew grabbed my hand as I did so.

'You're not serious,' he said, gripping me tight.

'Matthew,' I replied, now thoroughly at the end of my tether with him. 'If you don't stop putting your hands on me, I'm going to chew them off, understand? Of course I'm serious. Why else do you think I'm here?'

He let go of me, and had the wherewithal to look chagrined. 'I'm sorry,' he said. 'I'm just…I mean, this is just a lot, Megs! Not what I was expecting at all.' He swallowed, and looked into the tunnel again, and I could see it made him nervous.

'I know,' I said, more kindly this time. 'I

know, but I still want to look. I want to see where it goes. There is something...something I have to do.'

'But you aren't even wearing any trousers!' Matthew pointed out, and we both looked down at my bare leg dangling through the newly exposed hole. I hesitated.

He had a point.

'Or shoes.'

I glared at him, although he was perfectly within his rights to point this out.

'Fine.'

I retracted my leg, stood up.

'But I'm coming straight back down here after I've put some clothes on.'

Matthew folded his arms, the torch beam careening off over his shoulder as he did so.

'Well you can forget going down there alone. Why don't we do it in the morning, when it's safer?'

'No,' I said, simply. 'I'm going tonight. Now.'

Matthew threw his arms up in exasperation. 'Fine!'

'Fine,' I echoed.

'Good.'

'Good.'

I headed for the cellar stairs. 'I'll be back in a moment,' I said, and mounted the steps.

Matthew just stood there, shaking his head.

'You know, this isn't exactly what I had in mind when I drove all night to see you!' He shouted after me. The cellar took his voice and threw it around the large, cavernous space beneath the house, so that it echoed back tenfold.

I said nothing, because there was nothing to say. My going into the tunnel was as inevitable as night following day, and oh, what a day, what a day it had been.

He would follow me, I knew he would. It was just who he was.

Until he went to a place I couldn't go. But that would be later.

For now, I would walk ahead.

The tunnel sloped downhill gradually. As we walked, I tried to shake off the terrible nightmare. The voice of the thing beneath the tree was still firmly lodged in my mind, and I felt almost breathless as I remembered the beach, and the bodies, and the giant silhouette in the distance, marching along the tideline towards me.

But worse than that, much, much worse, was the crystal I'd held in my hand. Because it was impossible to think for even one moment that I'd brought it back with me, from a dream.

Which meant one of two things. Either I was hallucinating, or the nightmare wasn't a nightmare at all.

Unable to reconcile myself with either

possibility, I turned my attention to the tunnel. After a while I became sure that we were headed down through the bedrock under *Taigh-Faire's* foundations, away from the house and out towards Gruinard bay. It was hard to measure distance in the dark, and the uneven path beneath our feet made it difficult to stride out, but the further we went, the more sense I had of how far we had walked. I concluded that the ground we'd covered didn't match the distance between my house and the beach, as the two were adjacent to each other. We had travelled much, much further than that. The ground sloped more and more under us, and our ears popped in unison. The tunnel went *underneath* the beach. Underneath the bay.

And the only thing of note in the bay that lay in the same direction we were headed was...

The Island.

We were walking beneath the sea.

At the end, I would find myself in the place that had been calling to me all day. I knew this, because every pace forward I took eased the pain in my head, just as it had before, in Laide burial ground.

The closer I got, the less it hurt.

The Island wanted me to visit.

I kept these thoughts to myself, however, unsure of how to even begin explaining all this to Matthew. He had stopped trying to reason with me, but kept close on my heels, his proximity betraying how uncomfortable he felt in the tunnel.

I examined the stone walls as we moved along. They were jagged, and I had to be careful to keep my arms by my sides for fear of scraping them against the rough rock. Occasionally, although the torch's light was too poor to make out much detail, I glimpsed crude markings on the walls. They were geometric patterns, mostly, spirals, circles and squares connected by rough lines. A few of them weren't. A few of them looked like ancient carvings of animals I didn't recognise, things with teeth and claws and tails, but not much else I could identify.

And one of them looked like the hill figure by the loch just outside of Laide. A giant figure, human by shape, but not by proportion.

I stared at that one for a short while, thinking of my dream. Thinking of the sand beneath my feet shaking as something large and heavy approached.

If I could come back down here again with a better light source, I would sketch these markings, study them in more detail at a later point. The mathematical shapes were as interesting to me as the picture of the giant. I had read something once about sacred geometry, for a newspaper article I'd researched. Sacred meaning attached to form, and shape. Was that what this was? Was I entering sacred ground?

I thought again of the tree, and the

strands of crystal radiating out from its base, spreading across the beach. I thought of the shapes they made.

It was all connected.

All of it.

We walked downwards, Matthew stumbling every now and then behind me, but still following, because despite his fear, he was as curious as I was, which was why we were as close as we were. And why he was the better journalist. Because he knew how to squash down his fear to chase a story. I was reminded again of how much braver that made him. I hid from things. He hunted them down.

I could probably learn a thing or two from him, I thought.

Down, and down, and down further still. My knees locked as the gradient increased. I leaned back to keep my balance, and Matthew did the same.

Then, after what felt like an hour of walking, the path rose upwards again. It felt like an hour, but was in fact only twenty minutes according to Matthew's watch, but the dark was so complete and the tunnel so long that time had become a fluid thing. Minutes stretched out like hours as we put one foot in front of the other, and then the other, and ever on, into our shared unknown.

And I was glad, suddenly, that Matthew was here with me for this. I was glad, because whatever compelled me along the tunnel came from a place deep within that I'd never felt before. It was a compunction, a driving, almost violent appetite for momentum that threatened to tear me completely away from my moorings, untethering me from my flimsy grasp on reality. Stopping was not an option, not when the pain in my head lightened and the sensation of answering a call, an important call, grew stronger with every step.

So yes, I found myself feeling grateful for his company. Matthew was my connection with reality, a reminder of who I had been before I'd unlocked the door at *Taigh-Faire*. He grounded me, a little. No matter how terrible his timing, he was loyal, and that meant something to me.

As if sensing my thoughts, he spoke.

'How far are we going to walk along this sodding tunnel before we realise it comes to a total and complete fucking dead-end?' He said.

I smiled, and shook my head.

Spoke too soon, I thought.

'It won't,' is what I said out loud.

'How can you be so sure?'

'Because it won't,' I repeated.

And because the universe provides, the tunnel suddenly angled a little to the right, and we rounded a sharp, jutting lip of rock, and came face to face with a terrifying, bone-white mask. At the same time, my foot kicked something on the path, something hard, something that clattered as I made contact. I stopped abruptly, Matthew running into the back of me with a soft curse, and we both stood there, yanking the torch beam over to illuminate the thing.

It was a skeleton.

'Shit,' said Matthew.

'I think this might disprove the dead-end theory,' I replied, a little more smugly perhaps than I should have.

It was a deer, by the looks of it, a stag, but huge, bigger than any stag I'd ever seen. Its skull was almost the size of an elephant's skull. It looked as if it were stuck. The antlers, which were broad and had an enormous span, were firmly wedged at our eye-level between the angled rock walls, filling the entire width of the top of the tunnel. Empty eye sockets stared balefully at us as we stood there, nose-to-nose. I saw, after a moment, that it was only the skull that was wedged in place. The rest of the skeleton lay on the ground beneath the skull, the vast ribcage completely filling the narrow space at the bottom of the crevice. I spotted hooves amongst the bones. This made me feel sad, for some reason.

I had a vision of the animal wandering along the tunnel, not noticing how it narrowed the further it went, then finding itself stuck, unable to go forward, or back, its antlers snagged on the uneven rock walls. I imagined it struggling, bellowing mournfully with its head jammed tight in the crevice, legs and hooves pawing at the ground with ever-increasing desperation and futility, and then I saw it give up, close its eyes. It died from thirst or starvation, and decayed right there where it hung, the skin blistering and rotting, the skeleton drying out, bones whitening, becoming brittle, until the body, no longer supported by sinew and muscle, collapsed to the floor, leaving only the head behind with a small section of vertebrae sticking out, intact, underneath. It was a powerful image, and I swallowed, feeling pity for the creature.

We would have to step over it if we wanted to move further ahead. This felt disrespectful, but there was no choice. No going back. Only forwards.

Matthew whistled, taking in the size of the dead stag. 'What the hell is it *doing* in here?' He asked, reaching out to touch the antlers.

'Not much,' I said, unnecessarily, and stooped so that I could pass beneath the skull.

'Seriously though,' he continued as we picked our way under the antlers and over the bones, trying not to pierce ourselves on the wicked bone spikes. 'How in God's name did it even get down here?' His voice sounded odd in the rocky space of the tunnel, as if he were speaking inside a tin can. It added to the surreal nature of what it was that we were doing, and goosebumps travelled along my skin in a sudden rash. There was death down here in the tunnel, and that was something I hadn't thought about, until now: that what I was doing was dangerous. If the tunnel branched out, or split, or twisted and turned, we could get lost, could fall, and break something. Our torch could run out. We could get stuck too, maybe even die.

I swallowed, then shrugged it off. 'Maybe it wandered down here from somewhere else on the mainland, I don't know. This tunnel has to go somewhere, right? So it must have come from whatever lies at the other end.'

Still, I kept my theories about the Island to myself.

It was then that we came to the cave, suddenly, as if it had been waiting for us to pass the hurdle of death before revealing itself. One minute we were treading the rocky path in the dark, trying to keep our balance and sense of direction intact, and the next, the crevice widened, rounded out, our feet had more room to move along the floor, and we found ourselves standing, unexpectedly, in a small, dark cave. Beyond the mouth of the cave, I could see stars, and hear the sea. I could smell it too, that now oh-so-familiar rich, salty aroma.

And, as we caught our breath and peered out of the cave into our new surroundings, we heard, faint in the distance but sweet as a prayer, the sound of music.

The Island was welcoming me.

12. ANTHRAX ISLAND

'So where the hell are we now?' Matthew said, walking to the mouth of the cave and sticking his head out. He stumbled on something as he went, something that clattered and crunched underfoot, and he looked down.

'Okay?' I murmured, preoccupied by the music I could hear in the distance.

'More bones,' he muttered. 'But I think these are just sheep bones.'

My eyes adjusted to the different light levels, and I saw them all over the cave floor.

'A hell of a lot of sheep bones,' I replied, and then we both shrugged. After the giant stag, it was hard to be impressed by something as mundane as sheep bones, even if there were a suspiciously high number of them.

The music swelled, and a faint rhythmic beat could be heard underneath it. Matthew cocked his head to one side, trying to figure out where it was coming from.

'Is someone having a party out there?'

I crossed the cave floor, gingerly stepping around the sheep bones, listening as the shrill cry of a lone violin rose high into the air from somewhere over our heads, beyond the cave. I came to stand next to Matthew, and poked my own head out of the cave mouth. I saw that I'd been right. We were standing in a small, rocky hollow on one side of the Island.

I was finally here.

I smiled. It was a small smile, but it was something. It helped to dispel the greasy sense of discomfort that had settled on me since the nightmare.

Since the face under the tree.

More importantly, my headache had once again disappeared. I felt light in its aftermath. I could bear anything, once the headaches stopped.

Despite the hour, which was late, it was not full dark outside the cave. I could see Gruinard bay all around us, bathed in the washed-out light of a strengthening moon. The sky was now a rich, deep indigo, coming down softly to meet the darkness of the horizon. I could see the lights of Laide along the shore of the mainland. I could see the large wooden frame, glowing a ghostly, strange pale grey against a star-pierced sky. I could even see the cemetery, the burial ground where Granny lay, the hulk of its collapsed chapel crouching amongst the headstones. From here, the collection of little stone markers marching down to the sea looked like chess pieces on a far-away board.

And I could see, further along the coast, the small white fuzzy blob sitting up high that was *Taigh-Faire.* I realised then, quite how far we'd walked. Under the sea, across the entire depth of the bay. I pointed to the house, for Matthew.

'What's that?' He said, squinting. His vision was not as well-adjusted to the night as mine.

'That's my house,' I answered, slipping a hand in his. I felt at peace, suddenly, but couldn't explain why. The effects of the horrible dream began to fade. It was as if I had arrived at a place I was supposed to be.

He swallowed, caught off-guard, and then squeezed my fingers in response.

I let my eyes scan along the coastline of the mainland. A large building I had not noticed before took my attention. It faced the Island directly, but was heavily screened from the rest of the mainland by thick fir trees and vegetation. It was festooned in bright security lights, and I could just make out a tall barbed-wire fence topped with curling razor-wire snaking all around it.

I frowned.

'I didn't know that was there,' I said. 'You can't see it from the road at all. What is it?'

'Military, probably,' Matthew replied, following my gaze. 'NATO and the Ministry of Defence are fairly active around here, or used to be. There are small bases like that scattered all along the coastline, have been for many years. During the Second World War, they did a lot of testing in these parts. Bioweapons and the like.'

I didn't like that idea. I didn't like the thought of a large, faceless organisation burrowing into the shore, abusing the ecosystem, playing war games. There was something so wild and unspoiled about the Highlands. A military presence here felt like a violation, a betrayal of the land.

So much for getting to know the neighbours, I thought.

I leaned out a little more to see what else I could spy, and Matthew put a warning arm out to bring me up short. I looked down. Water lay directly below: the cave opened straight out onto the sea. I craned my head and neck out further. I could see we were bracketed on both sides by sheer, craggy grey stone. Easy enough to climb up, if we were careful. I shone the torch across and angled it upwards, trying to spot a clear route for feet and hands. As I did so, I noticed iron hoops hammered into the cliff edge, forming a short, rudimentary step ladder up the rock face.

Seeing this made me wonder about the giant stag. Because it became glaringly obvious, on seeing those small metal rungs, that the animal hadn't climbed down this ladder to get into the tunnel. Which meant it hadn't come from the Island.

So where had it come from? Did the tunnel branch off somewhere, connect to the mainland from a different location? I imagined a network of underground passages, sprawling across the shoreline and under the bay like a system of arteries and veins beneath the skin, all of them leading to one place: the Island.

I chewed my lip. The sound of drumming surged around us again, mirroring my heart beat. The music was hard to ignore, just as the Island had proven hard to ignore. Multiple threads, pulling at me. Multiple hooks in my soft, willing flesh.

I let out a deep breath. I found that I was nervous, and excited, and terrified and compelled all in the same instance. I didn't let go of Matthew's hand, and he didn't let go of mine.

'What do we do now?' He asked, and the music died down a little, as the wind took it elsewhere. 'Turn back?'

I took a moment to reply.

'I suppose we should find out where that party is,' I said, eventually. There was no way in hell that I was turning back, not now. I was here for a reason. It was time to find out what that reason was.

Matthew balked. 'Why? This has to be private property, Megs. We'd be trespassing, surely.'

'Why not?' I asked, in an uncharacteristic display of bolshiness. 'What's the worst that can happen? We've come this far, why turn back now?'

Matthew blinked, as if not recognising me for a moment. 'Because...well, it's the middle of the night, for one thing. And trespassing on private land in the dead of night isn't my idea of fun, thank you very much.' He drew breath, getting into his stride. 'And even if it *isn't* private property, that party could be anything. Anything at all! It could be a drug-fueled rave. A blood-soaked orgy, or a weird, sacrifice-oriented pagan festival presided over by ravenous, kilt-wearing cannibals. With that in mind, I vote to turn back.'

I looked at him.

'Kilt-wearing cannibals?' I said, deadpan, and his mouth twitched.

'Alright, alright. I have a point, though.'

I laughed at him, and it felt good to laugh after everything that had happened.

'Matthew...' I said, growing serious once again. I let the sentence tail off, and gave him a steady look. His bluster collapsed in on itself.

'You're going to go and explore, aren't you,' he replied, wearily, and it wasn't a question.

'Atta boy,' I said, and let go of his hand.

We left the cave, climbing up the iron

rungs in the rock face slowly, Matthew shining the torch for me until I reached the top so that I could see where I was putting my feet, then following behind. Always following behind. The deep, complex feeling of excitement and dread spread throughout my body as I hauled myself onto the Island proper, and scrambled upright. Ferns and bracken brushed up against me as if in welcome. I spread out my arms, feeling suddenly off-balance, despite being on firm ground. It was as if I were standing right on the edge of something impossibly high, and vertiginous, not a cliff edge, but the lip of a vast chasm, perhaps, or the edge of a tall tower, staring down, only the very tips of my toes in view, and a huge, faceless void beyond.

As if I was on the verge of toppling into that void, but clinging on. Barely.

And yet, it was somehow right that I should be here, it was somehow right that I should fall. The longer I stood, the more at home I felt. The tension in my shoulders and across the back of my neck- tension that I didn't realise I'd been carrying until now- eased with every passing moment. The woman who had driven up-country through the night from the South only a day ago seemed like a complete stranger to me suddenly. I stood, and let that feeling sink in. Was it possible that I'd been looking at this whole thing all wrong? That Tim had actually done me a service by letting me go? He had cut the rope that moored me, and now I was adrift, and there came a sudden, unexpected freedom with that.

Freedom. When was the last time I could say I had felt truly free?

This thought was so profound it rocked me to the core. I'd been thinking of my separation in all the wrong ways. Here I was, on the Island in the moonlight with music playing all around, my friend and lover by my side, and nothing and nobody to tell me what to do next.

Matthew pulled himself up to stand next to me, breathing heavily, and I was overwhelmed then, overwhelmed with the desire to act, to do something reckless, to share my newfound freedom with another.

And so I kissed him, suddenly and forcefully, in the dark. I grabbed him and kissed him as if I were a teenager once again, and, after a moment, he responded. We stood like that for some time, locked together by my need, by his longing, and I began to think back to the Christmas party. To the feelings that night had given birth to, feelings I'd repressed for years ever since.

Everything happens for a reason, my mother used to say.

We came up for air. Then, I took his hand, and led him towards the music.

A thin path took us across the roof of the

cave and over piles of slabbed rock that littered the shoreline. The path then forked, one branch leading down to a small, man-made spit of boulders that stuck out from the body of the Island like a long, thin proboscis. This was illuminated by lanterns that hung from poles jabbed firmly in amongst the rocks. Later, I would learn the Gaelic name for this spit, *Sròn a' Mhoil,* the word *sròn* translating rather literally to 'nose' or 'trunk'.

There were three small row boats moored to the 'nose', with what looked like fishing nets and a lobster pot bundled inside the largest.

'Boats,' I said to Matthew, pointing. He nodded, and seemed nervous. The lanterns and boats were a reminder that we were not alone.

The other path forked away from the spit, and travelled inland. I traced its route with my eyes, found what looked like an old shepherd's hut sitting just beyond the spit, roofless, long abandoned. Behind it, a dark rise of mossy, boggy land came to an abrupt stop.

I let out a small exclamation.

Looming beyond was a wall of skinny, spindly, white-trunked trees. These were the pine trees I'd seen from the mainland.

Up close, they were an arresting sight.

They rose high above the Island like giant needles, almost piercing the stars with shimmering spines that sprouted from the very tops of the trunks like porcupine quills.

'Well, would you look at that,' Matthew breathed, and I nodded in agreement.

'I am,' I said.

The trunks were unusually white, whiter even than silver birch trunks, as if each tree had been given a fresh coat of brilliant, snowy paint. They made for an eerie display in their massed uniformity, and looking at them for too long made me feel nervous. They stood so still, so straight. Trees usually swayed, moved about, branches and leaves in constant motion. These trees were different. Untouched, somehow, by the atmosphere around them.

'They circle the whole Island, by the looks of it,' Matthew observed, and from what I could see, he was right. The trees made a large dense ring around the Island's interior, screening it off completely from the world outside. They had to have been planted that way deliberately, for the sole purpose of privacy.

The drum beat returned, momentarily surging up from behind the pines, and I felt a distinct tug on the threads. The hooks sank in, deeper.

I pointed my torch to the stand of pines, and squeezed Matthew's hand. 'That way,' I said. 'Look, this other path goes right in through the trees.'

He resisted, sounding tired.

'Do we have to? Really?'

'We do,' I said, simply.

We took the smaller path, treading carefully. I kept a hold of Matthew's hand, marvelling at how much stronger I felt with his fingers laced through mine.

'Megs,' he said, interrupting my thoughts with a hushed whisper.

'Yeah?'

'There's a sign, look.'

I trained the torch to where he pointed, and saw a large, white metal sign held up by thin iron legs that were concreted into the ground. The signboard had rusted considerably, but the text was still clear and bold, printed in red capital letters.

It said:

GRUINARD ISLAND

THIS ISLAND IS GOVERNMENT
PROPERTY AND UNDER EXPERIMENT

THE GROUND IS CONTAMINATED
WITH ANTHRAX AND DANGEROUS.
LANDING IS PROHIBITED

BY ORDER 1989

I recognised it immediately, and stared at it in confusion.

I had seen this sign, this exact same sign, in my nightmare.

I had stubbed my toe on a half-buried

lump of concrete on a beach. It had been attached to a rusted metal placard, just like this one. There had been only one word visible upon it: PROHIBITED, stamped in large, red capital letters.

It was the same sign.

I worked my mouth, speechless. This sign, the crystal in my hand. What else from that awful, awful dream was going to find its way across the boundaries of reality and into the waking world?

In my memory, a great, long-legged beast strode across the beach towards me, and I felt cold.

'Matthew,' I whispered, but didn't get to finish the sentence, because Matthew was having a miniature meltdown beside me.

'Shit,' he said, and then *'Shit!'* Panic took hold of his voice.

'What? What is it?'

'What is it?! Didn't you read the sign?'

I shook my head. I'd been so busy worrying about the dream that I'd forgotten to actually take in the words printed on the sign. I read it again.

THE GROUND IS CONTAMINATED
WITH ANTHRAX AND DANGEROUS.

'Oh,' I said then, faintly.

'You know what this place is, don't you?' Matthew scrubbed his hands over his face and through his hair, subconsciously dry washing himself like a rat as he struggled to articulate what had upset him so much.

Our earlier conversation came back to me: *Military... testing... bioweapons... NATO...*

I couldn't quite fit the pieces together, but I didn't have to. Matthew did it for me.

'This is Anthrax fucking Island,' he said. Then he took a hold of my arm, wheeled about, and marched us right back up the path down which we'd come, walking as fast as his legs would carry him.

13. THE BOY

I let myself be hustled for a minute or two, pre-occupied by another memory from the dream: a cloud of brown mist drifting over an unreal ocean where roofs poked out of the surf like turtle shells. A mist that seemed to hang like a swarm of insects in the air before suddenly dispersing.

Anthrax?

Then, I came back into myself, and put the brakes on. I felt that quick, fierce anger flare at Matthew. He was doing it again. Manhandling me.

'Where are you going?' I snapped irritably, and wrenched my arm free of his overprotective grip.

He spun, and his own temper flared.

'Are you serious? Away from Anthrax fucking Island, that's where!' He was shouting, now, the generous limits of his patience well and truly surpassed. 'You know, where the government dropped a shit-ton of deadly anthrax spores during World War Two?' He then clamped his sleeve over his mouth and nose in a vain attempt to block out any poisonous, microscopic spores that might still, after all this time, be floating around in the air.

Sheep bones, I thought, and the skeletal remains in the cave made sense, now. There had been an awful lot of them.

'I can't leave, Matthew,' I said, and a note of desperation made its way into my voice.

'What?'

'And I think it's a bit late for that,' I continued, pointing to his makeshift face mask.

My observation did not go down well, and Matthew erupted.

'What is wrong with you, Megs?! What the fuck is going *on* with you?'

'Come on Matthew,' I said, trying to appeal to his sense of reason. 'World War Two was a long time ago, now. And if there *were* any spores left in the atmosphere, we would have breathed them in already, so there's not much point in covering your face. We're dead already, by your logic.' I tried to peel his hand away from his mouth, but he reared back, furious.

'You're unbelievable, Megan! I drove nearly six hundred fucking miles to come and make sure you were okay, to check on you after Tim threw you out, and this is what I get. A wild fucking goose chase in the middle of the night through a sodding, endless tunnel to an abandoned military experiment riddled with a deadly toxin that will probably kill us both in less than a week!' His chest heaved with emotion, and triggered my own ire. I lashed out in response.

'I didn't ask you to come, Matthew! I didn't ask you to come and find me! In fact, I think it would have been fairly obvious to anyone except you that I needed some privacy! That maybe, just maybe, I wanted to let the dust settle on my previous relationship before launching straight into the next one!'

That hurt him, I could tell. 'I came because I care about you,' he replied, sullenly.

And I found that I was mad, then, really, really mad. I had business on the Island, and this nonsense was just getting in the way.

'I know you care about me, I *know* you do! And I care about you too! But driving up here, uninvited, without even asking me what I wanted...can't you see how...how *selfish* that was?'

'I would have asked, but your phone didn't work!'

I threw my hands up, exasperated. 'I won't even start on how you went about finding my new phone number, that's beside the point. We both know it wouldn't have mattered if you *had* called. If I *had* told you to stay away. You would have come anyway.'

'Because I *love you!*' He shouted at me, finally lifting his sleeve away from his mouth.

The anguished words hung in the air, and I swallowed back tears. We were both silent for a moment, giving the words the space they deserved.

Then, I spoke.

'I love you too, Matthew.'

He stilled. I continued.

'I do. I love you.'

I placed a gentle hand on his face to reinforce the point.

'But right now, I have something I have to do. Can you try and understand that? I don't know what it is, I don't know what I'm doing here, but I do know that I have something to do, something really, really important. My house is connected to this place by a goddamned tunnel, Matthew! That has to mean something.'

The fight went out of him.

'You love me?' He asked, and at that moment he was so vulnerable that I regretted everything. I regretted my treatment of him over the years. I regretted the wasted time with Tim. I regretted it all. I had been an idiot.

And then a new voice came out of the tree line behind us.

A young voice. Boyish. Cheerful.

'It's not contaminated anymore, you know,' it said, and Matthew and I both started, in shock.

'Who's there?' Matthew cried.

'You shouldn't be here. It's private land,' the voice continued, and now it was accompanied by a shape. A small, slender shape, emerging from the dense shadows between the pines. He held an old-fashioned miner's lantern up before him, made of polished brass. A lit wick glowed blue inside.

He must have been cloaking the light with something, I wondered, *else we would have seen him before.*

It was a boy, maybe six or seven years of age. Standing bold as brass on the Island in the middle of the night, unafraid, unassuming, just a small boy out for a stroll through the shadows when all small boys should be asleep.

'Who are you?' I said, completely flummoxed.

Matthew stared at the boy as if he were an alien. 'And what are you doing out here in the middle of the night?! Shit, could this situation get any stranger? I feel as if I've been drugged!'

'I live here,' the boy said, speaking to Matthew as if he were an idiot.

'You live here? On this Island?'

'Of course. It's my home.' The boy smiled, his voice excited, conspiratorial. 'We don't get visitors a lot. Mac doesn't like it. If he sees you, he'll be very cross.'

'Who is Mac?' I looked around, expecting someone else to emerge from the tree line any moment. Matthew tugged on my shirt, also scanning the woods.

'Enough, Megs,' he muttered grimly. 'We

should go. Now.'

But I wasn't done yet. The Island still had its hooks in me. I resisted.

'Who is Mac?' I repeated, more gently this time. The boy was very young.

The boy shook his head. 'Never mind,' he said, and then he came forward a little further, until he was standing right in front of us. Up close, I could see a thatch of straight, dark hair. His lantern cast deep shadows under his eyebrows and across his top lip, but for all that, he had a thin, happy face, clear skin, and a pleasant demeanour.

And he looked familiar, somehow, although I knew that to be impossible.

The boy grinned up at me, and something silent passed between us. Something unspoken and powerful. I don't believe either of us were conscious of it, but it felt very much as it had felt when I had first climbed out of the van and set eyes upon *Taigh-Faire*.

It felt very much as if, by looking at him, I were returning to something.

The boy saw my free hand, and reached out for it. He slid his fingers through mine as if we had been the greatest of friends for many years, and I had a crystalline moment of blinding recollection. His touch was recognised. He *was* familiar, a stranger I somehow knew, although not from my dream. I had held this boy's hand before, in the past, I was sure of it.

Or had I held it in the future?

That jolted me back to reality.

Where do these thoughts come from?! Again, it felt as if my brain were reading from a script I was not privy to. A part of me, the old, fearful Megs, wanted to pull free, the feeling of his palm and fingers against mine too much, too disruptive. The boy had other ideas. He held fast, his face earnest in the lantern-shine.

'Do you want to come to a party?' He said, the invitation falling from his lips sweetly, casually.

And I knew who was really speaking to me through the boy.

It was the Island, coaxing me in.

As if on cue, the music rose around us like a sudden tide. I felt it wrap around my body, trickle down my ears and throat, fill me up with cold, sweet longing.

And I found that I did. I *did* want to go to a party.

Because the Island would have it that way.

14. A PLACE CALLED WHITE PINES

The Island, however, cared little for Matthew, and he for it.

'Oh, no. No, no, no *thank* you!' He shook his head vehemently, and made once more as if to leave. 'It's a nice thought, kid, but no. We're leaving now. Megs, let's go. Please.'

The boy gazed at him. 'But it's a special occasion,' he said, his face falling in disappointment.

Meanwhile the music, so sweet, *so* sweet, had found its way inside my skull. Matthew couldn't see this, he couldn't hear it like I could. He *could* see my hesitation, and tried to break the spell by waving a hand in front of my face.

'Megs, come *on*,' he said, exasperated. 'We're done here. Let's go back, please. I'm begging you. I don't like this.' He sneezed, twice, and groaned.

I heard him distantly, as if through a far-away speaker. Objectively, I knew he was right. This place was strange, and this boy was strange, and we should have turned back hours ago, but what would he have me do? There were too many threads, too many hooks, and I was help-lessly bound.

No turning back, a voice whispered inside of me as the music continued to play. *You are exactly where you are supposed to be, and you know it.*

I looked down at my hand, intertwined with the hand of a young boy I somehow recog-nised and yet didn't. Whatever my business was here, this boy was a part of it, that much was clear to me.

I smiled at him, and he smiled back.

'Take me through the trees,' I whispered.

And, upon accepting the invitation, I felt the Island shudder.

The faintest of tremors, but yes. It was there. A ripple, a shifting of the earth, strong enough that I felt it through the soles of my boots, strong enough to shake the pine trees that waited up ahead. The pale trunks convulsed in a sudden, anticipatory ripple of motion. I saw a light shower of needles fall to the ground like rain, and Matthew covered his head reflexively.

Then the boy and I stepped out together towards the trembling pines, and I left Matthew no choice, really. He could come with us, or return to *Taigh-Faire* on his own, defeated. I knew I was behaving irrationally, I knew I was being unfair.

But my body was no longer under my own control.

I answered the Island's call, and Matthew, to his credit, did what I thought he would.

He followed me.

We crossed the tree line, and the stand of pine trees swallowed us whole.

It grew instantly quiet around us. The effect was startling: the music cut out suddenly, completely, and all that was left was a pillowy sort of quiet that pressed down upon my ear drums.

The path continued straight as an arrow through the wooded boundary. It was lit by more small lanterns that dangled from thin metal poles thrust into the ground. Candles flickered behind the glass of these lanterns, casting just enough light to see the ranks of white tree trunks clustered tightly all about us. And it was difficult to wrap my mind around, even in my current state: that so many trees could exist in such uniform perfection on what was, ostensibly, a small land mass that couldn't be more than a mile long by a mile wide. Because there had to be *thousands* of them, stretching out in each direction as far as I could see until the darkness took over, and I knew that the dimensions of this place were all wrong. The scale of the forest didn't work with the actual limitations of the land. I felt that we had been walking long enough that we should have crossed the Island and been standing on the opposite shore, staring out at the sea, and not much else.

Instead, there were just more trees. And so strange, so tall, so unnaturally straight, with that flawless, white bark and those spindly arms located way up at the very top. Otherworldly. Ghost trees.

I called out to Matthew over my shoulder, keeping my voice low, because it felt disrespectful to do otherwise.

'The trees...are they indigenous, do you think?'

Matthew glared at me, his booted feet kicking up a dense curd of pine needles as he walked. He still half-heartedly struggled to keep a hand over his mouth and nose, although he had to remove it periodically to keep his balance on the path, where tree roots and rocks made things awkward. 'Plants are not really my thing, Megs,' he muttered, savagely. 'Foreign policy is my thing. International trade agreements, at a push. The finer points of punctuation and the correct way to employ the Oxford comma. Unrequited love, pointless candle carrying. Not fucking trees.'

GEMMA AMOR

'It's just the colour of the tree trunks...they are so *white*,' I answered, ignoring his bad temper and hubris and reaching out to touch one, and then snatching my hand back at the last moment.

Because in another place, there grew a cherry tree in a bubble of glass, with a stone face nestled into the roots, and I knew now that the power of one single touch could be catastrophic, especially when you didn't understand the rules of engagement.

Hands to yourself, Megs, I thought, and another errant memory of myself with Matthew at the Christmas party flashed across my mind, skin on skin and breath on breath. 'Hands to yourself,' I had told him, right before we got down to it, but it had been a joke, a gentle, teasing challenge. I bit back a wild, bubbling laugh. I could not find a footing at all, emotionally. It was like someone else was sitting inside my brain, idly flipping through different feelings and memories without being able to settle on any one moment, or state.

I tried to make conversation with the boy, to distract myself.

'Other people live here with you? On this Island?'

The boy nodded. 'Oh, yes.'

'Behind these trees?

'Uh-huh.'

'You know, I can see this Island from my

house on the mainland, but I couldn't see any signs of you. Not even any smoke.'

The boy shrugged. 'Oh, we aren't allowed to mix with people on the mainland, not usually. Mac says we are...we are...' He stuttered, trying to find the word.

'A cult?' Matthew's voice needled us from the rear.

The boy remained oblivious to his sarcasm.

'No, silly. Self-sufficient!'

'And no-one gets sick?' I asked, voice dreamy and preoccupied. I wasn't asking for myself. I didn't care about the anthrax. I was asking so that Matthew would stop worrying about it.

'Oh, no,' The boy swung my hand about as we walked. 'Mac says that the government made everything safe again. It has been safe since 1990. When the town was founded.' He had the air of a boy reciting something from a school lesson. In his enthusiasm, he sped up, eager to move faster. 'That's what the party is for!'

'An anniversary?'

'Aye, of when our town was born!'

'The town?' I had imagined a collection of tents, or huts, a cottage or two maybe, like the ruined shepherd's hut near the spit. Not a town. The Island wasn't big enough for that. The boy must be exaggerating.

'Yes!' The boy said, exasperated at my inability to grasp his circumstances. 'The town!

My town!'

And the woodland cleared, then, in the same way it had arrived overhead: so suddenly that I was not prepared. One moment there were trees all around, the next, a bright moon shone down upon us, as if curtains had been thrown open to let the night back in. It illuminated the white tree trunks, and I could see they made a large, bright, surreal circle that stretched out before us, within which we now stood, tiny, insignificant, off to one side.

And the space inside the trees was enormous.

Too enormous. The Island was only a mile wide by maybe a mile long, at most. This space was easily double, if not triple that in size, a generous expanse of scrubland and sandstone which sloped up gently towards a central rise, capped by a bare sandstone summit. On that summit, a large, cone-shaped pile of stones stood proud, like a miniature mountain. On top of that, a tiny light flickered.

And, clinging to the slope beneath the summit, was a town.

Music returned, hitting me like a bat to the face, frenetic, loud, driven by a fast and relentless drum beat, and a million other sounds and scents made themselves known: people laughing, talking, children screaming, a dog barking, other animal noises, the unmistakable clattering of plates and cutlery, the chink of glass on glass, the smell of wood smoke, and of meat cooking, and other things I couldn't quite place. It was a vast, swirling whirlpool of noise, and light, and colour, and movement, and all of it sat in the space inside the pine trees, as if the Island were an eye, the trees an iris, and this was the pupil, the very centre of it all.

A whole town.

'Well, shit,' said Matthew.

'Well, shit,' I said, in complete and absolute agreement.

The boy grinned at us in pleasure.

'How is this possible?' Matthew scrubbed his hands through his hair once again in disbelief.

I knew what he meant. There were *hundreds* of people milling around out there, maybe even a thousand, and a comprehensive infrastructure in place around them. I saw a chapel, tiny, with a small bell tower on the roof, and an iron cross on top of that. Below it, row upon row of simple stone houses stood resolute before us, no bigger than one-up, one-down. They were built close together to form tidy, neat streets. Dark, slate-tiled roofs capped each abode. There were chimneys on top of those roofs, and I asked myself again: why hadn't I been able to see smoke from the mainland?

Matthew pointed, and I saw a pig pen, where three large pink beasts rootled around in the shadows. Beyond, lay what looked like several vegetable patches, although it was hard to tell from where we stood, which was some distance away. A cluster of fruit trees were planted off to one side of the vegetable gardens, and I could see wheelbarrows propped under the trees.

Self-sufficient, the boy had said, and I understood what he meant now. Across from the pigs and vegetable patches stood a building with a red cross painted on the side. A surgery, or hospital, maybe. Tiny but functional. Near that, there was a long, low structure that could have been a town hall, or market hall of sorts. I saw a series of storehouses next to it, open-sided, crammed with smoked meat, dried fish, barrels, poultry, root vegetables, bags of grain and other things hidden by the poor light. Beyond, more animal shelters with pens, for chickens, sheep and small, blunt-horned goats.

These buildings all radiated out in a spider-like pattern from the epicentre of a small town square. In the centre of the square, an old-fashioned cast iron water pump sprouted, with an ancient stone bench placed next to it, upon which a row of old men sat smoking and drinking from old-fashioned beakers. Set up around each of the square's edges were rows of tables, stools, barrels and lanterns. Bunting hung above all of this, a gay procession of little coloured flags that ran around the square's perimeter.

And there were people everywhere. Dancing, singing, laughing, embracing each other, drinking, eating.

This was where the party was happening.

'What is this place?' I said to the boy, and as I said it, I felt the thundering train of fate stop dead at my feet, a hair's breadth away from my face. There was a moment, where I waited for his reply, teetering on the edge of that great chasm I'd been flirting with for what felt like an age. In that moment, all I could hear was my blood pounding in my ears.

The boy smiled proudly, and pointed to a painted wooden sign hammered into the ground a little way off.

It said, simply:

WELCOME TO WHITE PINES.

And I knew, at last, why I was here.
It was the town.

15. PARTY

I let it all sink in for a moment.

So many. So many people, cavorting around the main square of this idyllic, neatly organised stone-built town without a care in the world. And they all lived here, on this Island. In a town that by all laws of physics and practicality, shouldn't fit into the small, yet somehow huge, space amongst the pine trees. Like that fairytale world of snow and ice in the back of the wardrobe, or the land filled with Cheshire-cat smiles only found through a looking glass. A hidden, unexpected place, full of wonder.

White Pines.

I wondered then. Did Fiona and the other mainlanders know about this place? Could that explain her hostility towards the Island?

'Come *on*,' said the boy, impatiently, shaking me out of my stupor. He began to walk eagerly towards the party, desperate to show us where he lived.

Matthew made a grab for me. 'Megs!' He hissed.

I had grown adept at avoiding his hands. I stared at him, unimpressed. 'Please stop doing that,' I said, wearily.

'Just think for a moment, would you?' He was back in protective mode. 'We can't go in there, we're total strangers! We haven't been invited. It's one thing to crash a party, Megs, but none of this feels right. I'm tired. It's late. I want to go back.'

'But...' I gestured to White Pines. '*Look* at it, Matthew. It's...incredible.'

His mouth pressed into a hard, thin line.

'And what about this Mac character?' He asked, glaring at the boy, who was trying to hustle us along, bored by our hesitancy. 'We can't just walk into that lot uninvited in the middle of the night, we'll be lynched!'

I decided to try logic, because at this point, Matthew was beyond reason. I'd pushed him too far.

'Matthew. What's the worst that could actually happen?' I asked, as gently as I could.

'This is not what I came for, Megs,' he said, frustration running through his entire frame. 'I came...I came for *you*.'

'I already told you I loved you, Matthew. What more do you want from me, right now? At this moment?'

'Isn't it obvious?!' He cried.

I shook my head, and turned silently on my heel, and followed the boy.

'God on a fucking biscuit!' I heard him say, and I didn't have to look to know that he was following us up-slope, towards the party.

His fears appeared to be unfounded. We came to the square and the boy cut a path for us around the edge of it, skirting alongside the throngs of people gathered. We attracted a few glances, a few stares, but no-one challenged us outright. A few people frowned and made as if to come over, but we kept moving quickly. The citizens of White Pines were too concerned with having a good time to worry much about outsiders in their midst.

And having a good time they were, with joy riding thick and palpable in the air. People jigged and swayed and tapped their feet together, toasted each other with beakers of dark liquid, and twirled each other around in glee. The music had hit its stride, and was thundering along like an approaching train. I saw four musicians near the water-pump, two sawing at strings, and one hammering at an ancient, tattered drum kit. There was a piper too. The sounds he coaxed from the pipes under his armpit were extraordinary, as if he had a bag of souls in his hands instead of air, and each note was a different voice singing their own, distinct song. It was so arresting that I paused to watch as he played, keeping close to the edge of the square so as not to be conspicuous. He was completely lost in the music, cheeks puffed out, his foot stamping a fierce beat upon the ground. Sweat ran down his face and into his thick beard.

The boy, who had gone ahead a little, realised I was no longer following, and doubled back to see what was taking me so long. I ignored him, mesmerised by the piper and his call.

The tempo shifted up a notch. The piper unhooked the pipes from under his arm, set them down, and scooped up a long metal flute. Swaying with rhythm, I watched as his fingers flew up and down the instrument, and then, as I was staring right at him, he disappeared.

One second he was there, the next...not.

The sound of the pipes cut out abruptly, and yet no-one else seemed to notice. The strings kept sawing, the drum kept beating. The people of White Pines danced on, and I began to question my own sanity.

A split second later, and the piper was there once again, switching instruments, hands returning to work the chanter of his pipes furiously, the sound of wailing reeds making a mockery of my thoughts.

Fuck, I thought, reeling.

The piper caught my eye, and gave me a funny look.

Maybe I'm brain-damaged, I continued, arguing with myself internally as people danced and jigged around me. I shook my head as if to clear water from my ears.

Maybe I have a tumour, or I hit my head and

didn't realise, and that's why things keep disappearing on me. It would explain the headaches, the nightmare. Maybe it has nothing to do with the Island, after all. Maybe I'm just sick.

Perhaps that's why Tim replaced me, I wondered then.

Maybe he could smell it on you, the sickness.

They say men leave when their wives grow ill.

It was an absurd and incredibly unkind thought, even for a wife scorned, which I wasn't, really. We had grown apart, that was all. He had fallen for someone else. And so had I, although I hadn't been willing to admit it to myself. Playing the victim in all this was far easier.

And even if I was sick, it still wouldn't explain the tunnel under my house, the one that led right here. It wouldn't explain the dead dog either, or the giant deer stuck underground, or the capstone in my cellar, and the symbol that glowed when I pressed my hand into it.

It wouldn't explain the sign that I had seen in my dream, the one that stood real and proud outside this circle of trees, a faded warning, unheeded.

It wouldn't explain the anomalies of space that this town presented.

The boy looked up at me quizzically, and I felt Matthew come to a rest behind me. Both of them were wondering what was wrong with me. I continued to gaze at the piper, who eventually averted his eyes.

My mother used to say that in difficult times, when confusing situations arose and it was hard to see a clear path to the truth, the simplest explanation was often the most likely. I had already bitten myself once to see if I was still dreaming. I didn't fancy repeating the experiment, and so, the only thing left to do was to accept the fact that I was awake.

Which meant accepting that the man playing the bagpipes had disappeared, momentarily, into thin air.

Accepting this also meant accepting other things. Like a crystal in my pocket. A god beneath a tree.

A giant man.

A beach where death littered the shoreline.

Could any of it be real? It went against everything I had come to believe was possible over the course of my life. And yet here I stood, in the middle of a town that shouldn't be here at all.

'Megs?' Matthew sounded worried. I shook myself. I needed to move on, before I attracted too much attention to us.

I nodded, and the boy led us on.

I realised how long it had been since I had eaten anything when I smelt roasting meat, and spotted a lamb on a spit. Wooden barrels stood on trestles next to the spit, crude taps hammered into the end. People clutched more of those chunky, robust beakers, and decanted brown, rich-smelling liquid out of the barrels. Thick blue smoke hung in the air, blending with the cooked meat smoke. I saw several of the older men of the community puffing on long, curled clay pipes. This reminded me of the smoke that had risen from Murdo's cigarette, back when I had first met him on the road to Laide. Back when his murderous dog had still been alive.

Don't think about that now, I warned myself, but a little bloom of crimson popped into my mind nonetheless.

We made our way along the outside of the square, occasionally bumping into people and apologising whilst trying to be as unremarkable as possible. At one point, a drunk woman crashed into us, righted herself, threw her arms around Matthew, kissed him soundly on the cheek, then danced away. He flinched as if he'd been shot.

I started to sweat, and swallowed, feeling a little unsteady on my feet. Seasick, almost. The music was starting to get to me. There was so much colour, and movement, so much revelry. And beneath it all, there was an undercurrent of something. Something indefinable, unsettling. The closer to the centre of the Island we got, and the closer to the steep sandstone summit in the middle of the circle of trees, the more I felt it.

We finally made it to the far edge of the square, and the crowds thinned out immediately. The boy pulled us into one of the narrow streets along which thirty or so stone houses were lined up like dominoes, and began skipping cheerfully along it, a particular destination obviously in his mind.

'Where are we going?' I asked him, breathlessly trying to keep up, and he pointed to the furthest house on the street.

'I want to show you where I live!' He said, and Matthew and I exchanged glances.

'Okay,' I replied. Matthew kept silent.

Up close, the Island dwellings were impressive examples of building design and craftsmanship. Simple and solid, they were constructed from thick stone blocks topped with slate shingle roofs, each shingle tightly laid to keep out the weather. They had thick walls, to help trap heat, and small windows. Each house had a sturdy, brightly painted front door made from solid, smoothly planed wood. These were topped by thick stone lintels like the one over my own front door at *Taigh-Faire,* but there were no triangular symbols, not here.

Impressed, I finally caught up with the boy, who had paused to retie a loose shoelace. 'These houses are beautiful,' I said, and I meant it. The stonework was accomplished and attractive, and each house slotted tidily alongside its neighbour in the way that houses in military barracks are slotted together: to conserve space, and to foster a sense of unity, of belonging to something.

'Mac and my Daddy designed them together,' the boy said, puffed-up-proud in that way that children are of their parents' achievements. 'We all helped to build them. The whole community, although Mac says there weren't as many of us back then, and I was just a baby so I don't remember it.'

I nodded, and then thought of something. 'Were the trees here when you built this place?' Why I was asking a child this, I didn't know, but I had this nagging, unshakeable urge to know more about the trees.

'Oh, we planted those too. Mac had them sent over from America!'

This answer only gave rise to many, many more questions. I opened my mouth to ask the next one, when the boy interrupted me.

'We're here!' He said, and suddenly he was pushing open a bottle-green door.

'I'll wait outside,' Matthew said, and I sighed.

'Whatever makes you happy,' I replied, as neutrally as I could, and followed the boy into his home.

The door gave way immediately to a small, smoky kitchen, with a large wooden table taking up most of the space inside. At that table a woman stood, hastily plucking a chicken carcass and throwing the feathers into a basket on the floor next to her feet. Engrossed in her work, she didn't see me at first.

'Where have you been?' She asked, crossly, yanking another fistful of straggled feathers out. 'I need help running more ale down to the square, you know I can't manage that wheel-barrow on my...'

She looked up and tailed off as I came in, stooping so as not to hit my head on the low door lintel. Her shock at seeing me was as profound as mine was on discovering the house wasn't empty. I came up short, and the woman's face went pale- with fear, or anger, I couldn't tell.

'Hello, Ma!' The boy said, pleased with himself and oblivious to the mood. 'I found some people outside the trees!'

Ma, an attractive woman in her forties with a mass of dark brown hair pinned to the back of her head, dropped the chicken to the tabletop, and frantically wiped her hands on the rough apron she wore.

I cleared my throat, apologetically. 'Hello,' I said, and the woman's eyes blazed at me.

'What are you *doing* here?!' She hissed. 'You can't be here, especially not tonight!'

Matthew chose that moment to change his mind. He came into the house behind me, sensing trouble.

'Miss, I'm so sorry,' he said, from over my shoulder. 'I've been trying to tell them-'

'There's *two* of you?' She rounded furiously on her son. 'What are you *thinking*, Luke? Bringing strangers here? On Anniversary Night?!'

I realised that I had never even asked the boy I knew-yet-somehow-didn't his name. Luke.

Luke whined, face reddening.

'They were outside the trees, Ma, I told you! They looked lost, and I found them. She seems nice.' He gestured at me, and I fought back a small smile. The boy turned up the charm and gazed up at his mother with wide eyes.

'I was just trying to be nice. I thought they'd like to come to the party!'

Luke's Mother cuffed him upside the head, not too hard, but hard enough to let him know he'd behaved badly.

'You are an idiot boy!' She scolded. 'Mac will skin you alive if he sees them here! He will skin *me* alive, too!'

'I'm sorry, Ma.' Luke hung his head, and his lip wobbled. My heart turned over for him. I never liked to see children cry.

The woman glared at him. 'I'll deal with you later, laddie,' she said, darkly, and turned to us again with a pursed mouth, thinking.

'We don't like mainlanders here,' she said, eventually. She spoke as if we were naughty children, too. 'How did you even *get* here? Did you swim? Bloody tourists!' She swore under her breath. I didn't need to know Gaelic to understand that it was an uncomplimentary word aimed at our stupidity.

'Well...' I took a deep breath, but she cut me off, holding up a hand.

'Never mind, I don't want to know. However you got here, you have to leave. We don't allow strangers on the Island.'

'This place...this town...' I swallowed, at a loss for words. 'It's incredible.'

The woman ignored me. 'I won't tell anyone you were here,' she said, 'But you have to leave. Now.'

I nodded. 'Okay,' I replied, disappointed. I had been brought here for a purpose, and now I was being sent away before I could figure out what that purpose was. But this woman was adamant, and our presence made her uncomfortable. I sensed she was afraid of Mac, whoever he was, and I didn't have any desire to bring trouble down upon the head of a complete stranger. We were, as Matthew had pointed out earlier, trespassing. I sighed. Maybe I could come back another time, when there wasn't a party. Maybe the community would let me stay a little longer then. After all, I wasn't just any mainlander. There was a tunnel leading to this place from my house. The Island and I were connected. Surely that had to mean something.

'Okay, we'll leave.' I put my hands up in

a placatory gesture, and looked at Matthew. He rolled his eyes in relief.

'Listen, you don't understand,' the woman said, her tone softening as she tried to explain. 'I'm not being unfriendly. It's just...well, we have rules in this community. And the last time we had trespassers here, it didn't end well. We have an agreement with the mainland. Of sorts. They don't like us, and we don't like them. So we keep to ourselves. It's better that way. We're not hurting anyone here. We're just living peacefully, self-sustained, do you understand? We don't want any more trouble.'

'What kind of trouble?' Matthew too had begun to sweat. The small house was warm, and it felt very crowded with us all in the same space. Behind him, hung on the wall, a crudely framed mirror stretched floor to ceiling, a clever way of amplifying the narrow window light in an otherwise dark and stuffy room. I could see Matthew's reflection in the mirror, the side of his face. It was lined with stress.

His reflection flickered.

Like the piper.

Like a candle flame, so that he was half-there, half-not.

Then, as I watched, his profile disappeared completely, and I stared at the mirror in horror, not knowing what I was seeing, or what was happening. A second or two later, and he flickered back into existence, frowning and pinch-mouthed with strain.

I put a hand out and touched Matthew experimentally. He felt solid. Real. He looked at me, noticing my face, which must have been pale.

'What?' He muttered, and I couldn't think of anything to say.

Luke, unaware of any of this, pulled on his Ma's apron, pleading.

'Ma, can they at least have a drink to take with them? Try some of Dad's beer?'

Luke was a kind boy.

His mother sighed, and put her bloody hands on her hips, downy chicken feathers still glued to them. 'It might help you to blend in more, I suppose,' she said, with reluctance. 'I'm amazed you made it this far without being caught.' Then she whipped an arm back out, aiming for Luke's head once again.

'And I'm still furious with you, child!'

The boy ducked, avoided a second cuff to the ear, and collected two chunky beakers from a nearby stone sink. There was a small barrel like the larger ones in the square standing under the kitchen table. He filled each beaker with a thick, brown ale, then handed them to us. I accepted mine with a nod of thanks, still staring at Matthew intently, in case he vanished again. Unaware of my scrutiny, he shook his head.

'How do I know it's really beer?' He asked, suspiciously.

Luke's mother levelled him with a single, flat look.

'We're a community, not a cult,' she said, her voice level. Matthew had the grace to look embarrassed. He took a sip of his beer by way of apology, and a begrudging expression of enjoyment came over his face.

Luke's mother watched this, and opened her mouth to say something, then changed her mind and snapped it shut again. Then, she waved us away.

'Bugger off, before you're caught,' she said.

'Thank you for this.' I held up the beaker. I didn't feel like drinking, I felt like the world was slipping sideways. But I thanked her anyway. I wanted her to like me.

I wanted to be able to come back.

The woman marched around the table to the front door, and held it open for us. She was done being polite. She wanted us gone.

'Keep out of sight. You can leave via a different path, it'll be safer. It goes up behind the càrn.' She pointed in the direction of the mound that rose above the town. 'As long as you stay quiet, and low. You hear me?'

'The what?'

She pointed again to the summit that rose above the town, which was wreathed in shadow, except for that single solitary light on top. 'Càrn. Cairn,' she said. 'On the summit. It's called *An*

Eilid.' Then her voice grew softer.

'Take my blessing, if you're going up that way. *Cuiridh mi clach air do chàrn.*'

'What does that mean?' I asked, taken aback by the sudden emotion on display.

She pointed once again at the cairn. 'I'll put a stone on your stone,' she said, then pushed us out the door, and into the street, with no further explanation.

I managed to wave quickly at Luke before the door slammed shut, and he waved back, looking forlorn.

Then, we were alone again.

'Why is everyone around here so bloody enigmatic?' Matthew complained, sipping at his beer and obviously still enjoying it despite himself. I stared at him and sank deep into thought. I hadn't imagined it. I knew I hadn't. I'd seen him disappear, right in front of my eyes. The same as the piper in the square.

As if reality had thinned out for a second.

The simplest explanation is often the best, I recalled.

It didn't help that people in these parts spoke in riddles. It was starting to get to me. Fiona had been the same way, back at the Post Office in Laide. Like she was holding onto a great secret, one I was not allowed to know. As if you had to be a member of a special society or a club to fully understand what was being said, what was going on.

'Why do you keep looking at me like that?' Matthew asked suddenly, rousing me from my study.

I can't get a clear picture, I thought, eyes sliding away and staring over Matthew's shoulder, instead. I fixed onto a beautifully painted shiny red door on a house near Luke's.

This place, the people in Laide, and the tunnel beneath my house...the dream...so many puzzle pieces, yet none of them fit together.

'Megs? What's going on? You keep...disappearing off somewhere.'

I blinked. 'Can you do me a favour?' I asked, feeling hazy.

'What?'

'Pinch me. Really, really hard.'

'What? Whatever for?'

'Just do it.' I held out my arm. 'As hard as you can.'

He shook his head, then half-heartedly pinched the skin of my upper arm.

'Harder,' I said. 'Much harder.'

'You know, in a different situation, this would be almost kinky,' he grumbled, but he obliged, reluctantly. I could tell he was torn between hurting me and doing what I wanted. He squeezed my arm again, hard enough that it hurt, but not hard enough to bruise.

Nothing happened.

'I am still awake, aren't I?' I asked him then, doubting everything.

The sounds of the party snaked about us once more.

'We should go,' Matthew said quietly, and he looked worried.

We cut through the streets, and headed uphill towards the cairn.

16. LOVE NOT WANTED

The path that Luke's mother had spoken of ran behind the street where Luke lived. It meandered behind the rows of houses, up alongside the tiny chapel I'd spotted earlier, and around the back of it. Then it climbed up, and passed directly beneath the ancient stone pile capping the rise.

We sipped our beers as we followed the path, partly through thirst, partly because we needed some mild relief from the strangeness of everything. The ale was a rich, dark brown and tasted of hops and nuts and something else that felt familiar on the tongue. After a while I realised the flavour, which had elements of aniseed and liquorice to it, reminded me of the boiled sweets Granny had always tried to force on me whenever I saw her. If I looked around the house, would I find an old, dusty tin of those sweets stashed away in a cupboard somewhere? Probably.

Again, I wondered at my memory, which was so happy to recall the little, paper-wrapped candies I had hated, but not the Island that lay across the bay from Granny's house. Not the white trees, or the community nestling within. The important things.

Then I remembered what Luke had said. This community had only been here since 1990. Which meant the Island was uninhabited when I was a child, and probably still contaminated with anthrax. Obviously, Granny would not have brought me here if that were the case.

It also meant the trees would not have been planted, which was why I couldn't remember them. I thought about that. Like everything else, it didn't make sense. Those trees, if planted so recently, should still have been young, little more than saplings. The pines we had walked beneath were enormous, stretching high up ahead, and well-established. And there were so many of them, it was hard to believe they had all been planted by hand by a few people.

So why was I so drawn to this place? What was it that had called to me, so desperately? If I hadn't been here as a child, it couldn't be nostalgia at play. It felt wrong to be leaving the Island without an answer to this question.

We reached the base of the cairn, slightly out of breath. It was big, much bigger than I'd realised, and made of hundreds of stones, neatly stacked on top of each other into a conical shape. At the very top, someone had set a small lantern, and I was reminded of the everlasting candles that burned in churches. Matthew and I could see that the trail circled the mound of rock before heading down the other side of the slope behind it, back towards the pine trees. Once inside the tree line, it should be easy enough to find the path we had come in on, and trace our steps back to the spit, and the cave.

Matthew looked up at the pile of carefully arranged stones, and sighed.

'You know, in Mongolia, these things are called ovoos,' he said, voice neutral. 'You walk around them, like a ceremony. Make circles around the base, clockwise I think. Nice little ritual.'

'I like that,' I said. The tension between us had eased, and I was glad for it. Now that I had agreed to leave the Island, he was more relaxed, less frustrated. Or maybe it was the beer. Either way, it made life simpler.

The pile of stones loomed above us, that single lantern flickering like a pilot light on top.

'It's massive,' I said, only fully appreciating the size of the thing now that we were close to it. Like everything else here, scale and space were fluid concepts. Deceptive, tricky things. Maybe that accounted for the escalating queasiness in my belly. Or maybe it was seeing people flicker in and out of existence under my nose.

Or maybe it was simply the beer. I bit

back a slightly crazed giggle. It was strong beer, for sure.

'Perhaps there's an ancient Pictish lord or warrior lying in state beneath it,' Matthew mused. 'Wouldn't that be something?'

I had an intense flashback to my dream. To the stone god cradled by the roots of a cherry tree. A pocket of sour saliva filled up my cheeks. It stung, and I felt a cramp of discomfort in my stomach.

I turned and looked back down the slope, back past the chapel, past the ranks of stone houses spread out across the Island rise, to the town square. The party. The people. From here they looked smaller, like ants. I could hear their merriment, rising up into the night. Everyone was so happy. Everyone belonged. I envied them. I wanted to belong too.

'Can we go now?' Matthew asked.

I felt immensely weary, then, overcome by the Island, by circumstance, by confusion, by everything that had brought me here. My stomach roiled and cramped again, maybe reacting to the ale, and I sagged, then dropped down into a crouch, before finally sitting on a sprig of heather at the base of the cairn.

'I'll take that as a no,' Matthew said, dryly.

'I just want to sit here for a bit first,' I said, feeling forlorn and exhausted. 'Sit, and drink this incredibly strong, home-brewed beer, and maybe watch the stars for a moment or two, and the people down there having fun. And then we can go. Alright? It's been...' I tried to put everything I had seen and experienced that day into words, and failed. Instead, I summarised.

'It's been a long, and *very* strange day.'

'It has that.'

'And I don't feel very well.'

Concern clouded his eyes once more.

'Like...anthrax unwell?'

I shook my head vehemently. 'For heaven's sake Matthew, let it go. Look at everyone down there. Do they look sick to you? There is no anthrax left, you heard the boy. This is...this is something else.'

Unconvinced, he dry-washed his hands together in that fastidious, anxious gesture he'd developed since he'd arrived here.

'Sickness aside, you heard what the woman said, Megs. We should leave, before we get caught. That party can't go on all night, and when it is over, the locals aren't likely to be as tolerant as they've been so far.'

I nodded. 'I know. And we will. But can I just sit, just for a moment? Please?'

Matthew gave up, and joined me in silence, positioning himself to my left, just close enough that our knees brushed together.

We sat and watched the people down below. A formal dance had started in the square now, and the locals were going at it with gusto. The tune playing was 'strip the willow'. I remembered it from a childhood dance I'd been to once. It was hundreds of years old, repetitive, and easy to learn. A fun dance. Couples stood opposite each other in long, straight columns, and held hands, swirling around in a figure of eight up and down between the rows of people, exchanging partners at each turn. I found myself leaning forward as I watched them move, mesmerised by the music and the shapes the people made with their bodies. I saw patterns everywhere, then, circles and triangles and squares and a unique, geometric symmetry to everything. People moved, and left glowing trails of colour in their wake, in the same way that a plane leaves a line of cloud behind it in the sky as it flies. I rubbed my eyes, and the trails were gone. I felt so strange, so disconnected. Like I had felt in the burial ground at Laide. Had that really been me? It had felt so long ago, now.

Why was I here?

'I think about that night so often,' Matthew said suddenly.

'What?' I murmured. Shapes, lines, colours. Everyone connected, everyone tied by glowing threads.

Sacred geometry, I thought. *Everything has significance.*

We are all bound together.

Apparently it was not just the people of the Highlands who spoke in riddles.

Matthew carried on, undeterred.

'I can't stop thinking about it. How you felt, how you tasted.'

He was talking about the Christmas party.

I drained the last dregs from my beaker. Another cramp hit me, hard, and I winced in pain. I reached out to place a steadying hand on Matthew's shoulder, because I felt, even though I was sitting down, like I might fall over.

He took my touch for affection, and watched the people dancing, looked at the patterns they made with their bodies. Did he see them too? Shapes in the night. Everything connected by that interlocking series of lines and configurations. If he did, he chose not to comment on it. Instead, he pointed to something else, something beyond the square.

'What are those?' He asked. I looked, and saw two smaller mounds that I'd not noticed until now, now that I was up high enough to see the Island's interior more clearly.

I squinted, feeling tipsy.

'Not sure,' I said. 'They look like...more cairns?'

He nodded. 'Yeah. Smaller than this one. They look like boundary markers, or something. The town is built...yes, look! Wow.'

'What?'

'The town is laid out inside the lines you can draw from cairn to cairn.' He stuck out his index finger, and drew two straight lines across the air, from one cairn to the next. I watched him do this, and a great lump formed in my throat. I thought of a photograph, where a crowd of people stood facing this Island, their hands in the air. I thought of Fiona and Murdo, the pop of a rifle, triangles traced by hand into the blooded sky.

'See what I mean?' He asked.

And I did see. The land upon which White Pines stood was a natural, gently sloping plain surrounding the main cairn, where we sat. The smaller cairns were, as Matthew had said, like boundary markers. If you drew lines between them, they became corners. Inside these corners, the town spread wide.

But there was something wrong with this. Something numerically off. *Two corners isn't enough*, I realised.

I thought back to the lintel above the door at *Taigh-Faire.* To the capstone in the cellar. To Fiona's tattoo, and Granny's grave.

Three sides, three corners, four dots.

I thought about where we were sitting, under a pile of rocks set dead in the middle of the Island. I chewed my lip as I gazed at the other two cairns, and a slow tingle spread across my scalp.

Shapes. Symbols. Cairns. Sacred geometry.

'Back in a minute,' I said, suddenly scrambling up to my feet. I nearly tumbled straight back down, dizziness attacking me as I stood up-right, but I managed to save myself at the last minute by grabbing Matthew's shoulders.

'Where are you going?' He asked, taken aback by my unexpected momentum. 'What's wrong with you? Are you drunk already?'

'I just need to check something out,' I said breathlessly. I righted myself more slowly this time, and told Matthew to stay put.

'Are you sure? You don't look great, Megs, let me come with you.'

'Just stay there!' I said bossily. Then I ducked around to the other side of the cairn, and looked back across the rear slope, eyes scanning back and forth, looking for a little pile of stacked stones.

And I found it, sitting low and dark in the moonlight, just in front of the tree line.

A fourth cairn.

Three sides, three corners, four dots.

And I knew then, what this was. I knew that if I drew a map of the Island, a bird's eye view map, I would look down and see three dots. These would be the three small cairns located around the outside of White Pines. You could draw a line between those dots and make a per-fect, equilateral triangle in doing so.

Inside the triangle, the town of White Pines lay. And in the centre of that town, one final dot: the cairn where we stood.

As if hypnotised, my right hand came up

to the level of my face, and drew a symbol in the air. A triangle.

And it glowed softly in the night.

I gasped. The shape faded, but a faint white residue stained the insides of my eyelids as I blinked.

Everything is connected, I thought. And then I heard Fiona's voice in my head once again.

The Island deceives.

'Fuck,' I said, out loud. This was beyond me. This was all beyond me. I was falling into a world of puzzles, of enigma, where every rock and tree and boulder had a purpose I didn't understand, a significance so great I couldn't comprehend it.

The Island deceives.

And then something tapped me on the shoulder. Something heavy, and cold.

I started, whipped around, and came face to face with a double-barrelled shotgun.

For a split second, when all I could see were the twin eyes of the gun, I thought it was Murdo, come for me. Or Fiona. They had shot the dog, god knew why, and now they were here for me.

I fell back with a cry against the cairn. As I did so, my hands flew out, and made contact with the stones. A bolt of pure, raw energy raced through my body, almost ripping me in two. I convulsed, and heard a voice in my head.

An old voice. An angry voice.

A voice from my dream.

It was the god beneath the tree, chanting, speaking to me once more in that language I didn't understand. And I didn't want to understand, I didn't. I knew the god was saying terrible, terrible things, things I was too afraid to hear.

Are you down there, under the stones?
What are you?!

Bile raced up my throat. I scrambled away from the cairn, feeling horribly cold, my body wracked with aftershocks, as if I'd been electrocuted. The air around me felt charged, heavy with static energy, and *thinner*, somehow. Breathing became difficult.

And, as I crawled on my hands and knees, putting as much space between myself and the rock pile as possible, for the quickest of moments, the cairn was not a cairn at all, but a great, resplendent cherry tree, with branches that stretched high above me, and roots that dug down far below. I saw sand around it, and the sea beyond that.

And then the rocks were rocks once again, the sand was dirt, the sea was gone, and I found myself staring up at a man.

It was not Murdo.

He levelled his shotgun at me.

'You are not welcome here,' he said.

Mac, I thought, and then I vomited, right then and there on the ground in front of him.

17.

UNWELCOME

My body heaved and shook as I sicked up hot, acidic bile.

'Hey!' Matthew rounded the cairn, and quickly came to stand in front of me, shielding me from the gun in an act so automatically selfless, I didn't fully appreciate it until much, much later.

Would I have done the same, for him? It was a question that would come back to bite me many times over, in the days to come.

'Who the hell do you think you are, pointing that at her?!' My unlikely protector said, his body tight with rage.

The stranger stood steady, staring down at me from behind the gun's front sight.

I retched up the last of my stomach contents, wiped a thin dribble of acrid saliva from my chin, and got to my knees, panting. The voice in my head had died away, and as I grew more aware of my surroundings, I realised I had to calm the situation down before one, or both of us ended up shot.

But standing was difficult, and speaking even more so. I climbed to my feet and just stood there, swaying, trying not to throw up again.

What is wrong with me?

The man, who was clad in a simple linen shirt and fishermen trousers, kept the gun level and trained at my head, unmoved by Matthew's outburst.

'You're trespassing,' he said, and his voice had a faint Scottish burr, but it didn't sound like he was from the Highlands. It was subtle, but noticeable: he had spent time down south, like I had.

Behind him, there was movement, and three more people came out from behind the cairn. A silver-haired woman, a man the same age roughly as Matthew, and a young lad of maybe seventeen, eighteen years old. They stood next to the man with the gun, and the woman folded her arms as she took in the scene.

'We were invited!' Matthew made an effort to gentle his tone, looking to the newcomers and holding his arms up to show he was no trouble. 'There was a kid, a boy. He invited us.'

'A boy? What boy?' The man spat.

A small voice rang out.

'Me! It was me, Mac! I'm sorry!'

And for the second time that night,

Luke emerged from the shadows. His small face looked paler than ever, but he was unafraid. He squeezed past the cairn and planted himself next to Matthew, in front of me and in front of the gun.

It was enough to break me out of my stupor.

'Luke, no!' I said, and pushed the boy aside. A grown man putting himself in the line of fire was one thing. A small boy doing the same was another thing altogether.

Luke stared up at me with those huge, soulful eyes. 'This is my fault,' he said, and then he turned to Mac. 'I found them outside the trees. I thought they seemed nice. And I've never seen a mainlander before! I wanted them to come to the party.'

His face crumpled, and he began to cry.

'What are you doing here?' I said, trying to sound stern and failing in the face of his tears. 'Your mother told you to stay away from us.'

'I didn't want you to get lost. I snuck out again when she wasn't looking.'

I shook my head. 'She'll be worried sick,' I said.

The silver-haired woman watched this exchange, and decided to put an end to it. 'Come here, Luke,' she said, in a tone that brooked no refusal. 'Now.'

Luke did as he was told, still crying. 'Please don't shoot them,' he begged, as he passed Mac. 'Please, they are my friends.'

The man spat again. 'We don't have friends outside the Island, boy.' The shotgun stayed trained on me.

Matthew spoke in a low, furious voice, all attempts to placate the Islanders abandoned.

'Get that gun out of my face, before I lose my temper,' he threatened, and I put a hand on his shoulder, squeezing it tight in a warning.

'Careful,' I murmured.

'How did you get here?' Mac ignored Matthew's threat. 'I didn't see your boat moored on the spit. Did you swim?'

Fiona's voice rang out in my mind: *Your Granny used to swim in the bay every morning, come rain or shine...*

Matthew and I stayed silent. If he didn't know about the tunnel under the bay, and the cave, then I wasn't about to tell him.

'They were seen in the square, earlier,' the other man said. He had a tattoo on one cheek, the outline of a tiny fish. 'Just brazenly walking about like nobody's business.'

The silver-haired woman came forward, then, tucking Luke behind her as she did so. She frowned at me. 'You look familiar,' she said, peering into my face. It was barely visible from the light of the lantern on top of the cairn, but something she saw in me made her pause.

I kept my peace.

She turned to her companion.

'Mac, she looks familiar.'

Mac didn't care. Mac didn't like strangers. Slowly, and very deliberately, he pulled back on the trigger, and I heard it click, heard a mechanism slide into place.

'I'll ask you again,' he said. 'How did you get onto this Island?'

'We were invited,' I replied, repeating Matthew's words with my chin held high. And it was the truth. I *had* been invited.

Just not by the boy.

And this truth gave me courage. Because I knew Mac wasn't going to shoot me. It wasn't part of the Island's plan. Why show me the tunnel, why bring me here, just for that? It didn't make sense.

Down in the square below us, out of sight behind the cairn, the band rolled over into a different tune, faster, edgier, with livelier drums, louder strings, more pipes, everything hacking and sawing and clashing in a frantic rhythm. As we stood facing each other, like cowboys at high noon, the Islanders versus the intruders, I listened to the laughing clamour of the people of White Pines spiral up into the sky, thinking the same thing over and over without knowing why:

The Island deceives. The Island deceives. The Island deceives. The Island deceives.

It was then that the world fell silent.

18. SILENCE

Not a gradual tapering off of sound.

Not a quietening down, or a low murmur dropping away gradually as the party lulled. Not an ebb or flow of noise, dipping and rising with the breeze. There *was* no breeze. Everything was incredibly still, especially the air.

No. The noise...*all* noise...just stopped.

Dead.

As if we had been sealed, suddenly, in a sound-proofed room. I felt my ears glug, and pop. The hairs on my arms stood up. The skin beneath prickled. There was a faint tremor in my fingertips. The effect on us was devastating, like a bomb had been dropped. Not a single noise could be heard from the town below. No music. No children playing and laughing, no stamp and shuffle of people dancing, no shrieking violins, or banging drums, no pipes, no barking dogs, no snuffling pigs. Not even the sound of a fire crackling, or beer cups rattling together.

There was nothing, and the absence of sound was deafening.

I watched Mac's face as the quiet hit him. He finally lowered the gun, frowning at me. I licked my lips, which were suddenly very dry. An understanding passed between us. Something outside of the realms of normality was happening here. Whatever business he had with Matthew and I, it could wait.

He hesitated, then turned and walked back around to the other side of the cairn, the side that looked down upon the town square. The rest of us followed, because we knew something was wrong. We all felt it. Something was horribly, earth-shatteringly wrong.

Luke broke free of the silver-haired woman and came to me, slipping his hand silently into mine.

'What's going on?' He asked, in a small voice.

I squeezed his hand, not knowing how to answer, and we rounded the cairn together, Matthew close at my back.

And I looked down. Down to where only moments before, a festival had been underway. Down to where hundreds of people had swirled around in joyous harmony, to where a thriving community had been celebrating an anniversary.

They were not celebrating any more.

I felt heavy, and drunk. For a second or two, I did not know what I was actually looking at.

Then I realised that this was it.

This was the event.

This was why I was here.

Because White Pines had disappeared.

Dawn chose that moment to creep up on us, almost as if it had been waiting. I hadn't realised how late it was, hadn't seen the night tip over into early morning. The sky lightened, became a deep, bruised pink with purple accents. The moon waned to a thin, pale disc, now redundant.

And the sun, with horrible alacrity, pushed its head up above the tall tree tops. I saw rich, yolky light spill out across the centre of the Island, where moments before, the town of White Pines had stood.

To where the people, the children, the band, the houses, the cobbled square, the large tables set up with food, the barrels of ale on their trestles, the cast-iron hand pump, the storage buildings, the chapel, the sandstone bench, the vegetable patches and fruit trees and pigs in their pens, even the bunting, the discarded plates and cutlery and the spit-roasted lamb...

To where it had all been, and now, was not.

And before us, instead of White Pines, there lay something else. Something that spread out inside the circle of pine trees, something that occupied the same space that the town had, but was devoid of life, of movement, of landmarks, of distinguishing features of any kind.

It was a large, black scar upon the land.

A scar in the shape of a huge, perfectly proportioned equilateral triangle.

At each point, there sat a cairn. In the centre rested the fourth cairn, the largest, and the one underneath which we stood, stunned.

Three sides, three corners...

I couldn't finish the thought.

Lines, and shapes, and symbols, all around.

But there was nothing sacred about this geometry. This was evil. This was the geometry of abomination.

The silver-haired woman screamed, then, long and loud.

The scream hung in the air like smoke, lingering long after it had left the woman's mouth.

And the Island, now blank and empty like a slate wiped clean, listened.

19. ONE SECOND

My first thought was of the boy's Ma. The boy who held my hand, and stared at the scarred land below us, mute with shock. Had there been a father, too? Yes, he had mentioned his Dad, I was sure of it.

I felt him next to me, small, vulnerable.

Orphaned. Homeless.

The boy who would be gone, too, had he not followed us here.

His mother had been kind. Angry, but kind. She had given us beer, good beer, and directions.

And then I thought of all the other people I'd seen. The old men, sitting by the fountain, smoking. The kids that had been running through people's legs and around the square in feral packs. The women chattering with their arms about each other. The couples dancing 'strip the willow.' The piper. Even the drunk woman who had kissed Matthew.

Everyone who had existed inside the boundary of that triangle was now gone. Ceased to exist, as if they had never been there at all. Except for us. As if we were dreamers, and had suddenly woken.

Why us? Why leave us behind?

'What's going on?' Luke asked, again.

Mac dropped his gun to the ground. The silver-haired woman wailed again, and swayed as if on the verge of collapse. The man with the fish tattoo went very, very still, eyes almost popping from his head. The teenager swore and closed his eyes, then reopened them. He did this over and over again, as if in the grip of a seizure.

But it didn't matter how hard you looked, or how many times you closed your eyes and hoped that when you opened them, things would be different.

Because they weren't.

White Pines was gone.

A tiny white flake of something drifted past my nose. A flake of what could have been snow. It landed on my arm, and I let it sit there, too terrified to brush it away.

It wasn't snow.

It was ash.

'I don't understand,' Matthew whispered, staring at the empty wasteland where the town square had stood. The silver-haired woman had collapsed into Mac's arms, and was babbling hysterically. The teenager wiped tears from his face, which had gone from pale white to a blotchy, shocked shade of red.

Luke just kept holding my hand, confusion writ large across his face.

'It's gone,' he said, and I heard Matthew let out a great, shuddering breath as he heard the boy say this.

'Where's it gone?' He asked, and then he repeated himself.

'Please, where's it gone?'

I tore my eyes from the scar to look at him. And I had a moment of blinding clarity.

An ocean, where slate roofs poked out of the waves. A chapel, half submerged in the tideline.

A beach, full of bodies.

A cast-iron water pump sticking out of the sand. Other things that once belonged somewhere else.

It wasn't a dream, I realised.

If I'd had anything left in my stomach to bring up at that moment, I would have.

The man with the fish tattoo spoke up. 'No,' he said, as if quarrelling with a friend over something inconsequential. 'No, that isn't possible.' And before any of us could stop him, he started to march downhill, towards the place his town had been, saying over and over again in business-like tones: 'No. No, no, I don't think so.'

I had a moment then, when I felt something shift in the air, when a feeling of absolute dread gripped me tight as I stared at the retreating form of the man. I remembered the piper, snapping out of view. I remembered Matthew, there one moment and then suddenly, not.

'*Stop!*' I shouted, suddenly, as the man left the shadow of the cairn. 'Come back!'

'What is it, Megs?' Matthew said, voice thin with fear. 'What do you know?'

'Stop!' I screamed again, but it was too late. The fish-tattooed man took another step, still shaking his head and muttering to himself, and I saw a quiver, a change in the atmosphere around him, as if the air was flexing, shivering with a strange, uncontrollable energy, and then, in front of all of us, he simply winked out of existence.

The silver haired woman screamed again, and Mac made as if to repeat the same mistake. The teenager snapped out a hand, and grabbed his shirt. 'No!' He said, face piebald with fright. 'Don't, it isn't safe!'

'I don't understand what just happened,' Matthew whispered, and in that moment he sounded no older than the small boy who gripped my hand.

I looked down at my feet. *Why us?* I thought again. *Why are we still here?*

Then, I saw why, and grunted in surprise.

'What?' Said to Matthew, in a hushed

voice. It felt suddenly rude to speak out.

I pointed to the ground near our feet, and he looked down. Where we stood, just below the cairn, the land was still grassy and green. The grass made a definitive ring-shaped strip around the base of the cairn, about five or six feet deep. Outside of the shadow of the cairn, outside of the green circle, everything was charred, spent, and empty.

My right foot sat at the very edge of this green strip, my big toe a mere inch away from the dead ground. And I sensed what Matthew seemed to sense, at same moment: that stepping over that green boundary, putting even one toe into that black scar, would invite great pain and suffering. Like stepping into a bath full of scalding water.

I moved my foot back, with great care.

'Look,' Matthew whispered.

I was afraid to, but I did as he asked. I looked, and saw that there was something wrong with the air beyond the green circle, the air that filled the ashen triangle.

It flickered, as if it were static on a television set.

'Over there,' Matthew said.

He gestured at something lying on the ground. Half-full of beer and resting on its side, contents draining into the dead soil, a small dark puddle soaking the earth beneath it. A beaker. Matthew had thrown it away earlier, and it had obviously landed and rolled down-slope, away from the cairn.

We watched, and the air crackled, warped, and then the beaker was gone.

Without thinking, I reached towards the spot where it had lay, just as I had when I'd watched Matthew's reflection disappear in the mirror in Luke's house. I wanted to feel the ground, to see if it really was wet, to see if the cup had ever really been there at all, but Matthew, my shield against the impossible, stopped me.

'Don't,' he said, sharply, and I caught myself, snatching the hand back.

And I had a terrible thought.

Was it the town that had disappeared?

Or had we gone somewhere else?

My eyes scanned the scene, back and forth, back and forth. Could I make out even the faintest of outlines, foundations, remnants of buildings? No, not even any debris, rubble, or litter. It was as if everything within the triangle had been swept clean away by a giant brush. Nothing moved, except the air, which buckled like a sheet of metal under great pressure.

I looked around. I needed to test something. I picked up a loose pebble from the ground near the bottom of the cairn. I threw it at the space where the beaker had been, where now only air remained, air that moved with a strange intent. The stone sailed across the distance between where I stood and the dead place in a definitive arc, and then...

Vanished, mid-trajectory, before it hit the ground.

'That's...that's not possible,' Matthew said, sounding like the man with the fish tattoo. 'None of this is possible.'

'What was his name?' I asked, out loud, for it seemed important to know. I could not think of him as the 'fish-tattooed man' forever.

'Glenn.' The teenager had come forward to stand beside us. 'His name is Glenn.'

Present tense, I thought. *Is.*

What 'is' Glenn now? Alive? Dead? Something in between, like Schrödinger's doomed cat?

Luke clutched at my arm, his thumb now stuck in his mouth as he tried to comfort himself. The older boy gestured at the staccato beat of air, moving consistently, rhythmically, as if reality were tuning in, and out. From one place to another place, this place and then that. Wherever *that* was.

I had an impression of a veil being lifted, or a curtain pulled back, only fleetingly, momentarily, before it was dropped once again.

'What do we do?' Matthew said, voicing the question we were all thinking at the same time, but too afraid to ask.

'I think...' I swallowed, changed my mind. There was no point in telling them what I thought. They wouldn't understand about the beach. Not yet.

I chose different words.

'I think that if we leave the shelter of this cairn, go out there...' I trailed off, fully realising what it was that I was about to say.

'Well?' Mac's gruff voice rasped out behind me.

I shook my head. 'Well. I wouldn't, is all.' And I picked up another stone, a larger rock the size of my fist this time, from the base of the cairn. Another shock like electricity ran through me as I brushed against the mound of stones in the act. I gritted my teeth and ignored it. One anomaly at a time, thank you.

I threw the rock, further this time, arcing my arm back, hurling the stone as far as it would go, and the exact same thing happened as last time. It sailed through the air, crossed into the space within the triangle, came down in a curved trajectory, and then ceased to exist.

Gone.

'It must be a trick of the light,' said Matthew, trying to ascribe logic to a situation so far beyond description it was almost comedic. 'A heat haze? Or perhaps a fog of some sort. It's just not...'

'Stop, Matthew,' I said, rubbing my tired eyes with my four-fingered hand. 'Just stop.'

I heard the silver-haired woman speak, then. She had joined us at the edge of the cairn boundary. Her face was a portrait of shock, and grief. Her hands trembled as she patted her hair, a distracted, obsessive gesture that told me her brain was running in one direction, and her motor functions in the other. The other Islanders gathered around her, as if to catch her if she fell. They were a unit, I realised, like Matthew and I were. Part of a community. It made me unbearably sad.

'I only looked away for a second,' she said. Her hands kept patting that silvery pile of soft hair.

'Only a second.'

I swallowed, fighting too many feelings.

Clearly, one second had been long enough.

20. MAROONED

'So you're telling me...we're stuck here?'

Mac was a thick-set man, barrel-chested, stout-bellied, yet his stomach heaved up and down, and his eyes darted about frantically as he tried to come to terms with the new, insubstantial reality we now found ourselves trapped within.

I retrieved another rock, silently. I handed it to Mac. With a grim expression, he threw it out of the green grass circle. We all watched as it flew through the air, and then disappeared.

'You saw what happened to...' Even though I had just asked, the name evaded me, and I shook my head. I'm sorry, I can't...'

'Glenn.' The teenager stared at the ground, sadly.

'I'm sorry. To Glenn. You saw it. We can't leave. At least not that way.'

'What about the other side?' Matthew meant the other side of the cairn.

'Let me check.' The teenager, eager to

do something, *anything*, found his own stone, thought about it for a second, and collected several more. Then he walked clockwise around the base of the cairn, stopping every few paces to throw a rock into the triangle. He did this until he had looped the rock pile completely, and returned to the point where we stood, waiting.

Nice little ritual, I remembered Matthew saying.

Now empty-handed, the teen shook his head. Every single stone had blipped out of existence.

I thought of a desert island. We were marooned on a small islet in a sea of disquiet. Were there sharks out there in the water?

None of us felt brave enough to find out.

'We can't leave.' Mac repeated my words from earlier, only now it was more of a statement than a question.

I shrugged, feeling numb. 'Feel free to try.'

The collective realisation fell heavily on our disparate group. We *were* stuck. On this small mound of grass and rock in the centre of a black, dead triangle. For how long, was anyone's guess.

Mac glared at me then, as if everything was my fault. Deep down inside, in the part of me that wasn't shocked and exhausted and fore done, I felt the same. I felt inexplicable guilt. I felt the consequence of touching the face of a sleeping deity in my dream.

Because everything had gone to shit since I'd dreamed that dream.

Was this all my fault?

'We should wait,' I said then, as it was the only logical thing left to say. 'If we wait, this...whatever this is, it might end soon. Maybe everything will come back. Maybe it won't. I don't know. But this?' I pointed at the Island's empty interior.

'I don't want to set foot in that.'

Mac and I locked eyes, and I saw all of the blame and terror that he was struggling to swallow brim to the surface. He had a ruddy face, polished by cold winter winds and outdoor living. It grew darker as he let rage push his fear to one side. He took a threatening step towards me. Matthew moved once again to place himself in the other man's path.

'And what about water?' The Islander said, in a flat, livid voice. 'What are we supposed to drink while we wait? Or eat? What about food?'

I shook my head, out of answers.

Mac's voice wobbled. 'And what about my *town*, my *people?!*'

I thought then that he might fling himself at me, at the very least throw a punch in my direction, but he didn't. Instead he stared at Matthew and I with barely concealed hatred, then turned his back on us.

It didn't make much difference if he hated

us, I knew that. The only thing that mattered was that, for now, we were alive. That we had to *stay* alive, survive this event. I was convinced that sticking even one toe into the triangle would result in death, or worse. The cairn was safe, for now.

That was all that mattered.

21. WAITING

And so we waited for something to happen.

Waited for the air to still, for something else to signal a return to normalcy.

We waited in vain.

'Look!' Luke saw it first, and pointed.

Miserably, we huddled at the base of the cairn, and watched as the air quivered and snapped.

There is nothing left to take, I thought, for the unreliable air reminded me of snapping jaws, hungry for prey. *You've taken it all.*

But the Island wasn't trying to steal anything away, this time. It was trying to send something back.

Whatever it was appeared and disappeared so rapidly we couldn't make out anything beyond a quick blur, extinguished in seconds. I had the impression maybe of wheels, and possibly handlebars, like a bicycle, but it was over so soon I couldn't be sure. The triangle was a live thing, flickering and shuddering constantly. It gave us all headaches to look at, so eventually we stopped trying to make sense of it, and began to stare at our own feet, cushioned by safe, green blades of grass that didn't move unless we willed it so.

I began to work on a theory.

White Pines had gone, that much was obvious. But to where? To a place that was not far from here, not far at all. I could sense it. A place behind a curtain, behind a veil.

And the divide between that place and this was weak, flimsy. Weak enough to pass through, weak enough to cross over.

So the town was trying to come back, but only parts of it made it safely across the divide, safely beneath the veil. These were parts that the other place couldn't hold onto, for reasons I couldn't fathom. They popped into this reality, and were promptly snatched back into the other one.

As theories went, it was wild, I knew.

But then, I was only working with the evidence given me.

Headaches began to build. We were thirsty, and the sun was growing stronger. I felt my face burning, turning hot. The cairn cast a little shade, and we followed it about, like the shadow from a sundial, trying to keep out of the increasingly harsh glare.

Midday hit, and the cairn's shadow disappeared completely, the harsh noon sun affording us only a thin, dark crescent moon inside which we could not fit. The silver-haired woman took off her floor-length skirt, exposing worn, practical underwear and surprisingly lean, brown legs. She used her skirt as a sunshade, and left enough space for Luke to huddle beneath it with her. I swallowed back a lump in my throat when I saw this.

Mac had taken to marching around the cairn, hugging the stones tightly so he did not go near the edge of the green grass border. He walked as if marching to sentry duty, his shotgun resting on his shoulder. He was a man of action, and sitting still waiting for death or change apparently didn't suit him. In that respect, I sympathised.

There had been no time for pleasantries before. Now, I had all the time in the world. I seated myself quietly next to the silver-haired woman, introducing myself.

'I'm Megs,' I said. In another time or place, I would have offered her my hand. Now, the gesture seemed absurd. My name would have to be enough.

To my relief, she returned the courtesy. Her name was Rhoda. The teen's name was Johnny, and he was Mac's nephew.

Mac refused to make eye contact, or acknowledge me in any way. He just kept marching around the cairn, constantly moving, keeping ahead of his own existential dread.

We sat in shared silence for a while longer, and then I spoke up.

'The trees,' I said, and I didn't know who I was asking, or why it was so important to ask that question there and then. 'The pine trees. They aren't...from around here, are they?' My voice cracked with thirst, and I coughed and spluttered into my fist.

When I had recovered, I expected Rhoda to answer, but it was Mac who spoke up. He didn't stop walking for a second, but he was at least talking to me. I considered that progress.

'They are not. Indigenous.'

I nodded. 'Didn't think so. I've never seen anything like them.'

Mac did another loop of the cairn. Then, he stopped, finally. Sweat rolled down his temples, and he licked dry lips. He seemed actually happy to be distracted, and his eyes took on a faraway look.

'This Island had trees a long, long time ago. Pines, probably, larch. But it was barren when I bought it back from the government. Under quarantine for forty-eight years, it was.'

'Bought it back?'

'Aye, the land belonged to my family before the army bought it.'

I had completely forgotten about the anthrax. So had Matthew. We glanced at each other, and despite everything, a tiny flash of something almost approaching amusement sparked. How our priorities had changed.

Mac continued. 'Not much of anything left here after the army and the scientists finished with it. They took all the topsoil away in 1986. Dumped formaldehyde and seawater all over the place to decontaminate it. I bought it back off them for five hundred pounds, once they'd finished. Place was barren, then. My family should never have given it over in the first place. Shame. Shame.'

He shook his head. Something flashed into view on the charcoal ground to our right, beyond the green circle, and vanished a few seconds later. Was it me, or were the appearances getting longer? I felt like I could almost see that last object, as if it had hung around for longer than the blink of an eye.

'With the topsoil gone, we needed something for growing. Root networks bind the soil. Stop it from washing away.'

I'd picked up on it earlier, but I realised again that Mac wasn't from these parts. He didn't have the lilting Highlands accent I had expected. His voice was husky, distinct.

He continued. 'I ended up bringing my own soil, clean, uncontaminated, nutrient-rich. Best graded topsoil I could find, brought up from the South. We spread it everywhere, planted

that stand of trees. First thing we did, before anything else. Keep the wind at bay. Bind the soil
better. Stop run-off. Keep nosey-parkers like you
away from our community.'

I swallowed, and shook my head ruefully. Trees or no trees, my destiny had always
been this Island. God, I was thirsty. Matthew, of
the same mindset, stuck his tongue out. It was
coated in a white, sticky film. He made gargling
noises to try and get some saliva to move about
in his mouth. I let my eyes travel across the triangle, to the barcoded ring of pine trees beyond.

Now Mac had started, it seemed he
couldn't stop. 'Fastigiate Eastern White Pine, or
Pinus strobus Fastigiata.' He enunciated the Latin
carefully, and I had an impression that he was
well-educated. Horticultural college, maybe.
Perhaps he just read a lot. 'Native to America. I
had them shipped over especially, like the soil.
A couple thousand of them, young saplings, all
hand planted, most by me, some by Rhoda, the
rest by the community as it grew.' Rhoda and
Mac exchanged looks, and I saw love there, and
understood their relationship better with that
look.

Matthew put his tongue back into his
mouth, then stilled. He had spotted something
else in the triangle, but I still didn't want to
look.

'Only they didn't grow quite like they
were supposed to,' Mac continued. 'They grew

fast. Unnaturally fast, although this suited us, so we didn't complain about it. And they came up white, and skinny. Little tufts of needles on top. Fastigiata has a blue colour to the foliage, normally. Grows dense, like a Christmas tree. We thought maybe it was something in the soil. But they give us...' Mac trailed off, slapped a hand against his thigh in frustration. '*Gave us* some privacy.'

I had more questions. So, so many more questions. Why had he chosen to build a community here, with the history it had? Hadn't they noticed the disparity between the size of the Island and the available space they magically had to build upon? What and who were the cairns for? Did he know about the tunnel? Were there more?

All these questions would have to wait. Because I felt a hand in my hair, patting the top of my head to get my attention.

Matthew hovered by my side, zombie-like. 'Look,' he said. The air shivered like a sick animal all around us. Then, I saw it, lying on the ground. It was a child's hula-hoop, candy striped in white and red. It lay there for a full thirty seconds before disappearing.

I'd been right about something, at least.

After that, Matthew sank into a deep hole of depression as the atmosphere, his own helplessness, and shock at what had happened began to weigh on him. He roused himself every now and then to check on me, before retreating right back into himself.

Luke sat cross-legged on the grass next to Rhoda, keeping himself well back from the edge of the green strip as I'd instructed him to do. He pulled blades of grass and small sprigs of heather out of the ground with his small, deft fingers, and rolled them up into spongy balls in the palms of his hands, then made a pile of these in front of his feet. It looked as if he were subconsciously mimicking the cairn that loomed behind him. He sniffed every minute or so, and his lip wobbled frequently as he thought about his missing parents, his vanished house.

It grew brighter, and warmer still as mid-afternoon rolled in. Our timid, halting conversation dried up. We waited as the agreeable weather mocked us, and the pale pines looked on.

Nothing else happened.

Until Matthew raised a shaking hand, and pointed.

'There,' he said, in hushed tones.

We all leaned forward intently.

The air flickered again, like a heat shimmer on a hot tarmac road.

And inside the perimeter of the burned triangle, about ten feet away, something materialised.

Rhoda let out a strangled cry, and made to get to her feet. Johnny grabbed her, held her down.

'Don't!'

'But that's mine!' She said, and we looked.

It was a red door, or at least, the top two-thirds of a red door, still mounted inside its rustic door frame. There was nothing else attached to it, no wall, no masonry. No lintel. Nothing behind, or around it.

Just a door.

It stuck out of the ground at an odd, unnatural angle, reminding me of my Granny's headstone in Laide cemetery, leaning drunkenly as if the earth were subsiding beneath it. Only that wasn't right. The door wasn't sinking *into* the ground at all. It had simply materialised half-in, and half-out of the soil. As if the door had been sent back from wherever it had been, only to return to the wrong place. Instead of sitting at ground level, the bottom of the door now sat a foot or two *below* the earth.

A number also hung on the door, the number '4'. A simple brass door-knocker gleamed against the shiny red gloss paint. I stared, and bit back a wild urge to laugh. The door was so incongruous, so unnatural against the context of its empty, blackened surroundings that the scene reminded me of a Salvador Dali painting. A surreal, ridiculous nightmare.

'Where is the rest?!' Wailed Rhoda.

'Where is the rest of my house?!'

Johnny held onto her.

It was a good question. Where *was* the rest of the house?

Where was the rest of White Pines?

The urge to laugh died as quickly as it had arisen. 'I want to leave now, Matthew,' I whispered, and I saw him nod.

Wanting, and being able to, were two different things, however.

Thirty seconds later, the door vanished.

22. BEHIND THE VEIL

The sun travelled across the sky, bored by our helplessness.

We saw other things flit in and out of existence with an alarming, erratic rapidity. A child's bike. A chair. A long-handled wooden shovel. A steel bucket. Another door, green this time. It looked a lot like Luke's front door.

'What's happening?' The boy asked, for the hundredth time, as an upended tricycle juddered into life, then dematerialised. 'What's happening?'

'I wish I knew, kiddo,' I replied, also for the hundredth time.

'Is my Ma okay? And Daddy?'

Matthew heard this, and I saw his spine stiffen. He crouched down so that he was at the same eye-level as Luke.

'I don't know what's happening, pal. I wish I did, so that I could explain it to you. But we'll try and find out, won't we? We'll try our best for your Ma and Dad. We just have to stay brave, okay?'

Luke blinked back tears, and Matthew awkwardly ruffled the boy's hair. Then he spotted something glinting under the boy's shirt collar.

'What's that?' He asked, gently.

The boy pulled out a long silver chain. On the end of a chain, a pendant swung. 'My Ma made it for me,' he said. 'It's my lucky charm.'

'You hang onto that,' Matthew said, then. 'You hang onto it, tight.' He was thinking that it would be all the boy had left of his family. I bowed my head.

Mac spoke up.

'It's the town, you know. Trying to come back.' He said it in a dull voice. It was an eerie echo of my earlier thought process, and I found myself nodding.

'What?' Matthew looked at the man, not understanding what he meant.

But I understood.

Three more hours passed, three hours in which we didn't move. We watched the nightmare display of White Pines flotsam and jetsam, washing into existence on a tide of mysterious, indiscriminate energy, and floating back out again into the unknown moments later. It was exhausting and unnerving to witness. Thankfully, only inanimate objects came back. No people, or animals. I was more than grateful for this. I didn't want to see what would happen to a person who came back in the wrong place, buried to the waist in soil, or stuck under a rock, or worse. I didn't want to have to look at their faces when they disappeared again.

Mac, having tired himself out, now stood like a statue below the rocks, staring out at the triangle with a lowered brow. He reminded me of an eagle sighting prey. Every time the air flickered, he flinched, but that was the only sign of distress he allowed himself. Everything else about him was still, composed, as if he were forcefully holding all the pieces of himself together. *As a leader does,* I thought. *What must he be feeling? What must they all be feeling?*

A burgeoning need to urinate made itself known to me as the day wore on. I ignored the pressure building in my bladder for as long as possible, but after thirty minutes of squirming, I knew I couldn't hold it anymore. I signalled to Matthew that I needed to relieve myself. He roused himself, nodded, and sank back into his brown study. Mac continued his watch, back straight, eyes almost lost under his brow. Rhoda cried quietly into her hands. Johnny sat miserably on the ground beside her, head down, not wanting to engage with the world anymore.

Luke kept his hands busy, making little grass bullets to add to his pile. Every now and then he fiddled with the pendent around his neck, then tucked it carefully back under his shirt, patting it to make sure it was safe. He'd taken Matthew's words to heart.

I edged around the base of the cairn, to the opposite side of the rock mound, the side that faced the most northerly point of the triangle. I thought about the spiritual consequences of urinating on, or near, a sacred stone cairn, but I had no choice. Our bodies don't stop being our bodies just because the world is going to shit around us.

Besides, I figured I had already pissed off the god beneath the tree as much as I was able.

I sighed, pulled down my trousers, and crouched. A trickle of piss made its way downhill as I relieved myself, snaking through the green strip and across into the black, where, predictably, it vanished, like a thin, wet worm that had been unceremoniously sliced in half with a sharp knife.

My business finished, I stood up again and rearranged my clothes. They now felt days old, sweat-rough. My body ached. I looked at my hands, which couldn't quite get to grips with the zipper of my jeans. They shook as I held them out before me. The stub of my little finger seemed more pronounced than ever against the bleak, seared land behind.

Beyond the edges of the triangle, a circle of pine trees with flawlessly white bark watched my every move.

I hated them.

I turned to rejoin the group. As I did so, something caught my eye. Movement. A suggestive spasm, the air nictitating, telling me that something else was crossing back from behind the curtain. I waited for it, and when it materialised, finally, I gasped. Tears gathered in my eyes.

The Island had heard me, and called my bluff.

This time, it had sent back a wall, or a section of one. A drystone wall. About five feet long, by four feet high. Grey stones tessellated.

Amongst them, strange, brown, bedraggled things struggled, and squawked.

'Birds,' I breathed.

They were stuck *in* the wall. A whole flock of them, embedded into the stonework like nothing I'd ever seen before. Wings and feet twitched. Feathers trembled. Tiny, beady eyes darted about frantically. The birds were still alive, although dying fast. The wall had come back in the wrong place. Or the birds had. Or both had, simultaneously, smashing into each other to create this unholy spectacle, this macabre embrace.

'Little Brown Spuggies, my Ma used to call them.' Mac's voice came from behind me, and I jumped. How long had he been there?

We stood, aghast at the spectacle.

'Like flies trapped in amber,' he continued, and he was exactly right.

Like bodies in beach-glass, I thought to myself. *Like a cherry tree in crystal.*

Mac ran his hand across his eyes and coughed.

'What if it's not birds, next time?'

'What?' I didn't fully process what he was saying, at first.

'What if, next time,' Mac repeated, echoing aloud what I'd kept to myself earlier, 'It's not birds?'

'Don't,' I said, shaking my head to block out his words. 'Don't say it.'

'What if next time, it's a person?'

'Stop.'

'A child?'

'Stop it.'

'And they come back like...that?'

He pointed to the wall, which moved and fluttered and squawked and cheeped less with every second that passed. As the birds suffocated, and died, one by one.

I thought of a mouth gasping for air by my feet as slippery, deadly sand poured in. How I had dug down to free the face from the beach, and it had vanished under my touch.

Mac covered his face with his hands, then. He had used those hands to build a community. Now, they were all gone. I found it impossible to focus on anything else as he continued, just his hands, pressed into his large, red face.

236

'Like flies. In amber. Jesus Christ.' He said it from behind his fingers, and the air flickered in my peripheral again.

Then, we heard screaming.

23. PIG FLESH

Nothing else, I thought, frantically darting back to where the others were. I had visions of something awful happening to Luke, to Matthew, and knew I wouldn't be able to bear that.

I can't take anything else, please.

Behind me, the faint, weak chirruping of dying birds cut out, suddenly. I didn't need to look to know the wall was no longer there. That was just how things were now, on the Island.

The screaming continued, frenzied, chilling. But it wasn't human. I could see Luke, Matthew, Rhoda and Johnny, and they were all fine, unharmed. Confused, and scared, but fine. Relief knocked the air from my lungs, and I grabbed Matthew tight in a fierce hug.

'I thought something had happened to you,' I rasped, letting go of him and picking Luke up from his place on the ground. I hoisted the boy into my arms, marvelling at the deep, primal sense of protectiveness that came over me when I was around him. He buried his hot face into my neck, and I struggled to keep my composure.

'No,' Matthew said, and he sounded exhausted. 'It's coming from out there, somewhere.' Deep, dark hollows lay under his eyes. He was pale, and a sheen of sweat lay on his temples. The Island was taking a toll on all of us.

A strange wind picked up. I'd spent enough time watching the Island in the last few hours to know this happened sometimes, usually after something came back. As if the wind followed, from the Other Place. It carried the sound this way and that, changing directions as we tried to keep up, tried to find the source of the screaming. The land was barren, wiped clean of features, but for all that, whatever it was, wherever it was, the noise and its maker eluded us. All we could see was the level, charcoal plane of the triangle, and beyond it, the pines.

Gooseflesh crawled across my skin. The sound went on, and on. It was terrible. It was the sound of pain, and suffering. It was the sound of death.

'Where is it?' Johnny said, swallowing repeatedly. Luke shivered as the screaming grew louder, and I squeezed him tight.

'There!'

We shaded our eyes, squinted into the mid-morning sun.

'Oh, my God,' said Rhoda.

Something large and pink and horrifying thrashed around in the distance.

'What…what the fuck *is* that?' Matthew asked.

It didn't take Johnny long to figure it out.

'The pigs,' he moaned. 'Uncle, it's the pigs!'

'Aye,' said Mac, heavily, and there was nothing else to say after that.

The thing writhed and shrieked, growing harsher and more urgent with every passing minute. I realised it was moving towards us, edging its way over from the far side of the triangle's edge.

I narrowed my eyes. Whatever we were looking at was too big for one pig, surely?

Then it clicked. *Pigs,* Johnny had said.

The animals had been rootling around in the soil together in their pen when White Pines disappeared.

'Oh,' I whispered.

It wasn't just one pig that we were looking at.

The Island had sent the animals back, but in doing so, had crushed the individual beasts together, mashing them into a single, struggling, mutated form.

The misshapen ball of pig flesh screamed at us again, scudding across the ground on a mass of stiffly braced legs with trotters desperately scrambling for purchase, to no avail. We watched this display with a rising sickness in our hearts, as if a car crash were playing out in slow motion before us. The pigs bucked and rolled and scrabbled until eventually, having shunted themselves completely across one side of the triangle, they came to rest in a spot not far from us, a level stretch of ground that eventually sloped up towards our vantage point under the cairn. The elevation proved too much for the uncoordinated pile of limbs, and so there the beasts writhed, while we looked on, helpless in the face of their suffering.

'Fuck,' said Matthew, and he began to cry.

There were three hogs fused together, arms and legs and snouts and ears and tails all jumbled up as if they were once soft clay models and a small, impatient child had smashed them into a single lump in a fit of pique. One of the heads dangled, lifeless, its eyes rolled back in its skull, its tongue lolling from a slack jaw. The deafening screams the creature made came from the two other heads, conjoined pig-twins sealed together in the same skull, but with two different faces, two separate snouts. They gurgled and gnashed their jaws in agony, and I could already see life beginning to fade from their eyes. Just as the sparrows had struggled and died, so would the pigs, because what living creature could survive something like this?

I pressed my face into Luke's hair, wanting to scourge the image from my sight and memory, knowing somehow that I would never be able to.

And a gunshot ripped violently through the air, obliterating the noise of the pigs. The sound ricocheted around the Island's interior, and I clutched Luke tight, ducking down instinctively and covering his head with my hands.

Rhoda stepped forward. She had Mac's shotgun cocked and levelled, sight firmly fixed on the monstrosity. Gone was the weeping woman who shivered beneath the cairn. In her place, a tall, strong figure squared up to fate. I approved of the change.

The pigs screeched. They were still alive. With a grim determination, Rhoda reset her feet, blew out her cheeks, focussed, and fired again. The gun kicked back hard into her shoulder, but she took the impact, bracing against it, her silver hair clouding crazily around her head.

Her aim was better the second time around. The shotgun roared, and the squealing stopped, abruptly. *Thank God,* I thought. *It's over.*

When I turned back, there was nothing to see. Only a flicker.

The Island had taken the pigs away again.

Shaken, I looked at Rhoda, who broke the gun with practiced hands. Spent cartridges pinged onto the ground behind her. She blew into the exposed barrels, and handed the gun back to Mac.

'It's been a long time since I used one of those,' she said, and I put Luke down, gently, unable to carry him any longer.

'You have good aim,' I said, eyeing the heavy gun with respect.

'I'm not as good a shot as I used to be. I just couldn't stand to see them suffer like that.'

Johnny spoke up.

'We've had those pigs since the beginning,' he said, face tight and strained. He sounded almost accusatory. 'I hand-reared them from piglets.'

Rhoda patted her hair. 'I just couldn't take it,' she said. 'That noise.'

Mac put a hand on her shoulder.

'Me either,' he said.

24. PLAN

After that, the Island remained still, for the most part, except for the occasional flicker. Almost as if it had run out of energy.

The incident with the pigs had an unexpected side-effect, in that it served to finally unite us as a group. Brought together by Rhoda's decisiveness with the gun, we held a meeting, and tried to reason a way out of our shared nightmare.

'If we stay here, we die.' Mac stated this as a matter of fact, rather than something that was up for debate. And he was right, I knew that. We could not stay here forever, waiting to see what happened. Eventually we would starve, or die of dehydration.

But what waited for us beyond the protection of the cairn seemed a worse prospect than death, in my opinion.

I folded my arms. I was happy to play devil's advocate if it meant not ending up like Glenn, or the pigs, or the sparrows.

'If we go out there, we die.'

'You don't know that. It might not work like that.'

'True. Trouble is,' I said, digging my heels in, 'It's kind of hard to test, isn't it?'

There was silence as everyone thought about this. I used the opportunity to keep talking.

'None of us wants to be the first to put a foot in that triangle, do we? Not after the things we've seen.'

'But we can't stay here.'

I sighed. 'No. We can't stay here.'

'So what do we do?' Matthew looked haunted. Already beaten down, the fight had gone out of him completely after the pigs.

Mac and I stared at each other, thinking.

'I don't know,' I said, eventually. I felt as if I had been checkmated in chess.

Johnny cleared his throat, his eyes red-rimmed and puffy. He'd been crying.

'I've been timing things,' he said, holding up his wrist and showing us an old-fashioned watch he was wearing. 'I've been timing the things that come back.'

'What do you mean?' I frowned, watching Luke from out of the corner of my eye. The boy had fallen into a fitful sleep in the grass, exhausted, and was now dreaming. He whimpered like a dog, and jerked around. I moved closer to him, frightened he would roll himself across the green strip and into the triangle.

'I've been timing how long there is between each...appearance. Each thing that returns.'

'Why?'

'I remembered something from school.' I wondered if he meant school before White Pines, or whether the community had run its own school. I then immediately thought of all the children who had lived on the Island, children who were now gone, and felt winded, as if punched in the gut.

Johnny continued, choosing his words carefully, as if saying them out loud helped his own thought process.

'At school we learned about natural disasters, earthquakes, volcanoes, that sort of thing. And about warning systems.'

Matthew straightened up a little. Rhoda folded her arms, listening intently.

'Go on,' Mac said.

'I think what's happening here is a bit like an earthquake. It's a...a...natural phenomenon, right?' Johnny stuttered a little as he spoke, awkward and unused to being the centre of attention.

A natural phenomenon? None of us replied. What was happening on the Island felt like the most *unnatural* thing imaginable, like a perversion of nature rather than a display of it.

But the teenager was right in one regard. Whether natural or supernatural, the disappearance of White Pines was a catastrophic event. And in that respect, comparing it to an earthquake made sense.

And so, we let Johnny talk.

'No-one can know exactly when an earthquake will hit, right?' He continued, the bit more firmly between his teeth now.

'Right,' I said, beginning to understand what he was driving at.

'But every quake sends out these waves. And there are different types. Some waves move faster than others. Like...ripples in a pond.' He made a rippling motion with his hands, demonstrating two waves moving at two different speeds.

'Warning systems detect the early waves, the faster ones. They don't do much damage. It's the *slower* waves that cause all the problems. They come after.'

'So what are you telling us?'

Johnny rubbed his face. He was skinny, and lean, like Luke. His Adam's apple bobbed up and down on his neck as he continued on.

'I think the things that come back are like the early waves. The fast waves. They come back for a second or two, sometimes longer, then they go again. They're like...a warning.'

'A warning?'

'Yes.' He nodded, in earnest. 'A warning. That's the best way I can describe it. A warning for what comes after.'

'And what comes after?'

'The slower waves.'

Mac spat, losing patience. 'What's any of this supposed to mean? How does it help us?'

'It means that something...worse is coming.' Johnny shrugged, defensive. 'That's what I think, anyway.'

Rhoda shook her head, aghast. 'What can possibly be worse than what we've already seen? What can possibly be worse than losing...losing our home? Our people?'

I remembered a black beast on a nightmare beach, striding across the sand towards me.

That could be worse, I thought.

Johnny waved his watch at us again. 'I don't know! But I think we can use it. The space between things coming back, the fast waves, is getting longer. Remember when it first happened? Things came and went so fast we couldn't see, couldn't keep track of it. Then it slowed to every few seconds, then every two minutes, then every five, then every seven. The air doesn't...' He flapped a hand about in a flickering motion. 'Do *that*...as much as it did in the beginning.'

'Wait.' Matthew frowned. 'The gaps between waves are getting longer. Shouldn't that mean we are...safer?'

'One the one hand, yes.' Johnny picked up a rock, just like earlier, and threw it out into the triangle.

And this time, it didn't disappear.

A ripple of excitement passed around our group.

'Maybe it's going away,' Rhoda theorized, looking to the rest of us hopefully. 'Maybe if we just wait it out, like Megs said, it'll stop, eventually.'

I interjected. 'But the things coming back with each wave are getting worse, aren't they?'

Johnny nodded. 'That's what I'm driving at. I think the slower wave is on its way.'

I worked through the implications of that in my mind.

'Maybe...maybe Johnny's right. Maybe it takes more energy to bring something alive back. Maybe the Island needs more time, and is preparing itself.'

'For what?' Matthew said.

'Back from where, for Christ's sake?' Mac added, belligerent, his patience now entirely gone.

'Back from wherever everything has gone.'

Matthew began to pace around the thin grassy strip. 'But what you're talking about...it's...I mean...you're talking about...' He couldn't articulate his thoughts properly, and it was frustrating him.

'I don't know what I'm talking about, Matthew.' I was calm as I said this. 'All I have to work with are the facts. And the facts are this. There was a town, sitting right where that triangle is sitting now. And now it's gone. And it's taken all the people with it. Except it isn't gone entirely, is it? Things keep coming back. And those things are getting worse. First the birds, then the pigs. I agree with Johnny. It's like the Island is gearing up for something.'

I looked at Mac then, remembering what he had said earlier. He'd been right, too. What if the next thing the Island wanted to send back was human? Was Rhoda a good enough shot to put one of her own townsfolk out of their misery? Could she shoot a friend, a neighbour, a child, like she had shot the pigs?

'I don't see how any of this helps us.' Rhoda, oblivious to my thoughts, was in agreement with Mac. They were a tight unit, and suddenly, ridiculously, I thought about Tim, and how we hadn't been a tight unit. I wondered what he was up to, right now, at that very moment, as we debated our own survival with a teenager.

Johnny took a deep breath.

'I think...' He trailed off, losing confidence.

'Finish that thought,' I said, gently.

'I think that if we wait for something else to come back, then wait for it to disappear again, we might have a window. A nine minute window, maybe, perhaps even longer, before something else comes through. And we could make a run for it.'

I blew out my cheeks. I'd been afraid he would say something like that.

'But what about Glenn? I don't want to end up like him.'

Johnny shuddered, then regrouped.

'He made a run for it too soon. The space between the waves was too narrow. The air was constantly shimmering then, remember? Like...'

'Like static on a television,' I said, finishing his sentence for him.

'Yes. Does that make sense? It's like a door, I think, the triangle. Each wave that comes...that's the door opening. And when it's open, you get sucked in. You go somewhere else. Or, you get thrown out, sent back from the other place. Only you get mixed up with whatever was next to you at the time. Or with something that was nowhere near you when you were taken, but maybe it gets all jumbled up on the other side.'

My head was now full of sand, and bodies, and human debris trapped in puddles of melted beach-glass. How had this kid figured all that out?

And what if he was right?

It would mean...

Careful, Megs. Careful what thoughts you allow yourself to have. Was that my mother's voice, this time, or mine? I couldn't tell.

It's like a door.

It would confirm that my dream hadn't been a dream at all.

It would mean that the beach was a real place.

The Other Place.

It would mean the god beneath the tree was real.

And so was the black giant.

'The point is, when the door is shut, for those nine minutes, we have time to move. But we have to be fast. Really, really fucking fast.'

I looked to Rhoda, then, the eldest of us. The slowest of us. She met my gaze, and nodded, ever so slightly. She was a risk. She knew she was a risk.

Matthew squinted at the triangle, trying to spot a clear route across, trying to judge the distance with his eyes.

'It's not too far to the edge of the triangle,' he said, eventually. 'Not really. Not from here. Especially if we use the slope to our advantage. We'd be running downhill.' He pointed to the northern side of the triangle, closest to the path that led through the trees. The way down was steepest from that side of the cairn, and he was right. That could work to our advantage.

Rhoda looked down at herself, at her body.

'It's been a fair while since I ran anywhere,' she said, flatly.

'But if you *had* to,' Johnny replied, going over to her. He took Rhoda's arm, not letting her give up. 'If you absolutely *had* to, if your life depended on it. You would. I know you would. And we'll help you. Uncle Mac and I will help you.'

Rhoda frowned, and started patting her hair again.

'Megs,' Matthew whispered, in a tone that made me look up immediately.

'What?'

'Over there.' He pointed with a shaking hand, and I fixed my eyes on the place he indicated.

Air flickered.

Another wave was coming.

Johnny checked his watch. 'Nine minutes,' he confirmed. Just as he'd predicted.

The air moved again. And it felt different, this time. A strong gust of wind that was not from this reality rolled suddenly up the slope towards us, carrying a flurry of ash with it.

The door was open once more.

'Luke, wake up,' I said, then, feeling strange. I knew in my bones that something huge was about to happen, and I was breathless with its coming. The sleeping boy protested, but I hauled on him until he was off the floor, then gathered him into my arms again. He was heavy, but was the safest place I could think of.

'What is that?' The colour drained from Mac's otherwise ruddy face.

'I don't...I can't see, wait...'

A great, dark shadow guttered in and out of reality, in, out, in, out...

In.

I gasped.

25. DREAMS MADE FLESH

It was the thing from my dream.

Here, on the Island. Come out from behind the curtain.

Dreams made flesh.

The beach was real.

So was the giant.

Huge, it towered above us, the cairn and the pines trees, swaying on long, spindly legs like a reed in a stream. Bipedal, it looked as if it had once been human, a very, very long time ago, and had since forgotten what a human was supposed to look like, how one was supposed to behave, and move. It had a long torso, and a hard, flat stomach, and enormous, meaty arms. Enormous genitalia dangled between its legs, an approximation of a man's parts, but different. The flesh of its face drooped in a cascade of shiny folds, like gathered cloth. There were few discernible features amongst the curtains of loose skin hanging there, but I could make out three eyes. Milky-white in colour, they were attached to the end of three long, thin stalks. The stalks twitched and stiffened, moving like snakes, like medusa's hair.

As the giant acclimatised to its new surroundings, those eyes focussed on us.

26. RUN FOR IT

I backed up fast, clutching Luke to my chest, retreating until I hit the cairn. Another bolt of painful energy ran through me on contact with the stones, but I hardly noticed it. All I could see was the giant who had appeared out of thin air.

I realised I was screaming.

The thing's face split in two, folds of flesh parting way to reveal a mouth that was pink and wet and endless, and the monster screamed back at me, but only for a second, because then, the Island took it, and it vanished.

'Oh fuck,' I heard Matthew say. 'What the fuck was that? What the *fuck* was that?!'

Shaking uncontrollably, I clung to Luke.

'It's alright,' I whispered, more to myself than to the child. 'It's alright.'

'No it's not,' he whispered back.

I steadied myself. Took a deep breath, then another. We didn't have the luxury of feelings, not right now. We needed to move. Before the thing came back.

Because I felt certain that it would.

'Alright,' I said, addressing Johnny. 'Let's do it. Let's make a run for it. Before it returns.'

He nodded, looking at his watch. 'Eleven minutes,' he said. Then he picked up a rock, and threw it into the triangle.

'Just to make sure,' he said.

It flew high, then tumbled down and landed on the ashen ground, bouncing a few times. Then, it settled.

It didn't disappear.

The time was ripe.

Matthew shot me a terrified look. 'I'm scared,' he said.

'I love you, Matthew.' I replied, fiercely, and his chin rose up, just a little, when he heard that. 'I love you, and we're going to be fine, I promise.' I hoped it was enough, just enough encouragement to see him through.

'Okay. Luke?' I peeled the boy away from me, and set him on the ground. 'I'm going to need you to be brave now, do you understand? I need you to be brave, and run when we run. Hold onto my hand, and run, really, *really* fast. No stopping. If you stop, we die, is that clear?'

The boy said nothing, so I shook him, gently.

'Do you understand?'

'I understand,' he said, in a tiny, weak voice. He fingered the pendant around his neck, sliding it into his mouth and chewing on it anxiously.

Rhoda snatched up Mac's shotgun, and cradled it like a precious baby. Then, we gathered in a line, held hands, and made a chain, a chain of people thrown together by fate, by circumstance, by events beyond our ken.

'Nine minutes,' said Johnny, and we tensed, like athletes on the block.

'I love you too, Megs,' Matthew said, squeezing my hand. I could feel him shaking beside me. On my other side, a small boy clung tightly to my fingers, his little body still, tensed. Primed.

'Ready?'

Nobody replied.

'*Go!*'

And then we were moving, running, stumbling down the hill, going so fast I thought I might lose balance and topple over, so I leaned back, shifted my weight to compensate for the gradient. All the time, I was horribly conscious of the child next to me, trying to keep up with my adult strides. Luke's hand gripped mine hard, but was slick with sweat. Every step I took loosened the hold I had on him, and I was grateful that Johnny was on the other side of the boy. If for some reason I let go, he would have someone else to help drag him along until I could grab him again.

I didn't plan on letting go.

I heard Mac swear as he dragged Rhoda along at the end of our chain, heard him bark:

'Drop it!' and realised he meant the gun. There was a clank and a thud as the shotgun was discarded, and then the sound of feet on earth, the sound of heavy breathing, and I used the rows of white tree trunks beyond the triangle as a focal point. *Run towards the trees, try and keep in a straight line,* I thought. *Don't let go of the boy. Try not to count the minutes that have passed. Two? Six? One?*

Just run, Megs. Just run.

And we did, flying down the slope, moving in a ragged line across the ashen ground where people once lived, and laughed, and loved.

And then I looked down, and saw a straight, clean edge, where brown and black turned to green and grey, and I knew it to be the edge of the triangle.

'Nearly there, Luke,' I panted. 'Nearly there!'

A memory of a thing that hadn't happened yet assaulted me, out of the blue. A red jacket. A tearing sound. A fence. Barbed wire. A boundary.

A boy.

Have I been here before?

Have I done this before?

Is any of this real?!

Desperate, eyes only on the goal, I strained forward, pushing myself over the edge of the triangle. My feet hit safe, green ground.

WHITE PINES

The chain broke.

Luke's hand slipped from mine.

I spun. Matthew was just behind me. Beyond him, Mac dragged Rhoda along like a sack of potatoes.

Luke! Where was Luke, and Johnny?

There! He had stumbled, gone down. Johnny, his face a mask of panic, was trying to haul him up. Luke was frail, and frightened. He got to his feet and then tripped again. I swore, and ran back into the danger zone for them, grabbing at Luke, screaming at the boys to hurry, and again, that powerful sense of deja-vu knocked me near breathless, for a small boy screamed distantly in my mind.

Hurry! He said, and a red jacket hung motionless from a barbed wire fence.

I hustled them the last few steps until they were safe, safe outside the triangle's edge. Moments later, Matthew, Rhoda and Mac fell across the line too.

We made it, I thought, in disbelief. My chest heaved with exertion, and sweat poured down my body. *We made it out.*

And just in time, for I could feel the static in the air gathering, could feel we were only seconds away from a flicker, seconds away from another wave, from the door opening once again.

And in those seconds, Luke spotted something lying in the ashen triangle. Something silver, round, and shiny.

His mother's pendant. The chain around his neck must have broken when he tripped.

'I dropped it!' He cried, in anguish.

Then, he ripped free of my grasp, and ran back into the danger zone.

'*Luke!*' I shrieked, reaching for him, on the verge of falling back into the triangle, flicker be damned, but then Matthew, my Matthew, my brave, constant Matthew, pushed past me, forcing me back.

He went after the boy.

In three quick strides he had caught up with him, grabbing Luke by the collar of his dirty shirt, making to turn and drag him back to safety. They were so close I could almost reach out and touch them with the very tips of my fingers, and there was a moment, a split-second, where our eyes met, where I knew it was all going to be okay, we were going to survive, and I knew that I wouldn't hesitate anymore, I would tell Matthew I loved him every hour of every day, and that there was no such thing as a right or wrong time to admit that to anyone, to let that into your life, and I stood there with my heart in my mouth, unable to breathe, willing them back to me, and...

And the air flickered.

Matthew's face went pale. He lifted Luke into his arms, opened his mouth, began to say something, and then, they both vanished.

And I was left behind.

A towering scream ripped itself out of me. I fell to my knees.

Matthew had gone, and so had Luke.

The Other Place had taken them.

And that, as my mother used to say, was that.

27. DON'T WATCH

Except it wasn't.

Because the door was still open.

Air buffered.

Ash floated down before my reddened, raw eyes.

The monster didn't return.

Something else did, though, something mutated, tormented, like the pigs. A struggling mass of limbs and bodies, fused together.

And the screams that came from it, when it arrived, were human.

'Don't watch,' Mac roared, when he realised what he was looking at. 'Don't watch!'

But we couldn't help it.

Because there was a woman, a woman who was no longer a person in her own right, but part of a monstrous dance, an abominable waltz, her body mixed up with that of another person. Her face peered out in frantic terror from his abdomen. He looked down at the head poking out of his body, and opened his mouth wide in a noiseless cry of absolute terror and agony. Her torso appeared to have fused to his pelvis. One of her arms stuck out at a right angle from his chest, stiffly mimicking the arm of a cross, or a monument, and I could see a tattoo on that arm, a flower of some sort. Maybe a peony, I couldn't tell. Her legs came out awkwardly from behind the man's lower body, as if she'd rugby tackled him and run right through him instead of meeting resistance, creating the effect of a surrealist horse, a terrible centaur, with legs where legs shouldn't be. And the other body, the host body, tried to fight off its unwelcome parasite, limbs flailing about, hands tearing at the woman's hair and face in vain while she screamed, and screamed, and screamed.

We had no choice but to watch as the man died in front of us, then, his lungs squashed and ruptured by the catastrophic intrusion of another human form trying to occupy the exact same space that he was. He spat blood, burbled, and went limp. The pair of bodies crashed to the ground. The woman, who was still somehow alive, screamed, her legs working feebly in the blackened soil, her one mobile arm clutching and grasping for relief, and I looked away, because I couldn't watch this macabre shit-show any more.

And I wished with all my heart then that I was dead. I didn't want to live in a world where these sorts of things happened.

I didn't want to live in a world where Matthew was gone.

A hand dropped onto my shoulder. It was Rhoda.

'It's over,' she said, and she was right. The bodies had been swept away by the retreating tide, sucked back in through the open door.

I wept.

'We have to leave, Megan.' Mac's voice broke through my grief with a gentle firmness that commanded my attention, despite the state I was in.

'Leave me alone,' I said, gripped by the memory of the first time Matthew and I had kissed. 'Just leave me alone.'

'No.' He was insistent, a leader once again. 'We've made it this far. We need to keep going. Someone...we need to tell someone about all this. Raise the alarm. Come back, with help. We'll get them back, Megan. We will.'

'Tell who?' I replied, bitterly. 'Who is going to believe us?'

'Nobody, until we bring them here, show them what this place is.'

I swallowed, and broke down again, a fresh bout of tears coursing down my cheeks.

'It won't make a difference,' I sobbed, feeling hollowed out and empty. 'What can we do?

What can anyone do against...that?'

A twig snapped behind us.

'She's right,' a new voice said, a voice I recognised.

I turned. Saw a group of people assembled at the tree line.

Mainlanders.

Fiona stood front and centre.

'I told you not to go,' she said, her mouth a grim line. She was angry.

'Help us,' I pleaded. She had answers. I knew she had answers. She could tell me what this place was. Where all the people had gone.

She stared at me with dark, glittering eyes.

'The Island deceives. I told you that. I warned you. You should have known better. Now, you've woken her up.'

I don't understand,' I said, but it didn't matter if I understood, or not, because the Mainlanders surrounded us, and moments later I heard the swift, sharp sound of something heavy moving through the air, something that struck me on the back of my head, and I fell into darkness, and the ground came up to kiss me.

28.
CONSE-
QUENCES

When I came to, I was curled in a foetal position in the dirt, my head bowed as if before a great god. It took a moment for me to realise my hands were bound behind my back. My eyes were covered, blindfolded with a rough cloth. I could see a tiny strip of soil and heather beneath the blindfold, nothing more. My head throbbed. There was a ringing sound in my ears. I'd been hit hard across the back of my skull, and it hurt. A lot. Blood filled my mouth. I coughed, and spat, red phlegm spattering onto the strip of earth I could see.

The sound of feet shuffling came from behind me. I had a sense of someone leaning over. My blindfold was removed, and I was hauled to my knees. Blinking, I waited for my eyes to adjust to the sudden burst of light that came in after the blindfold was peeled off.

And the more I came to, the more I could hear.

And what I could hear was Johnny, crying.

My vision cleared at last, and I saw him. My mouth dropped open. We were back on the mainland. I knelt on the ground before the great wooden frame that I had first seen on my walk into Laide. The tall, inverted u-shaped frame with the strange carvings upon it. I'd paused, wondered briefly what it was for, and moved on. My shoes had been wet with dog-piss, and not long after, the dog had been shot.

I had forgotten about this frame.

But now, here I was, and I saw Johnny beneath it, arms and legs bound like mine were, and there was a noose around his neck, a noose made of rope, and he was shouting and sobbing, and trying to break free of his bonds, only he couldn't.

And I finally understood what the strange wooden u-frame was. What it was for.

It was a gallows frame.

Like something from centuries gone by. A gallows, proudly set here on the side of a quiet country road in the Highlands for all to see. An unashamed instrument of death. Of murder.

Then I knew, through a blinding flash of memory, that I had been here before. As a child.

I had been here with my Granny.

And there she is, that young-girl version of me, standing in a semi-circle of people that surrounds this hideous structure, onlookers all, watching as three silhouettes struggle like maggots on a fishhook at the end of three ropes, ropes which are slung across the top of the gallows frame, and come down sharply to one side. The ropes are anchored at the other end by people from the town, three of the largest, strongest men who grit their teeth in determination, neck muscles corded tight with exertion, while the counterweights giving them so much trouble jerk about, dying slowly.

My Granny is next to me, thin, yet solid. And I am not afraid, although I should be. Granny's presence is oddly comforting. As a child, I must have liked my Granny, I realised. As an adult all I could remember was her coldness, her bony frame, her quiet, strange manner. But here, in memory, she shows tenderness. Her hand is on my hair, stroking it, softly, a soothing gesture, and she is talking to me as I watch two men and one woman choke to death at the end of three ropes.

'Here,' she says, never taking her eyes from the frame. 'Eat this.'

And she pushes a paper-wrapped candy into my hand. I take it, peel off the paper, and pop it into my mouth, which instantly goes numb. The flavour is bitter, unpleasant, with overwhelming tones of aniseed, but the numbness is welcome. It spreads through my body, and I am calm.

And three people die in front of me.

The sun is behind them, slowly setting, meaning I cannot see their faces, which must be black and blue by now, but I can hear the sounds they make. And those are enough.

All else is silent, apart from Granny, who whispers something softly in my ear, something meant only for me.

'It's necessary, my sweet,' she says. 'No matter how it looks, remember that. It's necessary.'

And the girl, who still had five fingers on her right hand then, watches the execution. And in the distance, behind the dying folk, an Island sits in the bay, a familiar island, *the* Island, only this Island has no trees on it.

No trees, but there is something visible there, stalking across the landmass on long, terrible limbs. It is huge, and familiar, and it steps down awkwardly from the Island, feeling its way along the seabed carefully with its feet as it goes, and then it strides out across the bay, the waters barely reaching its ankles. It is vast and terrible, moving with deliberate and dreadful inevitability, and the girl is frightened, despite the numbness creeping through her system. The giant moves the same way that a cat moves when it is stalking prey. It is a predator, and even though she should be too young to know of such things, she recognises that. She squeezes her Granny's hand so tight she feels like she might break something, but her Granny holds fast.

The creature wades across the sea and reaches the shore of the mainland. Without pause, it steps up onto the sands of the bay and walks resolutely inland, approaching the gallows. The ground trembles and shakes under the weight of its feet. The men and the women who hung from the gallows are dead, now. They swing like grim window ornaments, ropes pulled taut like piano wire above them. It makes sudden sense to the girl, as she looks at the bodies. As she watches the beast approach. Why they are here, why they are all gathered, like this, a semi-circle of people watching, and waiting, in silence, and fear.

And awe.

The three lifeless corpses, gently swaying at the end of their nooses, are offerings.

Still warm, still fresh.

Offerings, and the giant is coming to collect. Later, three white marble stelae would be erected for them in Laide cemetery. There would be no bodies to bury, but slender, pale, tooth-like markers would be left behind instead, markers with a hanged man inscribed thereon. This is how it has always been, since the creature first came, and this is how it would continue to be, until the creature dies.

When that will be, nobody knows. The creature has been coming for many, many years, and does not show signs of ageing, or slowing down.

The girl knows this, the same way that all the assembled people know this. It is lore, and law. It is unlikely to change any time soon.

It is how they live.

The thing has reached the gallows frame, now. Up close, it is huge, it is an atrocious display of loose flesh and long limbs and foul odour, and the thing's questing eyes, mounted on stalks, obliterate the girl's sanity for a hot, urgent instant as she meets its gaze. She can feel her bladder give way, a small rush of warm liquid trickle down her legs, and she would feel shame if she could feel anything at all beyond the strange tingling sensation in her body.

A large hand comes up from the floor to grasp the body dangling in the middle of the gallows, the body of a young woman. The creature begins to shudder, and shake, a disgusting contortion of flesh and bone taking place in the area of its face which the girl realises is the jaw. A pink slit opens up wide within the horrible folds of skin.

And then the child's Granny covers her eyes with her gnarled free hand.

'Don't look,' she murmurs, softly. 'Best not to look.'

And the memory ended there, because the girl was me, and I came back into myself, kneeling before a gallows, a gallows from which a young man was about to be hung, but he would not be the first, or the last, I knew that now. I remembered.

I gasped, struggling with the weight of this knowledge. How could I have forgotten that which I had seen as a child? How? What had happened to me to make me forget something like that? Ritual sacrifice. A giant, foul beast. Complicity from those I had grown up amongst, if only for a short time. My Granny, a part of it all.

This is why Mother had broken free, moved us away from Scotland. She had been saving me from this bizarre, terrifying normality, where realities merged, and nightmares were real, and human sacrifices a community event.

I craned my neck around to look at the people assembled behind me. They were standing in a half-circle around the gallows, just like they had in my memories. Just like they had in the old, faded photograph in the Post Office. Did I know any of these faces, from long ago? Clearly they knew me. Did I belong here?

Was I one of them?

Fiona, one step ahead of the crowd as usual, watched events unfold before her like a queen holding court. She stood rigid and proud in front of the cowering teenager who struggled beneath the gallows, one hand raised to eye-level in expectation. My breath came fast and shallow. I knew what she was about to do. I knew what the hand was about to set in motion.

In memory, a dog's head exploded, leaving a red cloud in the air.

My heart pounded impossibly loud in my ears, and I could see the Island. Now that I was back on the mainland, it pulled at me. My head throbbed with pain, and I could no longer attribute it to the blow I'd received.

The Island wanted me back.

My brain felt like it was sliding sideways. Is this what it was like to lose one's mind?

Johnny's cries and struggles grew louder. I couldn't bear it. I couldn't stand to look at him, at his pathetic attempts to escape what I knew to be inevitable. I turned my face, and saw Mac and Rhoda beside me. They were also bound, kneeling and helpless. Mac had been beaten badly, his face a mess of blood and bruises. Rhoda had a black, swollen eye which wouldn't open properly. They both screeched and swore at the townsfolk of Laide, begging them to let Johnny go, trying to get to the boy, but unable to escape the mainlanders who held them back.

Their pleas fell on closed ears.

My eyes went back to Fiona. Her hand still raised, trembling with anticipation.

Johnny stopped struggling against his

bonds, and his face crumpled. He began to cry.

Fiona drew the sign of a triangle in the air.

'*No!*' I heard myself shout.

Then I heard the quick whip and buzz of a rope moving over wood, snapping tight as it reached capacity.

I heard a strangled cry, cut off before it could fly properly.

I heard the sound of a young man die, quickly but painfully.

Mac roared in fury, tried once more to get to his feet, tried to run to Johnny, but he was held back by men who showed no emotion whatsoever as the teenager died.

And that was that. It was over in minutes. I swallowed, raised my eyes to the gallows, and saw the boy dangling from the end of the rope, limp, hands loose by his sides. He was dead. I wanted to cry, but I had nothing left. Johnny had been a good boy, a clever boy. He had saved us.

For what? For this?

I was overwhelmed with guilt, then. I had this idea that my actions had started a chain of events that was killing everyone around me. No matter which direction I turned in, death followed me about, a dogged shadow on long legs.

And the memory of Matthew hit me like a sledgehammer, and I remembered that he was gone too, and Luke, that the Island had taken them. A huge sinkhole opened up inside my chest. I leaned forward and pressed my hot face into the dirt, and remembered I'd loved him, loved Matthew for years.

I wished they'd strung me up on that gallows frame, an offering to the beast, in place of the boy. But they hadn't. Instead, I was here, and I was being forced to witness this, and I had a good idea of why.

I was being educated.

Fiona turned to me, her expression cheerful once again. She stooped, and yanked my head back so that we were face to face. She cupped my chin fiercely with her hand, pulling it up so my neck was stretched uncomfortably tight. Brusquely, she ran a finger down my nose.

'You left us with no choice, dear,' she said, eyes fixed on mine. Her voice was not unkind. Rather, it was businesslike.

The shadow of the dead boy swung like a pendulum behind her left shoulder. The rope that had ended him creaked like an old tree branch as it sawed over the wooden gallows frame.

'This was necessary. In time, you will understand.' She sounded like my Granny.

Now that the show was over, the mainlanders started to leave, breaking off into smaller groups and walking the road back to Laide in dribs and drabs. None of them cast a second glance at the teenager they had murdered. None of them cast a second glance at me, or Mac, or Rhoda, as we knelt like bound slaves on the spoiled ground. It was as if they had taken part in a village fete, instead of an execution.

Fiona lifted me to my feet, placing a steadying shoulder under my right arm when I wobbled. She continued talking, her tone light and conversational, taking out a sharp pen knife from a pocket, unfolding it, and using it to slice the bonds that tied my hands behind my back as she spoke.

'You will not tell anyone about the things you have seen on the Island, or here.'

'Fuck you,' I spat, wincing in pain as blood flowed back into my wrists and hands. Pins and needles stabbed at me as circulation was restored, and I bit my lip.

Then, I hit Fiona, square across the jaw with my four-fingered hand. She recoiled, and I hit her again, and again, until a man I recognised stepped forward and cuffed me hard across my own cheek. I saw stars, somehow kept my balance. It was Murdo. He carried a walking stick with a forked handle, and had a new dog with him, a young, skinny pup. This one did not have a patch over its eye. It looked nervous, jumpy as it skulked around Murdo's feet, tripping him up as he moved. He rapped it gently across the ribs with the butt of his walking stick to move it out of his way, and the dog yelped, cowered. A pitiful creature, like myself. We were all pitiful creatures.

'The people...all those people...' I said,

panting and spitting fresh blood. My hand hurt.

'We can't do anything for them, now,' said Fiona, touching the rapidly developing red welt on her face. Her hair stuck out wildly from the neat bun on the back of her head, and I felt a small, grim satisfaction at that. It was a tiny win.

Mac hurled abuse at her from his place on the ground, his entire face puce with rage. Murdo brought his walking stick down hard on Mac's shoulder. I heard something crack, and Mac grunted. Murdo beat him again, hard about the head this time. I tried to stop him, but he was tall, and strong, and kept me at bay easily as he whacked the cane down onto Mac's shoulders, neck and head. Eventually the older man stopped struggling, and slumped, panting, his head hung low. Rhoda leaned into him, resting her face on his shoulder, whispering words of comfort that he no longer seemed able to hear.

Fiona continued as if nothing had happened, staring out to sea, watching. Waiting, and I knew for what, now.

The creature.

'You have to understand. What we do, we do for the protection of all,' she said. 'And if you keep messing around with things you don't understand, you'll upset the delicate balance we've worked so hard to build all these years. That your Granny worked so hard to build. And her grandmother before her. And hers before *her*. It's in your blood, see. It's not your fault you don't understand any of this. You were taken away from us at too young an age.'

She reached for my right hand, and gently pinched the stump of my missing little finger.

'Do you remember the night we took this?' She asked, and I stared at her, horrified. My voice came out choked, and dry.

'I...my mother told me it was an accident...'

I trailed off. Of course it wasn't an accident. There were no accidents, I was beginning to understand. Only accidental consequences.

'We took this on the eve of your eighth birthday. As is custom. Your mother was not best pleased. Despite knowing it was your fate. Your birthright.' Fiona sighed. 'Nothing we could say would convince her to stay, after that. And so you were removed from us. Which is why...' She shook her head. 'No. That isn't fair. This is not your fault. You weren't taught the things you should have been. No use crying over spilled milk.'

Mac coughed up blood.

'There were over a thousand of us on that Island!' Rhoda sobbed. 'All gone, now. Why didn't you tell us? Why didn't you tell us what you knew?!'

Murdo beat her across the back of the shoulders, too. She grunted, and fell flat on her face.

Fiona moved over to where the fallen

woman lay groggily in the soil. 'You *were* told,' she said, glaring at her as if she were a disobedient child. 'You idiot outsiders. When you came here, you were told to leave well enough alone. We tried to tell you, but no, you would have your secret community. Your wee paradise. With your trees and your pigs and your hippy, radical nonsense. We tried. We told you not to build on that Island. And now you know why.'

Rhoda remained uncowed, even as she lay there. 'Your fault.' She said. 'This is all your fault. Those people, *my* people, are on you. No-one else.'

Fiona rolled her eyes. 'Those people are gone now. The Island does not give back what it takes, at least, not easily. The only one who can come and go as it pleases over there is the Hunter, and it leaves us alone if it is fed.' She gestured to Johnny's corpse.

Mac chose then to rouse himself. He threw another choice word at Fiona. Murdo, primed and ready, lifted the cane high into the air again, but Fiona stayed his hand this time.

'No,' she said, and that infuriating smile grew upon her lips once more.

Mac faced down the pair, eyes wide. 'If you're going to kill me, get on with it,' he said, and Rhoda implored him to be quiet, to stop talking before he got himself strung up like Johnny.

Fiona cocked her head to one side, bird-like, and tutted.

'No, there is no need for that, not now.'

Mac was not giving up.

'I'll go straight to the police! The army. I'll speak to anyone who will listen.'

Fiona's smile grew, and I saw something distinctly sadistic flare in her eyes.

'You can't speak if you have no tongue,' she said.

Murdo was suddenly on Mac, then, crouching over him like a spider, kneeling on his legs, pinning his arms to the ground. Mac struggled but the other man was stronger, fitter. He held him down, and Fiona knelt, delicately sliding one hand inside Mac's open mouth, wincing as he tried to bite down on her fingers.

I tried to intervene. I tried to pull her away from him, but before I could get a proper hold of her, she'd jammed the penknife into Mac's mouth. He howled in pain, his mouth opened wide again, and in a fluid, practiced movement, she grabbed hold of his tongue with her left hand and thrust the penknife up with her right.

And I had another lightning bolt of memory strike from deep within the clouds in my brain. I was a child again, and I was being held down, much like this, an aniseed flavoured sweet burning in my mouth, and there was a knife, there was pain in my right hand.

My Granny looked on solemnly as I

screamed in agony.

Blood ran hot down my wrist.

Back in the present, Mac was choking, gargling. Fiona triumphantly pulled his severed tongue from his mouth.

Then she threw it to the collie dog, who pounced on it, and ate it down in three swift gulps.

29. ONLY TWO

Mac fainted. Blood poured out of his slack mouth, and pooled under his head.

Fiona wiped the knife blade on her cardigan sleeve. She looked down at the mess of a man beneath her.

'We curse the day you moved to the Island,' she said.

With that, Murdo and Fiona stood up in unison, dusted their hands on their jackets, and looked to Rhoda. Neither of them seemed terribly interested in me anymore.

I stood, rooted to the spot in disbelief.

Had we survived the Island, only for this?

The young dog licked its chops, and barked excitedly. It approved of the fresh meat, and wanted more.

Murdo stepped over Mac's body and went to Rhoda. He shot an enquiring look at Fiona, and it struck me suddenly that I'd never heard the man speak, not once.

Fiona nodded. Murdo lifted the old woman to her feet. I thought she might try to fight, but she went willingly, a shocked, vacant stare now on her lined and weathered face.

'Where are you taking her?' I wanted to intervene, I wanted to go to Rhoda, and help her, but I remained frozen in place.

'Away for a while. As insurance.' Fiona shot me a look. I had no idea what she meant by it.

'Insurance for what?'

Fiona began to walk slowly back towards Laide.

'Go home, Megan,' she said, over her shoulder. 'Go back to *Taigh-Faire*. Get out of here before the Hunter comes back, for its offering. Take that stubborn, foolish man with you. There's nothing else you can do for now. Except look after him.' She waved dismissively at Mac. 'We'll talk again soon.'

The Hunter. The giant.

She was right. It could come back at any moment.

Rhoda shuffled away, her unlikely captors on either side of her.

Johnny's body creaked in the background.

'You can't keep me here!' I shouted after them, my voice cracking. 'You know that, don't you? I won't stay here!'

Fiona stopped, but didn't turn around.

'No,' she said. 'I don't know that. The Island has plans for you. So do we. You were taken away from us once. We won't let that happen again.'

'I'll leave. If it kills me. I'll leave, and I'll talk.'

'We'll see,' Fiona said. And on she went, calmly walking along with the confidence of a woman who had just ticked an irksome task off of a long to-do list.

A breeze picked up, riffled through the heather and bracken around me. Johnny's corpse swayed.

I looked down at Mac.

And then, I thought, an unbearable sadness filling me up slowly on the inside, *there were only two.*

30. ESCAPE

I ripped off a long strip of fabric from the bottom of my shirt, balled it up, and used it to try and stem the flow of blood from the stump of Mac's tongue, all the while checking over my shoulder to see if the nightmarish thing from the Island would appear, would come marching across the water, ready to feast on Johnny's body.

It never did, and Mac, now a deadly shade of pale, never woke up. The strip of cloth soaked through and became sodden with blood within moments, and I threw it to one side in disgust. He needed a hospital, I couldn't help him here. I had to get him out of this place, away from these people, away from the Island.

I knew I wouldn't be able to carry him back to *Taigh-Faire* by myself if he was unconscious. He was a large man and a dead load. I hadn't eaten or slept for a long time, and had little strength left in me.

I made a decision. I would leave him here, return to *Taigh-Faire* as quickly as I could, collect the van, and come back for him.

I rolled him onto his side and arranged him in the recovery position, propping his head so that the blood would run down and out of his mouth instead of back into his throat, choking him. He looked as if he were already dead, he was so pale and cold, but I could hear him breathing, a shallow rattle that urged me on.

'I'll be back,' I whispered, knowing he couldn't hear me, but needing to say it anyway. I got to my feet. 'I'll be as quick as I can.'

I hoped I would be quicker than the Hunter.

I shuffled back along the road as fast as my exhausted body could take me, to *Taigh-Faire.* When I got there, shattered, stumbling, breathing hard and ragged, I realised I had to break into my own front door as I didn't know where my house key was. I did this with a rock, cutting my arm in the process, but hardly noticing. I barged in and began frantically searching for my van keys, before remembering I'd left them in the van, dangling by the wheel. I lurched back to the drive where the vehicle was parked, and climbed in, fumbling and swearing and trying to turn the key with hands that wouldn't cooperate.

All the while, I could see and feel the Island, hovering in the background. The memories of what had taken place there tormented me.

I got the engine to spark, reversed out of the driveway, and drove like hell to get back to

Mac. I was so relieved when I saw him still lying there by the side of the road that I would have cried, had I any tears left. I leapt out, and somehow managed to half-drag, half-roll him up into the van, where he lay on the floor behind the front seats. There was an old blanket amongst the boxes I'd packed when I'd left home, which were still in the back of the van. I wrapped it around him, tucking the corners under the rear seats to anchor him in place so he didn't roll around as I drove. I checked his pulse. It was weak, but there. He was still cold, however, deathly cold, and his skin was still that awful greyish tone.

'Don't die on me,' I said, and I meant it. 'Please don't die on me.'

I got back into the driver's seat and took a last look at the gallows and Johnny's body through my windshield. My insides felt like stone as I took in the young lad swinging rhythmically under the frame. He seemed so slight and thin up there, as if already fading away, already losing water and body mass and drying out like a salted fish on a rack. I thought about cutting him down, I thought about loading him into the van too, taking his body with us, but I lacked the strength, tools or time. Mac needed my help now, not Johnny. Johnny was dead.

I rammed the van into gear and sped away from the gallows, following the road inland, my head now pounding so hard I found it difficult to steer properly. Luckily the twisting road was as empty of traffic as it had been when I'd first arrived. Back before I'd known the Island even existed.

Except I had always known. I'd known, and repressed it. A traumatised child, carrying a terrible secret, for all these years. I hated the mainlanders for what they'd done to me. I hated them, and my Granny, for taking my finger. For feeding the beast. For making me a part of their terrible, bloody narrative.

I hated them for keeping the Island's secrets for so many years.

I glanced at Mac in the rear-view mirror. He lay stone-still on the floor of the van, eyes closed. I had no idea if he were alive or dead. I pressed my foot on the accelerator, hard.

And, for a moment or so, I thought I was going to make it.

I thought I was going to be able to get away.

But the Island, as Fiona had said, had other ideas.

The further inland I drove, the worse my headache became, as if a band of metal had been wrapped around my skull. The band grew smaller and tighter with each passing mile, and the crushing pain intensified.

I managed ten miles before my nose erupted in a messy spatter of gore, and then, I began to leak tears of blood. I didn't even realise it was happening until my vision clouded, until the world turned an alarming shade of red. I reached up with a shaking hand to touch my damp face, and my fingers came away bloody. I looked in the rear-view mirror again, screaming when I saw the twin tracks of crimson streaking down my cheeks. The van swerved wildly, and I yanked the wheel over, correcting it, narrowly avoiding driving into the verge and rolling the van in the ditch that lay beyond.

I kept driving.

So, I was bleeding. So, my head felt like it was about to explode. So what. I would not let the Island win.

After twelve miles, all the blood vessels in my eyes burst. I felt them go, a collection of tiny pops and twitches, and then my sight grew dark. The pain in my head intensified so fiercely that it was like hitting a great invisible wall at full speed. I had a moment to realise I'd been defeated, a moment to realise I was blind and still speeding along the road at seventy miles an hour, and then agonising pain ripped me to pieces. The world went from dark to complete, definitive black as I fainted at the wheel, unknowingly crashing the van into a larch tree on the side of the road.

And thus ended my first, and last, attempt to escape my fate.

Or, my duty, depending on how you looked at it.

31. DEFEAT

I woke to find hands on me, unbuckling my seat belt, supporting my head, sliding me out of the driver's seat, carrying me carefully away from the vehicle. I opened my eyes groggily, but couldn't see a thing. All was black. My head was a thing of pain, a block of excruciating agony.

I moaned, and heard a dog bark, a young dog. I knew then that it was Murdo who pulled me from the bent and crumpled wreckage of my van. He carried me as if I weighed nothing, and there was something almost gentle in the way he held me. Gentle, or reverent, like I was important. But I didn't want to be important, not to these people. I wanted to be left alone. I wanted to die. Death would be better than this endless, endless fucking nightmare I found myself living in. I struggled weakly, like a babe in swaddling robes, but I had no strength. No sight. No spirit.

No fight left.

There was no escaping from any of it, I realised. No escape. No running. No hiding. What would be the point? The things I had seen would follow me around until the day I died.

I was defeated.

I sagged back into Murdo's arms. Fine. Let them take me back. Back to Laide. Back to *Taigh-Faire*. Back to the Island.

Anything to stop the pain in my head.

Anything.

I heard voices as I was carried away from the wreckage, several male voices and one distinct, familiar female voice.

Fiona.

A car door opened. I was lowered. More hands came to help me, supporting my head, my back, taking my feet. I was loaded into the back of a car, laid across the seats. Firm fingers checked the pulse in my neck, and then on my wrist. A jacket was draped across me. It was heavy and warm.

The voices moved away. I called out, weakly, but there was no reply. I tried to move, but someone had pulled a seatbelt across me, pinning me beneath the jacket in a tight, secure cocoon, and I was too weak to find a way out of it. My head felt like an alien entity on my shoulders: huge, and swollen. I groaned. What were they doing? Why had they left me here?

I just wanted it to end. I could not bear such pain for much longer.

'Take me back,' I whispered to the empty air. 'Please. I can't take it anymore.'

There was no answer, but I heard the boot

door pop. Something clanged against the side of the car. I heard it thunk, metal on metal, and there was the faint sound of liquid sloshing around, too. Fiona's voice murmured a series of instructions I couldn't hear from somewhere nearby.

I smelled something unpleasant. It burned my nose. I realised it was petrol.

Why petrol?

Mac. I had forgotten Mac!

With a slow, breaking horror, I realised that Mac was still inside my van, the van I had crashed.

The petrol smell intensified.

'No,' I croaked, 'You can't!'

I knew what they were doing. They were pouring petrol on my van. They were going to set it alight, dispose of the evidence.

And Mac was in the van.

I dug deep, found a tiny grain of strength, began to flail and kick and shout. Every movement set off a violent wave of agony in my head, but I gritted my teeth and bore it. They were going to set fire to Mac.

They were going to set fire to Mac.

'You can't!' I cried again, with my ruined voice. 'You can't! Please!'

Eventually, a car door opened near my head. I sensed a face near mine. It smelled of peppermint lozenges and hairspray and floral, dull perfume.

Fiona.

'Mac,' I pleaded.

'Is dead,' Fiona replied, and the door slammed shut again.

The last of the petrol splattered over my van. I heard more murmured conversation, and then Fiona's voice, issuing an order. I wondered if she had her hand raised. I wondered if she were drawing the shape of a triangle in the air next to her head.

There came a whooshing, rushing sound, the sound of fire catching. I could smell smoke, acrid and foul. The rushing became a roaring, and the voices of the mainlanders grew closer to me as they stepped back from the blaze.

Mac, I thought sadly, and then the pain in my skull set me adrift, and I floated away on a sea of black. Distantly, I felt people climb into the car, and felt the engine start. The fire had taken, the job was done.

Mac was gone.

No loose ends.

The car rolled onto the smooth surface of the road, did a three-point turn, and headed back to the coast.

They were taking me back to Laide.

The Island still had plans for me.

32. ALL IN GOOD TIME

I thought I would wake in my bed at *Taigh-Faire*. Instead I opened my eyes and found that I was lying in a small cot bed in a tiny, low-ceilinged room painted a bright shade of white. My vision had returned, although it was cloudy and spotted, and there was blood crusted around my eyelashes. My head throbbed, but then that was nothing new. The pain was more tolerable, now, which meant that I was closer to the Island once again.

A creak and shuffle caught my attention. I lifted my head slightly. A blurry figure sat at the end of the bed, reading. I blinked, trying to clear the clouds from my sight. Eventually, I could see enough of the shadow to know it was Fiona.

She lifted her head from her book, saw that I was awake, and carefully closed it, tucking a bookmark in to keep her place.

'Oh, good,' she said, as if she were my kindly aunt and not the world's most monstrous woman. 'You're awake.'

She stood up, set the book on the chair, and went to a window nearby, where thick yellow curtains were drawn. She twitched the fabric back with a quick, sharp movement, and light spilled into the room. I hissed, squeezing my eyes shut. My dry and cracked lips parted.

'Are you my keeper, now? Is that it?' I croaked.

'No,' she said, calm as ever. 'Believe it or not, I wish you no harm. Can you sit up?'

Her hand slid under my neck, and she hoisted me into a sitting position even as I recoiled from her touch.

'Get off me,' I spat, as she plumped a pillow, shoved it behind my head.

'There you go,' she said.

I opened my eyes again. Through the small window I could now see the sky, hedgerow, fields, and the square boxy structure of Laide Post Office. I remembered that an old cottage had been set into the road, right opposite the tarmac forecourt of the building. *This must be where Fiona lives,* I realised.

'Is Rhoda here?' I hoped against hope that she wasn't dead. She was all that was left of White Pines now that Mac was gone.

Fiona left the room, ignoring my question.

She came back a little while later with a glass of water and a steaming bowl of soup on a tray. 'Here,' she said, setting the tray on my lap. 'Eat this. I made it.'

'What's in it?' I peered into the bowl.

'It's just chicken. It's not poisoned.'

'If it were poisoned, I might prefer it,' I said.

I slept again after I'd eaten the soup, hugely disappointed to discover that it was indeed not poisoned. When I next opened my eyes, it was dark outside. The curtains were drawn once again, but a small table lamp illuminated the room so that I could see. Another figure sat at the end of my bed, a male figure. A black and white dog stood next to him, wagging his tail slowly, nose in the man's lap.

Murdo.

I watched him warily, and he watched me back. Eventually, I found the courage to speak up.

'Don't talk much, do you?' I said.

He opened his mouth by way of response, and his taciturn nature suddenly made a lot more sense. I fought back a surge of sickness.

Murdo didn't talk, because he had no tongue.

I remembered how expertly Fiona had ripped Mac's tongue free from his mouth, how casually she had tossed the bloody organ to the dog for it to dispose of. Clearly, she was something of an expert. What mistake had Murdo made, to warrant having his tongue cut out?

What other violent rules did this woman govern by?

I held up my right hand for him to see. My missing little finger for his missing tongue, as if we were trading disfigurements like war veterans.

He closed his mouth, and went back to watching me, stroking the dog's head with a large, heavy hand.

I rolled over in bed, blocking him out of sight with a pillow.

And thought of Matthew.

On the morning of the second day of my enforced bed rest, I woke and found that I could see with almost perfect vision again. Ignoring the 'carer' who sat at the foot of my bed- a female mainlander I did not recognise, who eyed me with mild curiosity as I roused and sat upright- I decided to experiment with my legs. If I could see, then I could escape. I could not bear to stay under Fiona's roof for one more moment, one more second of my life.

I folded back the bedsheets, and found I was half-naked underneath them. No matter. I was beyond giving any thought to things like clothes and bodies and decency. Not when a beach existed somewhere, littered with body parts. Not when a town full of people had vanished before my eyes. Not when a huge fucking giant haunted the land. If I had to leave this house bare-arsed, so be it.

I swung my legs around and down, tentatively putting weight on them and then slowly standing, hanging onto the side of the bed in case I fell. The room spun a little, but I remained upright. Straightening, I spotted my clothes folded up on a dresser behind the carer. I went to them, never once acknowledging the mainlander, propping myself up against a wall as I laboriously slid one leg into my jeans. She tutted as she watched me, and made as if to help me.

'If you lay one finger on me,' I said, half-in, and half-out of my jeans, 'I'll bite your fucking throat out, do you understand?'

She tutted again, and left the room, presumably to alert Fiona.

I dressed, and found, as I poked my head out of the bedroom door, that there were only two rooms upstairs in the cottage, the one I'd been sleeping in, and a tiny, sparklingly clean bathroom. Which begged the question: had Fiona let me sleep in her own bed? I shuddered at the thought. It was hard enough living under her roof without knowing I'd been sleeping between her sheets, resting my head where she rested hers. It made me feel dirty, thinking about it.

I realised I needed to urinate badly, so I shut myself in her bathroom, locking the door, finishing my business as quickly as I could in my weakened, wobbly state. I washed my hands, watching as dried flakes of blood from under my fingernails disappeared down the plug hole. My reflection in the tiny mirror over the sink was haggard, shocking. I was thin, and had a large, steering-wheel shaped welt on my forehead. My eyes were pink, bloodshot, and my hair was a matted, greasy nest. There was more blood on my teeth.

When I emerged, I expected to be met by Fiona, arms folded across her breast, a pleasant smile upon her lips, ready to usher me back to bed. Instead, the cottage seemed empty. Quiet. I stood on the top of the stairs, listening for a while.

Then, I called out: 'Rhoda?' Maybe she was being held here, too.

Nothing came back.

Carefully, I made my way downstairs, barefoot, and paused at the bottom of the staircase. More silence. There was no trace of the carer, and no trace of Fiona. She was probably holed up at the Post Office, I realised, selling stamps and counting out change. How I hated her.

More than I hated the Island, even.

The layout downstairs was much the same as upstairs, only instead of a bathroom, a tiny galley kitchen sat, right next to the living room. I looked around, searching desperately for traces of Rhoda, and knowing it would not be that simple.

I'll find her, I promised myself. *Whatever it takes.*

I found my shoes waiting for me by the front door, and decided to steal the bright red jacket that was hanging on a coat rack next to it. It looked cold outside, breezy. As much as the idea of wearing Fiona's clothes disgusted me, I knew I was sick, and weak. I comforted myself by making a promise to burn the jacket when I was done with it. This resolve triggered a memory of the sound of my van burning, burning with Mac still buckled inside.

I had failed him.

I had failed Matthew, and Luke, and Johnny, and Rhoda, if she was still alive, which I was beginning to doubt. I had failed the community of White Pines. Thinking about it, about all those people who had simply winked out of existence, made me feel dizzy. I locked my knees, took a moment to gather myself.

Get away first. Mourn later.

My mother's voice sounded very wise, and very far away.

Opening the door, I was confronted with the ugly little concrete forecourt attached to the Post Office. Beyond this, lay the familiar green hills, the sickly-sweet blue of Gruinard bay, and the road, which forked, the lower fork heading back to *Taigh-Faire.* I looked to my right, where the higher fork wove its way out of Laide and inland. A little church I'd not noticed before sat on the side of the road, set back aways. It was like everything else in Laide. Tiny, functional, a thing from another time. A sandwich board sat out front, the words 'ARE YOU READY TO MEET YOUR GOD' written across it in capital letters.

And I thought, remembering the stone face beneath the tree: *I already have.*

I began to walk. It took a lot of effort. I'd been in bed for days, and hit my head hard when I'd crashed the van. Keeping in a straight line was impossible, and I was winded after only a few steps. But every step I took brought me further downhill, further towards the bay, and further towards the Island. And this made me feel lighter, stronger. It eased the ache in my head. Things seemed brighter, more in focus. Flowers had a richer hue. There was more detail in the trees, more depth to the sky.

The Island was happy I was returning, it felt like.

I wondered if I would ever be able to dig it out of my brain.

Am I stuck here forever?

I got half a mile down the road before Fiona caught up with me.

'Where are you going, Megan?' She asked, eyeing up the jacket I'd stolen, but saying nothing.

'To find Rhoda,' I replied, simply. I did not look at her. I was worried I would claw her eyes out with my bare hands if I did.

Fiona sighed. 'There is something I have to show you, first.' She tried to put her hand on my elbow, steer me to a stop. The gesture reminded me of Matthew.

I violently pulled back.

'Don't touch me. Don't ever touch me again,' I hissed.

'You can't help them,' she replied, calm as always. 'I know it sounds cruel, but the Island has them, now.'

I balled up my fists in anger, but kept my arms pinned to my sides.

'You can't wipe that many people from history without someone noticing. They must have relatives, friends, people who will want to know what happened to them. People will come here. They will ask questions. You can't hang every single one of them. Or burn them all alive.'

Fiona began to walk again, slowly. 'White Pines was a self-confessed colony of isolationists, Megan. A community of people who threw off modern technology. They removed themselves from the world, voluntarily. They didn't have telephones, or write letters. Many of those people had already said goodbye to their friends and relatives and told them not to expect any more contact. They wrote *themselves* out of history years ago, when they moved to the Island. Mac is to blame for that, not me. Or you. Their secret will be much easier to keep than you think. Very few people knew that community existed in the first place.'

'But you knew. You knew, and you let him build there, knowing what that place was. Knowing about that...that...thing!'

'Nimrod,' Fiona replied, simply. 'We call it Nimrod. We have, for centuries.'

I laughed bitterly. 'Biblical. It's a biblical name.'

Fiona sighed. 'In the Old Testament, Nimrod was a great hunter. Some say he helped build the tower of Babylon, in defiance of God. Maybe that's why we call it that. Because when I look at it, I think "how can there possibly be a God if such a thing as this exists?" But the name is of no consequence, really. What is of consequence is that it hunts us. Feeds off of us. It has for many, many years.'

'So why stay?!' I stopped dead, overcome with confusion and anger. I could not wrap my head around it. Any normal person would want to live as far away from that thing as humanly possible. How could these people live here with the threat of that creature forever looming over them?

'Because this is our home, Megan, and we do things differently around here. These are our roots.'

It was a typically cryptic Fiona thing to say.

'I don't understand.'

'That's because you've been away from us

for too long. Your Granny never forgave herself for letting you slip through our fingers.'

'Don't talk to me about my family.'

I moved off, still intent on trying to find Rhoda. Even if that meant searching every house in Laide.

Fiona kept pace with me.

'In the beginning, our ancestors tried to kill the beast, you know. Tried, and failed. All they ended up doing was making it angrier. There was much suffering, as a result. Those were dark days. We still talk about them.'

I said nothing.

'And then, we came to terms with it. Some of us even began to worship it. And we learned how to manage it. We gave it what all gods want. We gave it sacrifice. And now, it no longer hunts us.'

'You feed it,' I spat, thinking of the gallows, of Johnny's body, an offering strung up in the wind. Was it still there, creaking as it swayed to and fro? Had they taken him down? Had Nimrod come for him? Was there a new pale marker with a hanged man standing proud in the cemetery?

Fiona stopped, grabbed my arm again, and this time, I let her. I met her eyes. They burned with something bright and complicated.

'It doesn't hunt here *because* it is fed. Our grandmothers learned that through bitter experience. The place it comes from? Who knows?

But it is a Hunter, of men, and women, and children, and livestock. It is a plague, but we can contain it, if we follow the old ways. That is our burden. That is our duty. We keep it fed, and we keep it here. And in doing so, we stop it from roaming further, wandering inland. Do you understand?'

I looked at her, and she was ablaze now, back ram-rod straight, body held tight with all the zealousness of a pastor delivering a sermon.

And it occurred to me then that Fiona had knowledge. Ancient knowledge, passed down from generation to generation. Knowledge I needed desperately, if I was to survive any of this.

'Walk with me,' she said.

I followed.

'How often does it come?' I asked, sullenly.

Fiona shrugged. 'Whenever the gateway on the Island opens. Nobody ever knows when it's about to happen. Sometimes, a long time passes. Ten years, twenty years, more. Whole generations have come and gone without seeing it. Other times, there are only days between visits. The Island is tricksy like that. It likes to keep us on our toes. So we keep a watch on it.'

I remembered Murdo, with his old dog. They had been standing on the side of the road, watching the Island, when I'd come across them.

Sentry-duty, I realised.

'And it can't be killed?' This piece of information was beginning to sink in.

'Not with fire, not with guns, not with anything we've ever found.'

'So you feed it,' I said.

'Usually, we have volunteers. A lottery. It is an honour to be chosen. But sometimes, on occasion...well. On occasion, lessons have to be learned.'

She was talking about Johnny.

'He was a young boy,' I said, bitterly. 'He had his whole life ahead of him, you crazy bitch.'

'Maybe,' Fiona said. 'But what's done is done.'

I fought the urge to hit her, hard, as I had done beneath the shadow of the gallows frame. I needed to find Rhoda, and I needed to know what Fiona knew, so I fought against myself, and won, but my hands twitched by my side.

'The dog,' I asked, then, trying to steer myself away from violence. 'Why did you shoot the dog?' It had been tormenting me since the moment she'd pulled the trigger.

Fiona looked surprised, as if she'd forgotten the event.

'Oh, that. Well.' She took a deep breath. 'Murdo thought you were a tourist, when he first saw you. We don't like tourists around here, for obvious reasons. He set that dog on you, set it to piss on your boots. But he should have seen you for who you were. Should have known better.

He made a mistake. Mistakes cannot go unpunished, that is how things are around here. I had to teach him a lesson. He will be more careful in the future.'

'And who am I, exactly?' I asked, white-hot rage burning slow and deep inside me.

'All in good time,' she replied.

We walked on.

33. HISTORY

After a while, I realised we were headed to Laide burial ground.

'Why are you taking me to the cemetery?' I asked, still intent on finding Rhoda and getting her away from these crazy people.

'To introduce you to your family,' Fiona said, pushing open the burial ground gate and motioning for me to follow.

It felt like an age since I had last been here, hunting for my Granny's headstone. The sea lay blue and calm beyond the headstones. The ruined, roofless chapel sat lopsided and meek just as before upon the green grass.

Behind it, in the bay, the Island lay low.

Waiting.

I looked to my left, found the rows of little white markers marching down the hill.

At the end of the farthest row, a brand new marker had been set into the ground. I could tell it was new, for it was whiter than all the rest.

Johnny.

Fiona led me to the chapel remains. I saw

the sign again: *CHAPEL OF SAND OF UDRIGIL.* We moved around the sign, and stepped inside the ruin. I nervously eyed the decaying walls, which looked as if they could crumble and land upon me at any point.

'What are we doing here?'

Fiona retrieved a long metal pole from where it was leaning against one corner of the structure. It had a hook at the end. I stepped back, thinking for a second that she was going to run me through with it, but she smiled, this time in genuine amusement, the smile actually touching the corners of her eyes, a thing I had never seen from her before.

That smile only served to make me loathe her more.

Turning her attention to the ground, she felt around for something with one foot, tapping the earth at intervals until the soft *thump-thump* turned into a dull *clang*. There was something down there, concealed beneath a thin layer of soil and scree and undergrowth. Fiona crouched, pushed it all to one side with her hands.

There was a door, set into the ground.

The door was rusted metal, solid, with an iron loop-handle. Fiona slotted the hook on the pole into the handle, and twisted it, levering the door up as she did so. The door swung open, revealing blackness beyond.

'What is this place?' I asked, thinking: *so much of this new world I inhabit is under our feet, hidden from view.*

     Like the tunnel beneath Taigh-Faire.
     Like the bodies beneath the sand.
     Like the god, beneath the tree.

     'Your history,' she said, and we descended into the hole.

34. IN THE FAMILY

Stairs led down a short distance and ended at a pair of solid, wrought iron gates, chained with a padlock. Fiona fished a key out of her pocket, and wrestled with the lock. I couldn't make out much of what was beyond the gates, but I thought it looked like a crypt. I had a sense of space, and damp, and cold stone walls.

The chain slid free of the padlock like a slippery live thing. Fiona caught it, wrapped it around her wrist, pocketed the lock for later, and led me inside.

'Wait here a moment,' she said, moving off into the gloom. I heard a match being struck, saw a flare of bright, which quickly became the flickering flame of a lit candle. Then another, and then another, until the entire space was lit by candles, candles mounted on wall sconces. The candles looked fresh, not much burned, and I realised this was a well-tended place, cared for, like the cemetery above our heads: grass manicured, weeds controlled, headstones in good repair. The people of Laide minded their dead, minded their history, and that might have made me feel something had I not remembered, with a quick flash of hatred, that they kept their gallows frame in good condition too. *Custom and indoctrination are one and the same thing,* I thought bitterly as I took in the large, vaulted space before me. They weren't caring for their dead so much as keeping their traditions alive, and those traditions amounted to one thing and one thing alone: murder. Sacrifice. Whatever their motivations, whatever they wanted to call it, the end result was the same.

Life forsaken.

I thought of Johnny's face, purple and distorted by the noose that had killed him. I thought of him running across the Island, dragging Luke along with him, and I ached then, I ached for Matthew, and Luke, and Johnny, and Mac.

I miss you, Matthew, I thought, fighting back tears.

There were glass cases on pedestals standing to attention along the walls of the crypt. Clear, polished cubes trimmed with silver, catching the light from the candles and throwing it around the chamber so that strange little slivers of fire danced and flickered across the ceiling. The cases were lined up in rows, and I was reminded of the rows of white pine trees on the Island. They had the same air of regiment, and purpose.

'What are these?' I asked, because this is clearly what I had been brought here to see. Fiona just pointed at the closest case.

'Take a look for yourself,' she said, her face a strange, alive thing in the flickering candlelight.

I stepped forward, not liking it when Fiona was out of sight, or standing behind me. I could feel her eyes on the back of my neck. It felt horrible.

It was hard to see the contents of the cases at first glance, because of the play of candlelight on the glass. I had to stoop, push my face closer for a better look. Inside the first, which also looked like the oldest, I saw what looked like an ornate silver reliquary, a type similar to those I had seen in churches and cathedrals in Rome and Paris. Repositories used to showcase bones and scraps of skin supposedly taken from the bodies of dead Saints. Holy relics.

Sitting on a small velvet cushion inside the reliquary was a thin, small, yet instantly recognisable yellowed finger-bone.

It was the right size to be a child's finger-bone.

I looked down at my right hand, to where my little finger once grew. I had been eight years old when the mainlanders had taken it. Or so Fiona had said. I had blurry memories of it happening, the pain, the aniseed sweet, the blood. I remembered the capstone in my cellar at *Taigh-Faire,* how well my four fingers fitted into the holes at the triangle points carved into the stone.

I'd been mutilated for a purpose, I realised. My hand was a key, but not by way of design. By way of intentional deformity.

But that didn't make sense, because the tunnel under the capstone at *Taigh-Faire* wasn't the only way onto the Island. It was one way, sure, but the people of White Pines hadn't known about it. They'd used boats, maybe even swum.

My hand was a key, but what did it unlock?

Unless the tunnel went somewhere else. Somewhere other than the Island.

My mind swam with a million questions.

A small plaque was fixed to the pedestal beneath the reliquary. Upon it was a single name: *Agatha*, and then a date: *1642.*

The next case held another finger. *Mary, 1667.*

Then Helena, *1673,* and so on around the room: *Isabella, Marion, Tina, Annie, Peggy, Elizabeth...*all the way up through time until the present, to the last two cases, which were closest to the gates on the opposite side of the crypt to where I'd started. *Patricia,* the second to last plaque read. Granny.

And then my name. *Megan.*

I looked at my own finger bone, sitting neatly on a small velvet pad in glass and silver reliquary. No skin, thank god. Just the bone. It looked so small, so delicate.

That is a part of me, I thought.

And I am part of something.

Part of a chain of consequence and duty and deep-rooted obligation that I didn't fully understand.

'So these names...these women...they are all my ancestors?'

Fiona stood silently. She had a queer expression upon her face. As if she were jealous of my ancestry.

'Aye.'

I thought for a moment, running the dates through my mind. 'It moves from grandmother to grandchild, this duty?'

'Aye.'

'But the dates don't support that. Some of them are too close together.'

Fiona shrugged. 'Death comes to us all, Megan. Even the chosen ones.'

Her eyes flashed. She was jealous to her very core.

There were frames hung on the far wall of the crypt, beyond the reliquaries. I went to get a closer look. Inside the frames were pictures like the ones I'd seen in the Post Office on my first visit to Laide. More mundane village life scenes.

A harvest festival at the church, fruit and vegetables and bundles of wheat and barley stacked
high upon the altar. Fishermen dragging a catch
inland. A caravan on the beach. A small child
grinning around an ice-lolly.

And, in the middle of all these candid
shots of everyday life, a large framed lithograph.
I mistook it at first for a mandala painting: it
was bright, and intricate, painted around golden
ratios that both pleased and confounded the
eye. Tim had bought one not dissimilar to this
back from a trip to Nepal. It hung in the house
I no longer lived in. Tim's new lover probably
looked at it as she made him post-coitus coffee
in the small hours of the morning.

Not that any of that mattered, any more.

The first thing you saw was a large circle,
with a layer of intricate, geometric shapes nestled with symmetric precision inside. And then,
when you really looked at it, once you sorted
out the mass of lines and angles and curves, you
saw a large triangle drawn dead in the centre of
the circle, punctuated by four round dots. One at
each point. One in the middle of the triangle.

I was looking at a crude map of the Island.

The dot in the centre of the triangle represented the large stone cairn in the centre of
the Island. The cairn we had sheltered under
when White Pines had first disappeared, where
we had watched as reality warped itself around
us. The three corner dots were the three, smaller

cairns dotted around the Island's interior. The edges of the triangle were unambiguously precise, straight borders between the cairns.

Around the shape, the prolific white pine trees were represented by the circle on the lithograph, a circle within which everything else was contained.

My finger drew in the light film of dust that coated the glass over the lithograph. I drew a series of houses inside the triangle boundary. I drew a town square. I drew a chapel, and a pig pen.

I drew White Pines.

The lithograph was old, the paper it was drawn upon yellowed, and aged. There was writing around the outside of the geometry, but I couldn't make it out. Whatever the Island was, it had been that way for a long, long time, I knew that now. Mac had unknowingly built the town of White Pines within these ancient ley lines. I could see why. The Island had lured Mac in, placed a natural building site between the cairns: a flat, dry expanse of land with good bedrock upon which to build.

Fiona said she had tried to warn him, but how hard, I wondered. How would she have explained the danger he was in, explain it to him in a way he could understand?

Now all that was left of his community was a blackened, singed trilateral stamp upon the ground, where the air flickered and moved with a static charge.

I realised once again how beyond me this all was. There was a cosmic significance to the geometry on the wall that was awe-inspiring and terrifying in its breadth and depth of potential.

And maybe that's why Fiona had brought me here. To show me that we were all at the mercy of things beyond our ken. A foul beast that lurked, where, I knew not. An Island where reality didn't hold up to the same rules the rest of us had to follow. People, animals, infrastructure, all sucked out of existence in the blink of an eye. A beach where impossible images assaulted every sense.

Hesitantly, I raised my right hand, the index finger of which was now coated with grey dust, so that it sat level with my eye-line. I closed my eyes, and drew a symbol in the air.

And I felt it. A connection, like the feeling you have when you're falling in love for the very first time. It rolled over me and through me and filled up every tiny corner of me with longing, and a deep, primal need.

To go back.

To tread upon the ancient, tainted soil of the Island.

To kneel down, touch the ash that had once been a thriving town called White Pines.

Where are you, Matthew? I thought.

A single tear escaped, rolled down my

cheek. There was movement, and Fiona came to stand next to me.

I did not have to open my eyes again to know she was smiling.

35. ONE GOD AT A TIME

In a golden, guttering glow, two women stood, side by side. One was me. The other was a person I disliked with every fibre of my being. Because it felt as if she owned me, somehow. She owned me because she knew about me, about my history, about my role in a scheme I had not been aware of until now.

'What do I do?' I asked. 'What am I, to you? To the Island?'

'A Key. Just like your Grandmother was. And hers before that, and so on, as you've seen. And it goes beyond the bones in this vault. There were more, before Agatha.' She gestured at the first case I'd seen. 'According to records, many, many more. Perhaps for as long as humans have walked the earth. For as long as there's been an Island, there's been a Key.'

'A Key to what?'

'That is for the ancestors to tell you, not me,' Fiona said, and this made about as much sense as everything else she had told me.

'My ancestors.' I snorted.

'There is something in your lineage, in your blood that the Island responds to.' That odd flash of jealousy lit up her eyes again.

'I don't expect you to understand any of this,' she continued. 'You were never shown the old ways like those who came before you were. Your mother took you away from us instead. She should have told you about the Other Place. You cannot escape your calling, Megan. All of us come back to the Island in the end.'

'The Other Place?'

'You know, Megan. You've seen it. You've seen the beach, and seen the face beneath the tree.'

I shuddered. 'I touched it.'

Fiona flinched, genuinely horrified.

'What?'

'I touched it. I was...I thought I was dreaming, so I touched it.'

Fiona had to visibly compose herself.

'You should not have.'

'I didn't know.'

She passed a hand over her eyes. 'Now you do.'

'Is it a god?'

Fiona snorted. 'Who knows? We don't much care. We have a god, already. We don't need another.'

I thought about that. Indoctrination.

Tradition. Heritage. Propaganda. Belief. What did I believe in, now?

Nothing. Nothing that could be trusted. The only thing, person, I had truly trusted had disappeared, right before my eyes.

I was becoming more and more consumed by it. What had happened to him? It ate away at me, that question. It ached, a fresh, festering wound. Was he still with Luke? Was he alive, lost in another reality, or had he died horribly, as so many others had before him?

I jerked away from that thought process, not wanting to allow the possibility in. And as hard as it was to try and be practical about, thinking along these lines did me no favours, not in my present state. Whatever had happened to him, there was no Matthew in this reality, not now. There was only Fiona.

And it seemed that, like the Island, she had plans for me too.

'So what do I do?' I said, keen to cut through her spiel and get to the point.

Fiona straightened a stray button on her jacket. 'You need to go back,' she said, casually.

I stared at her, and tried to pretend I had not been thinking that exact same thing only minutes before.

'Go back? To the Island? Why? Why would I go back there ever again?'

'There are things you need to do, Megan. Things you are behind with. Duties. There is...a ritual.'

'What kind of ritual?'

'It's something that all Keys have to do. It's part of your inheritance, I suppose. There are things the ancestors must tell you.'

I glared at her. 'I wish you'd stop talking to me in fucking riddles,' I spat.

Her eyes flicked past me, and I frowned. We were no longer alone.

I turned, and saw that a congregation of mainlanders had gathered, Murdo amongst them. The young collie dog whined anxiously as his feet. The locals filled the small space outside the wrought iron gates, standing two-deep on the stairs leading down to the crypt, and spilling out into the chapel above.

They waited, silently.

They wouldn't let me wear clothes.

I blinked when Fiona told me I must go, but I must go naked.

'Why?' I asked, knowing it would make little difference to question her.

It's necessary,' she said, just like my Granny had told me when I was a child, as I watched three people choke to death on the end of three ropes.

'Why?' I repeated, stubbornly.

'Because that is how you greet your ancestors. You come as you are.'

I stared at her, trying to decide if she was fucking with me, or being serious. Fiona just smiled and waited. Was it necessary? Or was this another way of humiliating me? Asserting dominance? Making me pay for my 'special' heritage?

Was this necessity, or jealousy?

And what did 'greeting my ancestors' mean?

Either way, I knew enough about her now to understand the look on her face. She would not be moved, and so, naked I must go.

Slowly, I bent down, untied my shoes, and slipped them off, one by one. The mainlanders gathered in the entrance of the crypt looked at me doing this with blank faces, as if I were an insect climbing the wall. I felt momentarily sick at the thought of removing my clothes in front of them. The moment passed, and I stripped, slowly and deliberately, folding each item carefully. A woman came forward to take them from me. It was cold in the crypt, but I stood tall, proud, not allowing myself to shiver.

'Naked,' I said, at last, declaring my readiness.

'As you were born,' Fiona said, and they led me away.

36. BACK AGAIN

I was placed at the head of a slow procession. It marched ponderously out of the crypt, over the green grass of the cemetery, over the burial ground wall and down to the beach beneath, where a small motor boat was moored and waiting for me. The mainlanders followed behind me, two by two. I thought briefly about breaking from the procession and making a run for it, knowing how stupid and futile this thought was, but entertaining it anyway.

I did not run. What would be the point? I had nowhere to go. The constant headache that signalled the Island's hold over me was already wearing me down, stretching me thin, and reminding me constantly that I was stuck here. It was manageable while I was this distance from the Island, but if I tried to escape again, I might trigger a brain aneurysm, or stroke, or worse.

More than that, if I tried to escape, I would be leaving Rhoda behind. If she was still alive.

I consoled myself with the thought that at the very least, going back to the Island meant my head would stop hurting, if only for a little while.

And I could still feel that connection with the place, could still feel those hooks in me.

But going back also meant seeing things. Awful things. Things I didn't want to see.

And then, there was Nimrod.

'Fiona,' I said, as that sudden, terrible realisation hit me. 'Fiona, what if the Hunter comes back while we are there?'

'Nimrod has been fed,' she replied, not breaking her step for a moment. 'It should be a while before it gets hungry again.'

I thought of Johnny.

I was escorted through ankle-deep, freezing seawater, and deposited at the stern of the boat. Fiona sat next to me on a small wooden bench, close enough that every now and then, her clothed knee brushed against my bare knee, and I had to clench every fibre of my being in an effort not to flinch from her, or lash out, and push her over the side. I tried my hardest to be as she was. Calm. A blank slate. I tried my hardest not to display any emotion.

Murdo untied the boat and climbed in after us, his dog squeezing into the space by my feet. I stared at the collie as it hunkered down and rested its muzzle on its paws, remembering how eagerly it had eaten Mac's tongue.

Murdo fidgeted for a moment, and then the engine started. The mainlanders stood in a neat line across the beach, and watched us go, their right hands all raised, fingertips drawing geometry in the fresh Highlands air by their heads. I turned my back to them, and we sped across the bay.

Cold sea spray battered my naked body, and dark clouds spread across the sky. It looked as if it might rain today. The Island loomed large before us, and despite my best efforts, I began to shake. Not with the cold, but with the memories. I remembered every single thing that had taken place there so vividly. Every detail of that nightmarish experience was burned into my brain, forever. I was changed, forever, because of it. The Island had taken a soft, privileged woman and chewed her up, remoulded her into something else, something raw, and desperate.

A piercing cry shrieked out from above. I shaded my eyes and saw a large bird of prey with wide wings and white tail feathers wheeling over our heads. It banked, swooped lower, then made for the Island, where it began circling the pine trees, as if looking for something.

'What is that?' I asked, gratefully distracted by the beauty of the bird. 'A buzzard?'

'White-tailed eagle,' said Fiona. She watched it with a neutral expression on her face, hands stuffed in her pockets. As if she'd seen a hundred of these before, and would see a hundred more tomorrow.

'It's beaut-' I started, and then the words died. The eagle, having soared over the top of the pine trees to the sky above the centre of the Island, vanished, mid-flight.

I sighed.

We approached the Island differently to how I'd expected, cutting across the water at a right angle rather than aiming straight for it. The motor boat reached the closest shore and then circled around it almost entirely, past the cave where Matthew and I had once stood looking out at a dark sea with stars all around, past the iron rungs hammered into the rock, past bare stone and heather and bracken, to the man-made spit we'd found on my first visit to the Island. The one shaped like a long, peaky nose that pointed at the mainland.

I felt immeasurably sad as it came into view. I'd been here last with Matthew.

So this is what it's like when someone you love dies, I thought. *Like constantly trying to swallow a sharp stone.*

Except he's not dead. He's not. He's out there somewhere, in the Other Place.

Him, and Luke.

And the thousand or so people who had lived in White Pines.

Murdo steered the boat into the spit, and moored it next to the handful of others which still rested there, motioning for us to climb out. I put a tentative foot out onto the stony embankment. The stones were cold, and painful underfoot. Fiona moved around in the boat next to me, and my balance shifted suddenly. The stones slipped under my toes and I fell forward, awkwardly, landing on my hands and knees, skinning both painfully. Fiona did nothing to help. She climbed out after me and stood on the shingle, looking bored and waiting for me to get up again. I held onto the hate that warmed me as I scrabbled around trying to find a steady place to put my feet so that I could stand up again. I would need that hate, later. I would need it to fuel me, carry me through whatever awaited.

Murdo's large hands hoisted me upright. His touch on my naked flesh was difficult to bear, and I slapped his hands away in a panic. He stepped back and I noticed a long-handled shovel lying by his feet. He must have brought it with him from the boat.

'What's that for?' I said, panting slightly.

He motioned for me to walk.

I did as I was told, noting that my headache had gone.

We took the small path that led from the spit to the trees by way of the old, ruined shepherd's hut I'd seen before. I had not looked closely at it then, but now it was daylight, I could see a heavy stone lintel above the door frame, the same style as the one over my front door at *Taigh-Faire.* The triangle was there, carved deeply into the stone in the centre of the lintel. A little worn from the elements, but definitely there.

We passed the hut, and left it behind us. Fiona led, and Murdo brought up the rear whilst I tried to keep pace with them both on bare feet. When we hit the tree line of the pine stand, we stopped. Fiona looked up at the towering, white trees that stretched so high over our heads.

'The first thing we will do after today is cut these down,' she said, her lip curled in distaste.

For once, she and I were in agreement about something, for I hated the trees too, hated how they watched me.

A faint rustle rippled through the treetops as if in response.

'Careful,' I muttered. 'They're listening.'

Fiona, unimpressed, snorted and marched on. We followed her into the trees, into the preternatural quiet. The dense carpet of needles prickled and stabbed at the soles of my feet as I walked.

And then, much more quickly than last time, as if the Island was hungrier than ever for me, the forest spat us out. We emerged into the centre of the Island, and there it was, in all its horrifying glory: the big blackened triangle where a town had once sat, had once thrived. A place for people to live away from the pressures of a modern civilisation. Away from machines and noise and currency and politics and television and celebrity. A place to be at one with nature, and the outdoors, and practice self-sufficiency. A place founded by a man called Mac, who burned alive in a van on the side of the road.

We had come out of the trees at the bottom southeast corner of the triangle, not far from where one of the smaller cairns lay. A dot at a triangle tip. What were they for, these cairns? Boundary markers? Crude coordinates? Burial mounds? I didn't know.

But Fiona seemed to.

She led me to the nearest cairn. The blank, charred triangle behind it loomed blank, and threatening. I remembered running through that space, running while the air flickered. I remembered human screams. Things seemed quiet inside the triangle for now. Johnny had been right about the waves slowing down.

I thought of Nimrod, the Hunter of people.

We stopped next to the small pile of rocks.

'What now?' I asked, shivering with anticipation.

'Watch,' she said, and reached out her hand. She delicately removed a tiny stone from where it was balanced at the top of the mound. I heard a sizzling sound, smelt singed flesh. Fiona hissed and dropped the stone, wincing and shaking her hand. Her fingertips looked burned, and raw. She blew on them.

'Now you,' she said, pointing to the rock pile, which was one rock fewer.

'Why?' I said, knowing she wouldn't answer me.

She pressed her lips together tightly. Her eyes, one brown, one blue, bored into me.

I hesitated. The last time I had touched one of these, the cairn in the centre of the triangle, it had hurt. A lot.

'Do it,' Fiona ordered.

'What's under these stones?' I asked.

'No questions,' she replied, her calm exterior slipping just a little. She was not used to being challenged, only obeyed. 'Just do as you're told.'

I narrowed my eyes, and found a small stone near the top of the pile, as Fiona had. I let my fingers hover over it without touching, trying to establish how much pain I was about to experience.

Then, I picked it up, balanced it in the palm of my hand.

Nothing. No pain. No jolt of electricity. Nothing.

I set the rock down on the ground by my feet, and looked to Fiona for further instruction. She folded her arms.

'Keep going,' she said. I understood then that she wanted me to dismantle the cairn, stone by stone.

Murdo leaned on the handle of his shovel, and suddenly that made sense to me, too. What it was for.

They wanted me to take apart the cairn, and dig up what was beneath.

'What's down there?' I asked again, looking from one to the other.

Neither replied.

I set to work.

37. ROCK
BY ROCK

It took a while. Soon, I was grateful for the lack of clothes. The work was hard, laborious. I was covered in sweat within minutes. My cheeks burned, turned red from the thin light overhead. The cairn was made of maybe a hundred varying sized stones, smallest at the top, largest at the bottom, stacked on top of each other in a dense, tightly organised cone. I worked my way down from the peak, laying the stones carefully in a separate pile to one side as I removed them. It felt odd to do this, take apart something built with such care and precision. Odd, and disrespectful. I did it anyway.

My hands grew sore and chafed from handling so many rough rocks. My back burned with the effort of bending down and standing up, time and time again. Then, I found a rhythm to what I was doing, found myself in the swing of it, carting rock from mound to mound, back and forth, back and forth, back...

Until there were no rocks left.

Underneath, there lay dark soil. Not dark like the dead earth inside the triangle. This was rich and fertile soil, moist and coloured deep with rotting matter. Insects and worms wriggled around in it, rudely exposed to the light of day.

I straightened up, panting. My throat was raw, and I needed water, but there was none forthcoming.

Murdo simply offered me the shovel.

I took it, and dug.

It was incredibly hard work. I wore no shoes and could not use my foot to stamp the shovel into the ground. I had to use the force of my arms alone. Every cut sent a jolt of impact juddering up my forearms, across my shoulders, down through my chest and along my spine. I gritted my teeth, feeling blisters form on the palms of my hands. Down, and down I dug, bringing up scoops of earth and roots and twigs and insects and more stones, my arms straining under the weight of the soil and the effort it took to extract. I stopped to rest more than once, panting and sweating, legs almost buckling with exertion. Every time I did this, Fiona and Murdo stared down at me with cold, beady eyes until I resumed my labour.

Once the hole was deep enough to stand in, I did so, stepping down carefully, soil splurging up through my toes, shifting from one side of the hole to the other as I dug first one half and then the other, deeper and deeper, all the while sinking further below surface level.

And then I came to it. The shovel glanced off of something hard with a loud metallic clang, and I stopped digging.

'Is this it?' I asked, struggling to catch my breath. 'Is this why I'm here?'

Fiona towered above me, her feet level now with my head. I had to crane my head back to speak to her, and I had a feeling that she liked that, me being this far below her.

She kept her silence, and I handed the shovel up out of the hole to Murdo. I caught his eye as I did so, and had a shock. His usually impassive face was gripped with something that looked very much like fear. Or pity. Or maybe something else I couldn't quite put a name to.

Compassion?

I knelt to examine the thing beneath the soil, clearing away the last thin layer with my torn, bleeding hands. It took me a moment to figure it out, but then I realised what it was. Same stone, same size and shape as the one in my cellar at *Taigh-Faire.*

It was a capstone.

I cleaned the last vestiges of muck from the thing, and found the symbol staring up at me. The dots at the corners of the triangle had mud in them, and an earthworm slithered out of the hole in the centre as I sat back on my heels and stared at it.

'What is this?' I looked up at Fiona. She had taken possession of the shovel, and now she raised it slightly, as if in threat.

'Open it,' she commanded.

The message was clear. If I didn't do as she asked, she would hit me, hard.

A part of me knew it was an empty threat. She needed me. It was why I was still alive, why I was here, because she needed me and my special heritage for something. I knew this. *She* knew that I knew this.

And yet, I was still afraid of her.

I set my right hand upon it, working my fingertips into the holes, picking out dirt so that I could slot them in more comfortably. Once again I had that sensation that I was putting my hand into a long-favoured glove, one tailored exactly to my hand's shape and size.

My hand, which was a key, slid into the lock. There was a moment of stillness, and then the sensation of something moving, some catch beneath the stone being released.

And then I heard a whisper, right in the centre of my mind.

I clapped my spare hand to my head in agony. The whisper was *loud*.

The capstone rotated slowly, lifting up and away from whatever it lay on top of, twisting sideways on an invisible axis, until it stood upright upon its rim, looking for all the world like a giant coin that had been dropped from above and had miraculously landed upon its side.

I looked down.

And what lay beneath took my breath away.

38. SEALED

In a circular hole that was about six feet deep by three feet wide, lined with curved stone slabs that tessellated perfectly to make an airtight sort of tube once the capstone was lowered, lay the mummified, curled, compact body of a small human.

Brown, shiny skin stretched taut across small, bird-like bones. The skin clung to most of the body except for the hands and fingers, where it had rotted away, leaving bone exposed. The feet were crossed at the ankles, and I could see toenails, veins, tiny hairs. Arms clasped around knees which were raised to the chest, like that of a baby in the womb. Thin, slack breasts squashed up around the knees. I saw a nipple, hard and brown like a sweet chestnut. On top of a ladder-like column of vertebrae sat a round, small skull, perfectly intact. A mass of clumped orange hair still covered the skull. There were tiny flowers in the hair. They looked like daisies.

And a face, perfectly preserved. Eyes closed, cheeks sunken. Lips slightly parted over brown teeth. Frown lines across the forehead. Eyelashes, also orange in colour, red seeming to be the only pigment that had survived interment.

It was a woman. Ancient, tiny, frozen in time. She looked as if she were asleep, rather than dead.

My ancestor.

The cairns marked the locations of ancient tombs. Matthew had been right.

The Island was a burial ground.

That meant there were three other tombs on this Island that I knew of. Did I have to break into every single one? Was that the ritual?

The whispering voice still echoed around my skull. A strange vibration rattled my teeth, and my skin buzzed. I swallowed, scratching at my arms. What now? What was I doing here?

I looked up at Fiona once again, and the smile was back on her face. My heart flipped.

'Get in,' she said.

'What?' I didn't understand.

'Get. In.' Her eyes were huge, expectant. She gripped the shovel handle with white fingers.

'No.' My part in her game was over. I reached an arm up, tried to hook it on the edge of the hole, hoist myself up and out of it.

The blade of the shovel came down flat and whip-fast, and smashed into my fingers. I howled in pain.

'Do as you are told,' the woman said, in a voice of ice.

'No!' I cried, trying once again to climb out of the tomb. The shovel came down once more, this time on my shoulder. I heard something crack. My collarbone. I kept trying to hoist myself out, regardless. The mad bitch meant to bury me down there, cover me with stone and soil until my body dried out and became brown, waxy, still like the woman at my feet. I would not have it. I would not!

But every time I tried to get out of the hole, the shovel came down upon me, over and over again, until I was sobbing, covered in bruises and welts and long, nasty gashes which welled up readily, spilling my blood into the ground like an offering.

And the Island drank deep, and shuddered in pleasure.

Then, Murdo reached down.

'*No!*' I screamed, bucking and straining, but he was strong. He took a hold of my shoulders, forced me down hard, and I lost my footing, slipping down into the hole with the ancient, sleeping body who waited for me at the bottom, and the mainlanders looked down at me for a moment as I sobbed and shrieked, and then they both made the symbol of the triangle in the air. Murdo reached across the hole, and I realised with horror what he intended to do.

'For the love of God, *no!*' I scrambled for

purchase, feeling cold bones and hard skin under me, but it was no use. It was simply no use.

Fiona and Murdo pushed against the capstone. It rolled ponderously back over the top of the tomb, and the light disappeared, and the sky was sealed from me, and my screams were swallowed by the earth, just like my blood.

39. SEE

I screamed until I exhausted myself, then crouched in the pitch-black tomb, panting. I tried to tell myself to take shallow breaths. The air was horribly thin, and stank of stone and peat. Soon, it would run out, and I would suffocate.

Something crawled across my left arm: a centipede, a worm, I couldn't tell. A thousand tiny feet tramped across my bare skin, and I would have screamed again, but my throat had seized up. So I hunkered in the earth, horribly aware of the mummified remains of a woman who may or may not have been my ancient ancestor, trying not to move so that her fragile bones didn't break beneath my superior weight. I could feel her ribs and vertebrae and finger bones and pelvic bone and shoulder blades all poking into me, and the meeting of dead flesh with my live skin was the worst sensation I could have ever imagined possible.

I moved to one side of the hole, so that the ancient corpse lay with its back to me. My hands brushed against her knobbled spinal column and the smooth, hardened skin of her back. I shuddered, and shrank as far back from her as possible.

All was deathly quiet apart from the noise of my own distress.

Relax, I tried to tell myself, over and over. *You have survived worse. Hard to believe, but you have.* I could hear my own pulse hammering in my ears. I gagged repeatedly on what little air I could. Had it been minutes or hours since the mainlanders had thrown me in the tomb? I couldn't tell.

A rambling internal dialogue started up in my head:

How long have I been down here? I can't die down here!

Relax.

How long?!

Relax.

There are bones sticking into me.

Relax. Think.

I know, I know. I'm trying!

Try harder. You are not going to die down here. If they wanted you dead...

If they wanted me dead, they would have hung me from the gallows by now.

Exactly.

They need me, for whatever reason they think they do.

Relax, Megs.

I won't die here. I won't.

Breathe slowly. Don't use up the air. Start counting.

I forced myself to count to ten, and began breathing in time with the numbers. I squeezed my eyes shut so that I wasn't distracted by the dark, by the all-consuming black. It was like being blind again, and I couldn't bear it. I couldn't...

I can't...

Relax.

My breathing slowed, little bit by little bit.

I saw Matthew's face, in that last moment before he disappeared.

He was brave, Megs. So are you.

I opened my eyes.

So, I was in a tomb.

So, there was a dead body down here with me. I had seen worse. I had seen the face of a woman emerge from the torso of a man. I had seen a three-headed pig. I had seen an entire town disappear in the blink of an eye. I had stared into the face of a colossal giant, a creature from myth, a thing that should not exist.

I had woken a sleeping god beneath a tree.

I can survive this.

Keep thinking. You were put down here for a reason, Megs.

Yes. So what is it that I am here to do?

I listened then, listened hard to the tomb,

to the sound of insects creeping and my own careful movements, to the sigh and creak of stones settling against each other.

I waited for another whisper in my mind, but it didn't come.

Patience. It will come, eventually.

I lay down, slowly, conscious of fragile parts alongside me, wriggling and working myself so that the woman's delicate, wizened back was to my chest. There was just enough space in the hole for me to lie beside her. She had been no taller than four feet, and was tiny in every other way aside from her height. Were it not for the breasts, I might have thought her a child.

My eyes adjusted, little bit by little bit, to the intense blackness all around. And in doing so, the dark seemed to soften. A muted grey glow blossomed around the sleeping form before me.

I had a sense that somehow, despite her sleep, the ancient one knew I was there.

I used my right hand, felt gently along the tiny frame, frightened at first that I would damage her, that she would crumble beneath my touch, but then growing in confidence as she didn't. I started at the head, traced down from the skull and followed the path of the right arm bones, the humerus, the ulna, and found what I was looking for.

The woman's right hand.

I felt for her finger bones, and found the small, delicate digits clenched tight, the sharp fingertips curled inwards.

Laboriously, my breath coming harsh and quick as the air in the tomb grew thinner and thinner, I counted them.

A thumb, and one, two, three...three fingers.

The smallest finger on the right hand was missing. Just like mine was.

We were the same. Same burdens, same ancestry, same tomb, same fate. She was a woman like me. She was an ancestor. Blood.

She was a Key.

She was family.

I gently laid my hand over the old one's hand, and rested my face against the back of her head. I felt a deep sense of sympathy for the dead, knowing, at least in some part, what burden she must have carried in her lifetime. The burden of knowledge. The burden of things seen that no one should see. My arms went around her, instinctively. I held the body as if it were a child, and I its mother, and we were drifting to sleep in the child's bed, a sweet fairy story still lingering in our memories.

A ringing sensation began to build in my ears.

The stone walls around us grumbled. I heard earth beyond the tomb shift and move. I heard the roots of plants flex and stretch, as if waking up after a long sleep. Bugs and beetles and worms of all descriptions suddenly poured out of every crack and crevice between the stone slabs, and ran across my skin in a confused flood, invading every part of my body. I bore it. Even when things began to squirm and crawl under my armpits and between my legs, I bore it. I let nature caress my naked back and thighs, I let the tremors fold themselves around me like a blanket, I let the worms play in my hair, and I gave myself to the ritual, whatever ancient and practiced thing this was that I was doing. I allowed my instincts to lead, and thought:

If I do die, this is as peaceful a way as any.

I'm sorry, Matthew.

I held my ancestor in my arms while the ground shook around us, and I thought about the capstone on top of us, thought about the weight of it, should it fall, should it be dislodged as the ground shook, and I thought about that sensation of life leaving me as it crushed me to a flattened husk, and I could feel my mind coming free of its moorings, slowly, slowly, drifting away, and it was such a relief, such a relief to let go of all of this, and maybe my skull would be full of earth too, at the end of all this. Like hers was. Maybe I could be a hollow, dried vessel full of worms and roots and rotted life and whatever strange power it was that lay deep in the land on this Island. Maybe I could just lie here, and feel the bones of those who had gone before me, and...

I felt them move.

Just a small shift, at first. A twitch of movement beneath my fingers. Then a spasm, more pronounced, along the spine, and then another. Arms flexed, feet twitched, the head rolled around in a jerky, uncoordinated awakening.

I pulled my own arms back, giving her space to move.

The ancestor shook herself free of sleep and unfolded, like a flower opening up in the spring. Then she rolled, so that she faced me, nose to nose. I lay still as stone, waiting, waiting. I was not afraid. Fear was for other people. I was a Key. I had gone to a place beyond fear.

The ancient one placed her mutilated hand upon my chest, and opened her eyes.

There was nothing behind the eyelids except for black. The soft, delicate orbs of her eyeballs hadn't survived the passage of time.

It didn't matter. I knew she was looking at me anyway.

I smiled, and she dug her bony fingertips into my flesh. They sank into my skin easily, like fingers sinking into sand, and left four deep holes in me as she withdrew once again. Blood welled up from the wounds, hot and eager. It soaked into the soil, and I felt the Island stirring once more, that great satisfied shuddering rumbling up to the surface from deep underground.

A strange sighing noise came out of her mouth. Hot, rancid air clouded into my face. The fragile mandible yawned open, then shut, shut and then open. Her teeth clacked gently against each other. I saw a decaying mass in her mouth: her tongue. It looked papery, like a wasp's nest.

A word slid into my ears like the maggots weeviling across my thighs.

'*See,*' the ancient one said, and her eye sockets began to glow a fierce, bright black.

And I saw.

Oh, *how* I saw.

40. ALL THAT SHE KNOWS

I saw everything that had gone before, and everything that was to come after.

I saw the Island, at the centre of everything we thought we understood, but didn't.

I saw ripples of consequence, of possibility, of potential, circling out into the sea from this simple crop of land, which was the epicentre, and those ripples manipulated the fabric of reality like the aftershocks of an earthquake, just as Johnny had said, folding time, flexing space, compressing distances hitherto incomprehensible until now.

I saw other ancient ones, sleeping in their circular tombs. Three of them in total, arranged strategically around the Island. The tomb where I lay, and two others. If you were to walk a path from tomb to tomb, you would create a shape with your feet, an equilateral triangle, a Euclidean boundary.

Within which another tomb sat, dead

in the very centre. And something slumbered there. Something older and wiser and more terrible than my ancestors. I couldn't describe it, couldn't fully understand it, but I could *see* it lying down there, in my mind's eye.

A face, carved from stone. Horrifyingly simple and crude, yet recognisably human. A face I had seen before, in another place. One garlanded with the roots of a cherry tree.

And beneath that, or beyond it, or behind it, or maybe *around* it, lay the Other Place. Instead of a cairn on a hill in the centre of an Island, a cherry tree stood in suspended animation within a giant glass bubble, marking a sacred place.

And all else beyond it was chaos.

The mummy vomited her knowledge into my brain, which was wide open with rapture and the glorious pain that came with finally being able to understand what my place in this world was, which was no place at all, because my place belonged *between* worlds, and once she knew that I knew this, she released me. I had a second to try and breathe, to try and drag some of the air remaining into my burning lungs, to try and speak, but before I could, the ancient one…

Crumbled to dust.

I cried out. Whatever purpose had kept the body intact all these thousands of years was now fulfilled, but I felt a keening loss despite this. The papery flesh, leathery skin and brittle bones disintegrated before my eyes, and the Island sighed beneath me once again. The rumblings outside of the tomb intensified. The stone tomb walls began to crack, splinter like teeth biting down on something too hard. Soil spilled into the hole around me, cold and damp and stinking, and full of insects, more insects. The earth surged in beneath me like rising water swelling up a well shaft, and I rode the wave of it, rolling into a crouch, and thrusting myself up, and out of the darkness.

The capstone over my head split in two with a thunderous crack.

I rose from the tomb in a fountain of shattered stone and dust and earth, naked as the day I was born, coated in mud and insects and blood and dead leaves and grass and roots, all of it plastered to my skin so that you could barely see the woman I was underneath. I rose, and I saw Fiona, pale-faced, mouth open, holding out a hand as if to ward me off.

This was not how the ritual usually played out.

'You're not supposed to...' she stuttered, backing away from me. 'You're supposed to wait until we let you out!'

I stood before her. Taller. Wiser. Changed. My ruined eyes leaked a thick bloody pus down my cheeks, and I let it dry in the salty air. The ancient one had taken my sight, but it was not like earlier, not like the car accident. I was blind, but I could still see.

I could see it all.

Fiona took another slow backwards step.

'This isn't supposed to happen. This isn't how it happens!' She shouted at me, and she wasn't smiling anymore. The old me cherished that I had finally found something to wipe that insufferable smile from her lips.

The new me cared nothing for such trivialities.

I walked towards her. The blood from my chest wounds trickled down between my breasts, over my tummy, into my pubic hair. I let it flow. They were marks of honour. Of belonging. Of family.

She cowered as I drew near. Murdo stood to one side, letting me pass. Awe was painted bright on his face.

There was a moment then, when Fiona was before me, a little thing, such a little, unimportant thing, and I thought she might prostrate herself, but her pride would never allow that. She stood, half-grovelling in my path, a malevolent, greedy insect, driven only by selfish need and ambition. I thought how easy it would be to place a hand on her head and crush her to a bloody pulp with just one gesture, but I had more important things to do, first.

I had more to learn from my forebears.

Fiona cried out, fell backwards, and

landed hard on her rear. I walked straight past her, ignoring her bleating cries that I was not following the ritual properly, and I trod the line of the boundary, walking the path around the edges of the triangle, around the edges of what used to be White Pines, green grass beneath one foot, burned soil beneath the other, marching along a thin frontier that was a veil between this world, and the Other Place.

I walked in a straight, perfect line to the next cairn, and laid my hand upon it.

41. JOB DONE

It was easy, once you knew how. All it required was a willingness to listen. The ritual was a passing down of knowledge, like the passing down of heirlooms. Like handing over an old, weathered cottage to a long estranged granddaughter.

And the more I spoke to these tiny, wizened kin of mine, the more I learned, and the taller I grew, and the sharper my senses became, even as I lost parts of myself with every step.

The first tomb took my eyes.

The second, my ears. I felt them go, my eardrums, as my ancestor whispered to me. A small explosion, one on each side of my skull. Pain, intense pain, and then a rush of new sound. And, as with my vision, it was as if all the noise I had been listening to in my life before this had been a false approximation of noise. And now, only now, was I hearing what the universe truly had to say.

The last tomb took my tongue. My ancestor leaned into me, opened her mouth, and kissed me on the lips. Her breath spilled into my mouth, and it burned, intense, bright, incredible heat, and when she crumbled into dust, I found I had nothing left inside of my mouth except for charred flesh.

The ritual repeated, leaving three shattered capstones behind me on the dirt.

I found myself back at the point at which I'd started, back to where Fiona and Murdo still waited for me, my steps sealing a path which became a closed loop as I rejoined them. Then, I turned my face into the triangle.

The final cairn sat proud on its summit in the centre of the Island.

Only one left.

Was I ready?

It didn't matter if I was not. Because the ritual wasn't complete. There was a god down there under the rocks, a god I had unfinished business with, and I did not wish to keep it waiting.

I put one bare, bloody foot into the triangle.

Something flickered in the air before me.

I held my breath. The cairn would have to wait.

Out of the air, the huge, long shape of the Hunter snapped into view.

Nimrod.

It swayed on its enormous legs, gelatinous jowls wobbling and quivering as it moved, its eyes trained on me from the ends of their stalks, and I found I wasn't afraid of it any more. I had become more than prey. I had become a type of hunter, too.

It waited, blocking my path to the cairn. We studied each other. I cocked my head to one side, and Nimrod did the same, its skin flapping and slapping with the motion.

It stretched one leg out before it, testing my reaction.

I took a step forward, matching it.

The Hunter shifted its weight, tensed its body, as if ready to start a race. It was excited, I could tell.

But I had no time for this. I had a ritual to complete.

Behind me, Fiona shrieked in fear. Murdo's dog began to bark, furiously.

I ran.

Nimrod roared, and one giant foot lifted high, then came crashing back down again. A thunderous tremor shook the earth.

Nimrod was fast, but I was faster. In a few quick strides, I caught up with Murdo and Fiona, both of whom were running for the tree line. They came up sharp as I appeared in front of them, and Fiona reared backwards, seeing something in my face that terrified her more than the creature who followed behind.

I put my hands on her shoulders.

I was the smiling one, now.

'How...how can you see me?' She whispered, and I laughed. There was eye-jelly on my cheeks, still. Blood in my ears. Ash in my mouth.

We do not need eyes to see, I thought, and I thrust my fingers into her hair. Fiona cried out in pain, but pain is a transitory thing, a necessary step towards what awaits us.

I dragged her back towards the edge of the triangle, and stood for a moment, contemplating the creature who lurched for us. Murdo's dog yapped and snarled incessantly in the background, crazed with fear. Murdo himself seemed turned to stone, frozen to the spot. He had not tried to help Fiona, but then I remembered he had no tongue either. Would he try and save the woman who had ripped his speech from his mouth? Obviously not.

It was a moot point, anyway.

Fiona thrashed and flailed at the end of my arm. Nimrod bellowed with hunger, and another foot came down, *whump!* The ground shook with another mighty tremor.

I tightened my grip on Fiona's hair, and kissed her lightly on the forehead, even as her fingernails raked at my face. A damp patch spread on the crotch of her trousers as she saw the last few seconds of her mean, miserable life play out before her.

Then, I threw her to the beast.

Nimrod pounced, pulling her up from the floor and yanking her body tight between its hands. Fiona's spine popped with a loud, definitive snap like the inside of a Christmas cracker. The eye stalks shivered in pleasure, and a pink, wet slit opened up in the giant's lumpy, doughy face.

The body of the mainlander was then folded in half, feet to forehead, and crammed unceremoniously into the terrible, wide-open mouth. There was a gulping, crunching noise, and Fiona was gone. The giant swallowed, moaning in pleasure, and its knees sagged and buckled with appreciation.

I watched, in awe. The creature shuddered as its meal slid down into its belly, and then squatted, dipping down towards the ground and back up sharply again, as if...

As if in thanks.

A shame, I thought then, cracking the knuckles on both my hands.

A shame to have to kill such a beautiful beast.

42. THE HUNTER BECOMES THE HUNTED

The air within the triangle tightened, snapped like a rubber band stretched tight across a cardboard box.

I didn't have long.

I looked to the cairn. The ritual was incomplete, but it would have to wait.

For I had an opportunity, and I did not care to waste it.

I turned to Murdo, who was still rooted to the spot like one of the many, many trees behind him. He was pale. His dog, now beside itself with terror, barked and growled and pivoted in frantic, frenzied circles on the spot.

I put a finger to my lips, as if soothing a small child.

The dog lay down next to Murdo.

The air behind me trembled. My window was closing. I could feel the wave, about to recede. I turned. Nimrod, flesh-drunk and swaying about on those long, crane-like legs, dimmed around the edges, as if the great beast were only a silhouette, a shadow, and the sun was retreating behind a cloud. It flexed its shoulders, and threw back its head.

I stepped into the triangle.

Nimrod vanished.

And I let the Island take me, too.

PART THREE: BRANCHES

43. GRANNY

I opened my eyes. I was lying on my back, staring at a blue, high sky. My arms were restrained, pinning me in place. If I flexed my hands, I could feel five fingers on both of them, not just one.

I looked down at myself, awkwardly lifting my head as far as it would go. My body was smaller, lighter, and thinner. Like that of a child's. My hair dangled down behind me. I realised I was on a long, stone table, raised off the ground. People moved around me, busy, talking in low whispers. In the distance, there was bird song. I was outside, and it was warm, summer-warm. A butterfly flew across my line of sight. I followed it with my eyes as far as I could, and then a face came into view, blocking the butterfly out.

It was a face I barely remembered, but knew just the same.

It was the face of my Granny.

'Hello, Megan,' she said, smiling gently. I could make out every single line and pore on her skin, see every hair, every spot and wart and whisker, every broken vein and mole that peppered her face.

She lifted something to my lips, something that smelled of aniseed.

'Eat this,' she said.

I obeyed, because I trusted my Granny. I opened my mouth, and she popped a boiled sweet onto my tongue. I sucked on it, shuddering with the bitter aftertaste, and after a moment or two I began to feel light-headed, and dizzy. A numbness spread from my mouth to my throat, and then to my chest and along my arms.

'Better?' Granny asked, and I nodded, woozily.

Then, she held something else up before me. It had handles, like a pair of scissors, and two flat blades with a circular hole cut into each one. I could see one of her eyes through the holes, as if she were wearing a strange, frightening monocle.

'Listen, child,' she said, and there was a sad expression on her face. I saw other faces then too. They made a ring around me, faces of men and women I thought I knew, but didn't really. Two in particular stood out, and I realised who they were: younger versions of Murdo and Fiona, watching me with grim expectation.

I started to squirm, but Granny pressed down on my chest firmly.

'This is necessary,' she said, gently. My right arm was freed from its binds, and held up in front of me by two men, one of whom gripped my elbow, the other my hand with his own cold, rough fingers.

Granny carefully slotted the little finger of my right hand into the holes in the blades, sliding the scissors-device down until it was just above the lower knuckle, and pausing as she held it in place for a moment. The contraption was cold and sharp against my tender skin, and despite the numbness creeping through my body from the boiled sweet, I could tell that whatever that was about to happen was going to hurt. A lot.

I cried out, afraid.

'I love you, Megan,' Granny said then, and bent to kiss me on my forehead. Just as I had kissed Fiona before feeding her to Nimrod. Is that why I'd done it? An unconscious tribute to my heritage?

Behind her, the circle of onlookers silently raised their right hands, and drew triangles into the air.

'In time, you'll understand what all of this is for. In time, you'll know. For now, try not to judge me too harshly.' Granny looked at me with love in her eyes. Love, and something else. Something that went beyond love.

Something that I would later recognise as duty.

Without any further ado, she squeezed the handle of the scissors together, and cut my

little finger off like a twig.
        And oh, how I screamed.

44. THE LAIR

I awoke upon the beach.

It was different, this time. Molten glass still lay upon the sand, but aside from that, all was peaceful, and calm. I could see no bodies. No houses in the sea, no burning car. The sand was clean, unblemished.

Except for a trail of giant footprints.

I could see Nimrod in the distance, then, loping away from me, enormous strides devouring the sand under its feet.

I got to my own feet, and began to follow. As I walked, I looked for signs of White Pines, but found nothing. I also searched for the cherry tree, to no avail. The beach looked just like any other beach back home.

Apart from the giant walking ahead.

I followed in the steps of a great, time-worn predator.

The giant followed the line of cliffs that edged the beach, oblivious to my presence, or perhaps not considering me a desirable meal now that it had just eaten. The tracks it left in the sand were deep, and as long as two fully grown men lying head to toe. There were scuff marks connecting each print, as if the creature dragged its feet after every step. It was heavy with food, and moved sluggishly, ponderously, as if tired.

I was not tired. My body had been forged anew, enriched with the wisdom of three of my forebears.

The beach eventually began to curve inland, and the cliffs with it. Suddenly, the giant disappeared around a corner. When I rounded the headland, it was nowhere to be seen. Then I saw a large, dark cave mouth set into the cliff face.

A giant's lair.

The cave mouth was a tall, jagged slit in the wall of cliffs that rose high above the beach. The cliff's colours were bright and distinct now that I was up close. Bands of orange lay atop layers of pink, grey, cream and yellow. The cave made a black slash across the banded colours, a hole from which a lone seagull emerged, wings spread wide. It unhurriedly soared over my head and out to sea, and I wondered if it was the same gull that had screeched at me from the roof of a drowned house in my dream.

Boulders lay strewn around the cave entrance. As I began to climb over them, I saw images painted onto each one in rusty red paint, crudely, as if daubed there by large, clumsy fingers. The paintings were reminiscent of the carvings I'd seen in the tunnel beneath *Taigh-Faire*. Animals I didn't recognise leaped about, drank from rivers, and slept in various poses on different rocks. Behind them, great men approached with spears and clubs. I recognised the motifs immediately. They were giants, hunting in groups, large, lethal clubs held high. I'd seen the same outline on the hill outside Laide, and beneath my house.

As I moved closer to the cave, there were fewer fantastic beasts to be seen. The paintings thinned out. Then, I climbed across a boulder upon which, instead of animals, a small cluster of undeniably human figures cowered beneath a giant. The beast was frozen in the act of plucking one from the ground, and smashing it into its mouth.

At some point, the creatures had stopped hunting their own natural prey, and moved onto other sources of food. People.

Why? I wondered. Necessity? Preference? An extinction event?

When had they stopped hunting in their own territory, and moved to ours?

The boulders rounded off, grew smaller and more worn. The paintings became even scarcer. On the last one I passed, I saw the distinct, upside-down shape of a gallows frame scrawled in red paint. Hanging from it was the limp body of a stick man. A giant loomed over the frame, ready to collect its tribute. Gathered at its feet, a congregation of small people, all of whom had one arm raised to the sky.

It can't be killed, Fiona had said, *so we manage it.*

I knew better, now.

As I got closer to the entrance of the lair, I started to notice strange, greyish lumps of congealed matter scattered like pellets amongst the stones. I crouched to get a closer look at one of them, poking it with my finger. It was dry and spongy, about the size of a large pillow. A white, sharp object stuck out of the grey stuff, the end splintered, and chewed.

Bone.

This was the regurgitated human matter that the giants could not digest properly, parcelled up, expelled as pellets and deposited here, outside the cave. Hair, bone, clothing, other things that glinted. Jewellery, perhaps. Maybe teeth with fillings. Other things I didn't want to look at too closely. The giant pellets were like owl pellets. I found another one, saw a rotting wisp of white lace peeking out from amongst the bones. And another, from which fragments of skull stared balefully at me. The more I looked, the more I saw lying around, in varying states of decay. There were hundreds of them around the mouth to the cave, each one representing a human life, snuffed out.

How many years had this thing been killing my species?

Were any of these people from White Pines?

Was there only one Nimrod?

One giant?

I stared at the entrance to the giant's lair, my body brimming with strange energy. I'd been given this strength for a reason, but was this it? Was this my purpose? With the ritual incomplete, it was hard to know.

I pushed the thoughts to one side, and went into the lair.

It stank. The giant may have been fastidious about leaving its bone-pellets outside, but it was not so fastidious about its excrement. Huge piles of it lay curled in stinking, brown coils near the mouth of the cave. Scuff marks in the sand showed that the giant had half-heartedly attempted to kick dirt over the shit once it had done its business, as a dog would. The resulting mounds of faeces rose to either side of me, and through the middle of this, a wide track ran.

I took the path, listening for signs of the giant, and hearing nothing. The further in I went, the darker it became, but to my ruined eyes, it made no difference. My sight came from another place now, a place deep inside. I could still feel what was left of my eyeballs crusted on my cheeks, twin streams of gore that had now gone hard and flaky, like dried egg yolk. I left them there. The Picts of old painted their faces with wode. These were my own battle marks, and I wore them proudly.

The cave was long, and ran far back into the cliff side. Huge stalactites stabbed down from the cave ceiling, only to meet with stalagmites stretching up from the floor. I was soon surrounded by towering, needle-like columns of mineral deposits down which water trickled constantly. It grew cold and damp around me. I moved along, and the stalactites gave way to massive crystal formations, great white spars of something that looked like quartz, easily ten to twelve metres long, the root of each one glowing a deep, vibrant blue. The temperature shifted, and became warm, humid. I would have sweated, in my old body, and grown thirsty.

I no longer lived inside my old body.

Eventually the cave widened out, the crystals thinned to small, sparkling lumps on the walls. I began to hear noises echoing down the path towards me. Heaving, grumbling, moaning noises.

Finally, I came to the lair. The cave walls swooped out to the sides, and a huge natural pocket opened up before me. Despite how far into the cliff we were, there was a faint, greenish light illuminating the hole, in the centre of which, a giant had made its home. I could see an enormous, sprawling nest of driftwood and dried seaweed and foliage and soft things the beast must have scavenged from the beach.

In the middle of this nest, Nimrod crouched before me with its back turned. Its entire frame heaved and shuddered, and it thrust its head forward and down rhythmically, emitting long, low, pained noises as it did so. The soft flesh of its face hung loose like soft, putrid dough, and its eyes trembled with exertion on those rigid stalks, as the giant heaved, and heaved, and heaved.

And I knew then what it was trying to do. It was trying to regurgitate what was left of Fiona, what it hadn't been able to digest.

I watched, fascinated, as the pink slit of a mouth opened, and streams of drool began leaking down to the ground. Then, something lumpish and wet and grey squeezed out from between its jaws, slowly at first, and then suddenly shooting out with a rush: a pellet of undigested bone, and hair, and clothing.

Nimrod caught it deftly with one of its massive hands, and crooned to itself in satisfaction, poking at the pellet as if fascinated with its own excretion.

I remembered the first time I had met Fiona, sitting in her little glass box at the back of Laide Post Office. I remembered her counting out money and politely quizzing me about where I had come from, even though she must have known who I was straight away. I remembered a tattoo on her wrist, and mismatched eyes. I remembered how she had slammed a spade down on my head, how she had ripped out Mac's tongue.

I thought, distantly, that this was a fitting end.

Nimrod played with the soggy pellet for a minute or two while I watched, and then got to its feet. It made to leave the cave, no doubt to deposit the bundle along with all the others, amongst the boulders outside the lair. I shrank to one side of the cave as the beast stalked by, those massive feet thundering past me in long, heavy strides.

Once the cave was empty, I realised I did not know what to do next.

How does one kill a giant? I thought. It was not knowledge that the Ancestors had thought fit to bestow upon me.

I looked up, thinking. On the ceiling of the cave, far, far above my head, white blobs had been daubed onto the rock. They glowed a faint, fluorescent green in the dark, the source of the light in the lair. Algae? Phosphorescence of some sort. The giant had used it like paint to decorate its home. I realised that the blobs looked like stars, like a galaxy of sickly, green stars, and that the creature must fall asleep looking at them.

Do giants dream? I wondered, and a wild

laugh bubbled up from the depths, rolling around the cave as it burst out of my mouth before I could swallow it down again.

There is a dark surge of air above my head. An enormous hand swoops in from above, for Nimrod never left the cave at all. Nimrod knew I had been following it, and hid behind one of the huge columns of crystal, waiting for me to reveal myself.

It had tricked me.

Nimrod was clever. My ancestors chose its name well.

The hand wraps around me.

45. UP

Up, up, up.

I felt breath, hot and fetid on my face.

I bit down hard upon the hand that held me. Rubbery, blistered skin broke beneath my teeth, and my mouth filled with the taste of it, a taste beyond description. I gagged, but hung on grimly, squeezing my jaws together as hard as I could. The creature roared, and I was pelted with the debris of its earlier meal: tiny scraps of flesh and bone, gobbets of hair, brain matter and flaps of skin that must have been stuck in its mouth, dislodged only now with the force of its cries. I saw, as it bellowed at me, that the giant had no teeth, which is why it couldn't digest the bones and other, tougher items humans wore. Like a bird, it could not chew its food, and so it regurgitated what its stomach could not handle.

Roaring back, I bit down again, and again, and again, until I was able to free first one of my arms, and then the other. Nimrod did not let me go, for I was a puny, biting human, a mere gnat, an insect, and the giant was a hungry apex predator.

But I cared not for such things. I was different now. I was an insect with a poisoned sting.

I cared only for a world where this creature did not exist.

I shot an arm out and grabbed one of the giant's eye stalks as it craned around me. The vast, white eye attached to the end stared at me with unrestrained, wild malevolence, and I wondered how well Nimrod could see through the thick, crusted cataract that festered on the end of the stalk. What did I look like through that diseased lens?

Like food.

I yanked the flexing tendon, and twisted it with all my strength. Nimrod's fingers tightened on my body, trying to crush the life out of me, and its pink, slitted mouth began to open wide, preparing to stuff me inside even as I fought back.

I squeezed, and wrenched, and pulled, and the eye-stalk snapped beneath my twisting fist, and suddenly I was falling, falling from a great height, for Nimrod had dropped me in pain. It clutched its ruined eye, which now flopped down like a wilted flower, and howled with rage. I had time to feel satisfied about that, to feel triumphant before I slammed into the ground, but as the floor rushed up towards me, the giant caught me, snatching me back up again mere seconds from death. Its hand went back to-wards its mouth, and I knew, in those last, final moments, as Nimrod opened wide and fed me into its massive, pink maw, what it was that I had to do.

46. DOWN

No teeth. Only gums, ridged like mountains. Only a scaled, hard tongue that rasped against my naked skin. Saliva, acrid and thick and gelatinous, soaked me in seconds.

The mouth closed. I took a deep breath as the last of the light faded from view.

Then all was hot, dark, and wet.

The creature swallowed, or tried to. The massive tongue surged up beneath me, squashing me into the roof of Nimrod's mouth. It hurt, like nothing I'd ever felt before. It was like being rolled flat by an enormous, fleshy rolling pin. I screamed, unable to help myself, and struggled, and then realised that I had only seconds to act before nature took its course and I found myself in the giant's throat.

The tongue curled, began to shunt me towards the back of Nimrod's mouth.

It was going to swallow me whole.

I rolled into a ball, head between my knees, arms over my head, tucking in like I was about to dive-bomb a swimming pool. The world spasmed around me.

Nimrod swallowed.

And I slid down.

I was in the colossal throat, being slowly pushed along towards the esophagus. I had no time to think about what waited for me at the end of that narrow passageway: a pit of acid, ready to digest me whole, ready to break me down cell by cell while I thrashed about in agony.

The throat narrowed, and I felt something sphincter-like beneath my bare feet, contracting and pulsing, ready to take deliverance of me before sending me down into Nimrod's belly.

This was it. This was the last stop before death. The point of no return.

I braced myself, shooting my arms and legs out, digging my hands into the slimy walls around me, stabbing my feet out and in as hard as I knew how. My hands were strong, with them I had unearthed thousands of years of history, with them I had dug three holes and held my sistren tight, with them I had...

The giant swallowed again, trying to force me down. A huge sound of distress rumbled through my body, and I pushed back as the wet walls constricted again, as they tried to subdue me, tried to deliver me to my death.

But I was strong. Stronger than I'd ever known.

I knew what it took to kill a giant.

I held myself stiff, and large, and I blocked Nimrod's airway, filling its throat with my body, and I made a seal, felt burning air trying to escape past me.

And eventually, Nimrod began to choke.

47. TO KILL
A GIANT

It took far, far longer than I could have imagined.

Every second that passed became a year. Grimly, I hung on, my limbs trembling with effort. I was filled with a strange, primordial strength, a power that came from four-fingered women who had walked the earth long before I.

Massive fists beat against the outside of my heaving prison. I dug in, clinging like a limpet to a storm-battered ship. The fists turned back into hands, and I could feel it as Nimrod then clutched at its throat instead of beating at it, the deep, shatteringly loud distress cries turning to high-pitched squeaks and whistles as I jammed myself tight up against the wall of its voice box.

And still, I endured. My hands made deep furrows in the lining of the giant's throat. I felt the massive larynx of the beast rattle and buzz with a peculiar, strangled whine. Nimrod's windpipe gripped me fiercely with a reflexive, uncontrollable contraction.

There was a sense of something shifting, a difference in orientation, as if the world were moving slowly sideways. I realised that Nimrod was sinking to its knees, still scrabbling at its neck as if it could claw its way through its own skin and get to the obstruction blocking the airway. An almighty jolt confirmed my suspicion, and I almost slipped from my place as the giant crashed down heavily to what I could only assume was a kneeling position. I held firm. I held strong. My body remained a seal against more chaos. Against more white stones in a little seaside cemetery. Against innocent bodies dangling from a gallows frame. Against years more of warped, indoctrinated self-sacrifice and missives of duty.

It all stopped today.

There was another shift, and we were lurching again, falling further downwards. The giant keeled over at the knees, slowly, like a felled tree making its final descent to the earth. Nimrod's movements grew weaker and weaker, and the keening whine trailed off.

I made one, last, final push, keeping my body flat and tight and sealing the vacuum in the ancient creature's windpipe.

And the giant, unkillable by fire, or guns, or any weapon a man could make, stretched out long across the floor of its lair, spasmed three times, emitted one final, pathetic, distorted whine, and died.

I waited. Nimrod was tricksy, a smart beast. I wanted to make sure it was really dead.

It was.

Slowly, carefully, I inched my way back along the giant's throat, back into the huge, disgusting mouth. The beast had twisted its head as it had fallen, smooshing its lower jaw into the ground and forcing a small gap between its lips in doing so. Its monstrous tongue lolled out of this gap, swollen and blue, making a bridge for me, a slimy path from the giant's mouth to the ground.

I dragged myself across this bridge, inching along by grabbing the creature's discoloured, chalky papillae and using them as leverage handholds, every part of my body burning in pain, and, then, finally, slippery as the day I was born, I rolled out of the mouth of the beast and crashed to the floor, where I landed on my back and lay panting in a puddle of giant phlegm, staring up at a ceiling painted with glowing green stars.

PART FOUR: LEAVES

48. WHAT THINGS I HAVE SEEN

I don't know how long I lay in the giant's hole, breathing in and out while the corpse of a vast, ancient predator grew cold and stiff beside me.

Eventually, I summoned enough strength to stand. I climbed to my feet, and stumbled out of the cave, to the beach, which had changed in the time I had been inside. New things decorated the sand. I did not know what they were: they were not from a reality I recognised.

I turned to look back only once as I stumbled away from the lair. Above me, perched on the edge of the cliffs where before there had been nothing, I saw a castle. Not ruined, but intact, well-maintained, the stone clean, and bright, as if built recently. It perched haphazardly on the cliff's brink, one perfectly crenellated tower teetering half-on, half-off the banded ledge, seconds away from collapse. I knew it was from my world, but it was not from my time, my era. Time must be fluid here in the Other Place, the past and present simply opposite ends of a single piece of string that had been knotted to form a loop. I squinted at the castle, and a shower of masonry rained onto the sand underneath. I could hear men shouting from inside the structure, and then I saw them, scrambling to escape the building before that part of it tumbled away. They ran, ant-like across the ramparts, dressed in strange clothes, and I thought of all the historians and archaeologists and scholars who would have wept with joy and wonder to see what I was seeing. History, in motion.

I did not stay to watch the castle collapse in its entirety. I did not stop to watch the men inside die, or gawp at the waterfall that suddenly poured from the sky not far from where the rubble landed, piling up in front of the giant's lair and effectively sealing Nimrod in, a fitting tomb for a terrible beast. The water tumbled from a wide hole in the air, and beyond, for a split second, the edges of the fall were visible, as were rocks, ferns, and trees. The hole then closed as if zipped up abruptly, and the cascade snapped off, mid-pour. The remaining water hurtled downwards to the beach with the same terrible finality that the castle had, and hit with a loud smack, before making its way across the sand and out to the sea.

A castle on the brink of collapse, a water-fall in the sky: these things were beautiful and terrifying, but I had seen worse. I had seen what happens when the boundary between my world and another flickers, when those who built their home in the wrong place suffered the consequences, and when those who had been kidnapped by the Other Place were returned.

I had seen such things, such dreadful, wondrous things.

And I still had a ritual to complete.

I stumbled across the beach, walking towards what, I did not know. I kept going until I could walk no more. Like the giant I had killed, eventually, I ran out of steam. My legs buckled at the knees, and I saw Matthew's face once again, floating before me, his final expression haunting me, always haunting me, but none of that mattered anymore, because here was the beach, here was the sand, here was my end, and I had made it a good one.

Of course, it was not that easy.

I found myself back in the triangle. A cairn rose up proud in the middle of it, waiting for me.

I stared at it hazily with one ruined eye.
I had...I had a ritual to complete.
But I couldn't.
I just couldn't.

Instead, I lay on the ashen ground, sticky and sandy and filthy, and felt the weight of what I had just done press down upon me.

I was a giant slayer.

Like something from a child's fairytale.

But instead of triumph, I felt...diminished. Bereft.

Changed.

My hands wandered across my face. My eyes were still gone. In their place, two sunken holes, cauterised, the lids deflated and empty on top. I felt for my ears, felt the dried, sticky blood that had congealed around each one.

Finally, I poked a finger into my mouth, and instead of a tongue, I found only the ragged remains of my frenulum, that small fold of mucous membrane that connects the tongue to the floor of the mouth.

Taken.

It had all been taken from me, a fee, a tax I had paid for the incredible power that had helped me kill the beast.

And now, the power was gone. I could feel it. My body was weak, twisted, and frail. I was human once again. My joints ached, my skin was tender and sore.

A tax paid cannot be reclaimed, not on the Island.

I opened my mouth wide, to let out my grief, but no sound came forth. As if to taunt me, a dog barked from outside the triangle.

I had enough time to turn my head, see Murdo and his pup, walking across the barren land towards me.

Then, I returned to the black.

49. LOCKED OUT

I tried to go back.

Once I had healed, and even before then, I tried, many times over. Because I needed to finish the ritual. I had to do more for the people of White Pines. I wanted to rescue Matthew, and Luke.

The Island had different ideas.

I made it as far as the pine trees, each time. I would enter the woods, determined, mouth set, fists clenched, and walk the path I had walked before. But no matter how long or far I travelled across the blanket of pine needles, through the preternatural quiet, I never came out of the other side of the trees. The pines never gave way, never spat me out into the Island's interior like before. It was just endless rows of black and white, the pale tree-trunks like stripes in a barcode, stretching endlessly in every direction. I once tied red string around each trunk I passed, hoping to mark my way like Theseus with Ariadne's ball of thread through the laby-rinth, but when I turned back to check my progress, the string had always snapped, come loose, and was trailing behind me like thin, for-lorn entrails dragging across the ground.

It took time for the message to sink in, but sink in it did. Eventually.

I was locked out.

Unwelcome.

The centre of the Island was kept from me as surely as if a door had been slammed in my face.

I had sight, still. I could not see the way normal people could see, but I had vision, des-pite my missing eyes. It was not as strong and clear as it had been when first gifted to me, but it was still there.

I could hear, too, although my ear drums had both been destroyed. The old ones had al-lowed me to keep those senses.

I could not, however, speak without a tongue.

Mute, I existed as a shadow, marking each day as it came and went with scratches on the wall of Granny's kitchen. I made them with a tea-spoon, deep and deliberate in the old, soft plas-ter, and tried not to despair. I tried to think of it as all being part of some great, as yet uncommu-nicated plan. But it was hard. Because Matthew waited for me. So did hundreds of innocent people, thrust into a reality they were never prepared for. I wanted to help. I *had* to help. It was my job, as a Key, as someone who could go to the Other Place and come back, alive, and unchanged.

But the Island would not let me in.

And so I remained a prisoner at *Taigh-Faire*, doomed to stare out of my Granny's windows at the small land mass in the bay and wonder about Matthew, about the boy, Luke, and all the other people taken from this world, and the angry god beneath the tree, and the dead giant once known as Nimrod.

50. LAYERS

The first year Matthew was gone was the hardest.

His face followed me around in my every waking moment, and for most of the sleeping ones, too.

The longer he was absent, the longer I had to dwell upon it, this grief, the longer I had to figure out that there are layers to loss. First, the flimsy outer layer, which, when ripped away without warning or ceremony, exposed a raw flesh beneath, a tender dermis that screamed the longer its nerve endings and capillaries remained exposed to the cold air. Eventually, the fragile network of feelings and regrets and anger and shame dried out, shrivelled away, and the pain-layer sloughed off to reveal acceptance: bitter, hard, like a crab apple. Over time, that eroded too, because everything decays, in the end.

At least, it does in this world.

If I struggled, so did Rhoda.

She appeared at my house the same day I killed Nimrod, blackened and bruised but alive, which was all that mattered to me. Fiona hadn't killed her, hadn't taken her tongue. For that, I was grateful. The people of White Pines still had a voice. I had some company, for the long, grey hours where the Island taunted me through the kitchen window.

I don't know, thinking back, how she bore it as well as she did. I know I didn't. I mourned for Matthew. I mourned for White Pines too, of course I did. For Luke, and his mother. For Mac, and Johnny. But I hadn't lived amongst them as Rhoda had. They had not been my community. Taking on her loss as my own was in poor taste.

Instead, I wrestled with guilt. Because if anyone could find them, help them, bring them back to this life, I knew it was me.

It should have been me.

I just couldn't find a way in.

To cope, we developed new rituals, as a couple. I wrote a lot. The word processor I'd carted from my old life in the South finally came into its own, helping me in a number of ways. First, because I could no longer speak. Rhoda knew sign language, but I never really got the hang of it, my missing finger not helping the cause. So I wrote, and left notes for her around the house, little letter trails for her to follow, so that conversation still flowed between us.

Second, because I had a story to tell.

And what a story it was.

We developed other habits as time wore on. Walks along the bay. Breakfasts eaten in silence. Evenings by the fire, where little was said, but lots was felt. Fishing in the bay. Endless games of chess. Preparing meals for ourselves and Murdo's dog, who turned up at our doorstep in much the same fashion that Rhoda had one day, after which, he never left. We didn't give the dog a name. He remained 'Murdo's dog' until the day he died, many years later.

Turned out, he was a good dog, too.

Food was never an issue, to my surprise. It was brought to us every week by a mainlander, who wordlessly left a well-stocked cardboard box of groceries by the front door every Monday morning. I never questioned this, and the locals never demanded payment. I assumed it had something to do with Murdo, that this was my reward for freeing them all from Nimrod.

And Fiona.

Little by little, as we went through the motions of living something akin to a normal life, Rhoda began to talk to me, about all sorts of things. She had been a teacher, once, and it made her happy to share information. She liked history, customs and tradition. She had respect for the past, believing in its power to shape the future. She still held stubbornly to some of the old ways from her childhood. On the first day of May, she washed her face in the fresh, early morning dew. She said it brought her good health, and as traditions went, it seemed harmless enough, so I indulged her and washed my own face, too. On the Island, she had been planting new traditions, new customs, like seeds, before her people were so rudely ripped away from her. The seeds never flourished, and so instead, she told me stories.

And I wrote them down.

As we sat together of an evening, flames leaping high into the chimney breast that really needed sweeping but hadn't been dealt with yet, I learned the history of White Pines from Rhoda, who found that staring into the fire and talking of easier times eased the pain a little.

And this is what I learned.

51.
DECLASSIFIED

Anthrax Island, also known as Gruinard Island, was, long before I had ever laid eyes on it, a largely uninhabited chunk of Torridonian sandstone, comprised of four hundred and eighty four acres of land that sat uninhabited in Gruinard Bay, halfway between Ullapool and Gairloch. I say largely uninhabited. In 1881, a population of six was recorded. By 1890, that number went back to zero. I wondered about those six people a lot in the years to follow: who they were, why they were there. Why they were only there for nine years. Did they know of the cairns, the gateway, the Other Place? Of Nimrod? Did they disappear like the people of White Pines?

Or were they punished for trespassing, sacrificed to the beast from the gallows of Laide?

Before that, in 1549, a clergyman by the name of Dean Munro wrote in his records that the Island was wooded, making it an ideal spot for smugglers and rebels and pirates to shelter on, concealed from the eyes of the mainland. Rhoda told me this was a big part of why Mac chose to reintroduce trees to the Island all those years later. He believed in history too, and the power of nature to heal. And he liked the idea of a private, secret place hidden from view.

In the 1940s, Gruinard Island became Anthrax Island when scientists from the Microbiological Research Department at Porton Down decided to bomb the tiny landmass with a particularly virulent strain of anthrax called Vollum 14578. This part I already knew. I wrote it down anyway, and embellished it with my own research. This was made much easier in 1997, when a video was declassified of the scientists at work. I managed to get hold of a copy of that video, through connections in my old life as a journalist. I watched it on a brand new VHS player, hooking it up to the ancient television set in the living room at *Taigh-Faire*.

Rhoda refused to watch. She said she didn't need to see it to know it had happened, and besides, she had seen far worse since.

I wanted to watch it though. A part of me knew that this was what Matthew would do, if he were still here.

Watch, learn, and extrapolate.

The grainy, wobbly film opened with an information placard, and quickly changed to idyllic scenes with blue skies, the camera sweeping around the beautiful scenery of Gruinard bay, as if the cameraman were shooting a video for the tourism board and not a biological research department. The Island, now of modest and completely normal proportions, came into view. I saw no trees upon it. The place looked naked without them. Wrong, somehow.

Sheep were unloaded from a fishing trawler and ushered along the stone spit by a man with a sheep dog. A collie dog. I wondered if it was a distant relative of Murdo's dog. I wondered why that mattered to me, but it did, for some reason.

I couldn't make out much of anything after that until men in brown suits and gasmasks took the sheep out to an open part of the Island, not too far from a large rocky summit in the centre that I knew very well indeed. *An Eilid*, Luke's mother had called it. The men in suits did not recognise what sat on top of it: a cairn.

The fourth cairn.

The only one remaining intact, now, after my botched ritual.

The resting place of an ancient entity.

Ignoring it, the scientists of the past tied sixty poor, doomed sheep to wooden frames set up for just this purpose. They moved quickly, in a business-like fashion. It was a chilling echo of what happened with the gallows at Laide.

A pole was then thrust into the ground. It had something attached to the top of it, something that was then released.

And then the spores were unleashed.

There was a sequence of images, spliced together with increasing rapidity. A brown mist, spreading across the Island. Sheep, anchored to their pens, oblivious to their painful fate.

And then there it was, that sign I'd been after. Hard to tell for sure, given the degraded quality of the film, but after rewinding and re-watching several times, I was almost certain. There was a flicker in the mist, a sudden parting of ways, as if the vapour hit a solid surface. The illusion was gone in the blink of an eye, but I knew what it was. It was something from the Other Place, flickering into view for just a second, mostly obscured by the gas, but affecting it.

Then it was gone, sucked back to the other side of the veil.

But White Pines had yet to be built, so what was it that had come back?

Maybe the Other Place wasn't static like I had thought.

Maybe, things moved more like a carousel, behind the veil. Like that story I had read as a child, the Magic Faraway Tree. A new reality with every rotation, glimpsed through a single gateway: the Island.

The video kept playing, a 16 mm colour display of death. Sheep carcasses were dissected, analysed. Some of them were then burned in a makeshift furnace. Others were dragged away and dumped in a cave I knew very well. Matthew and I had walked across their bones.

The scientists took their leave, and there was a period of quarantine for the Island. This lasted until 1986, when two hundred tons of formaldehyde and seawater was dumped all over the place in an effort to sterilise it, just as Mac had told me.

Four years later, the government sold it back to Mac for five hundred pounds.

He had no idea what he was taking ownership of.

52. NOTHING

I kept visiting the Island, despite knowing I could not find a way in. It felt like I had to try, and keep trying, or fade into the obscurity of acceptance, and so I did. Try, that is. I wandered amongst the pines like a will-o'-the-wisp, aimlessly rambling to and fro, trying to get out of the woodland. Never succeeding. Returning to *Taigh-Faire* frustrated, yet ready to try again the next day.

And then, on a morning no worse or better than any other in what had become an endless parade of lacklustre sunrises, the trees opened up for me.

It was so unexpected, that I couldn't quite grasp it at first. The shift from dark to light was so abrupt, so rude.

But there it was, before me, sitting quietly in the ring of trees. A flat, desolate plain, with a sloping rise in the middle, on top of which sat a cairn. Around this, a blackened triangle. Around that, a tall barbed wire fence. The mainlanders must have put it up after I killed Nimrod. The Island was clearly not closed to every-one.

I wasted no time. I passed the first ruined cairn without stopping to remember what had happened to me down there beneath its stones. I was angry at the Island for toying with me. I was aware that my time within the circle of trees might be limited. I had only one thing I wanted to do.

The fence was high, but there was enough space for me to crawl beneath. I squatted low, wincing as a barb caught the back of my shirt, then unhooked myself, placing one foot care-fully on unhallowed soil.

Come on, I thought. *Come on, you bastard!*

Nothing.

All was still.

I pulled my other leg out behind me, and stood up within the triangle.

Still, nothing.

Not even a flicker in the air.

Maybe I needed to get further in.

So I walked, where once I had run in terror. I walked as far into the triangle as I could without approaching the cairn. There was something about that final, unconquered pile of stones that I wasn't ready for, yet.

But I *was* ready for the Other Place.

I stood in the danger zone and waited. Waited for something to come back. Waited for the air to flicker and fail, for the curtain to lift.

And nothing happened.

I waited for two hours, like an idiot.

Absolutely nothing.

It didn't make sense. Why let me in, only to deny entry now? I was ready! I was ready to go beyond, again!

Was I no longer worthy? I had held the bodies of my ancestors in my arms, bled them of their knowledge, woken a god, slaughtered a beast, and now I was no longer good enough?

I bent down, touched the soil with my bare hands, felt an echo, a hum, an energy that set my teeth on edge.

But that was it.

Nothing else happened.

And nothing else continued to happen for the next ten years.

Days passed, and turned into weeks. Weeks became months. Months morphed into years, and time became a new enemy. Because I was older than I had been when Matthew had first disappeared, and somehow, that made his absence so much worse.

Arthritis set into my bones, and spread from joint to joint like mould on a damp wall. My hair grew grey, thick, dry. Rhoda's grew sparse and wispy. Murdo's dog slowed down, grew stiff-jointed like the rest of us, and Murdo himself, on the rare occasions that I saw him, became a stooped, worn figure. But the food baskets still came, every Monday. The locals did not forget their debt to me. Rhoda still bathed her face in the dew every first day of May, and every winter, we sat by the fire, and told stories of our past lives.

And nothing ever happened on the Island.
Until the boy came back.

53. REPLAY

It's been over ten years, yet still it feels as if the Island is waiting for White Pines to return. Time has stopped here. Nature has not reclaimed the land. Instead, the ground remains scorched. Nothing grows. Not even weeds. Animals don't forage here, birds don't fly over the big, blank space in the soil where houses used to stand. I can't even see insects flitting around on the breeze. There is no breeze, despite the fact that the sea is all around me.

No-one else comes here anymore, except for me. There is no reason to. There is nothing to see, no ruins to mourn over. No-one mourns.

But I still come.

Sometimes I take a small boat across the sea.

Sometimes, when I feel particularly numb, I swim across the bay, just like my Granny did. Sometimes, I use the tunnel, running my fingers over old carvings on the walls as I walk.

I come, and I pay my respects to the missing, and then I return to Taigh-Faire, and my seat in the kitchen, from where I can see everything and nothing, all at the same time.

And nothing ever changes. Hopelessness lies thick on the ground like snow. A tiny flicker here, perhaps an image there. Something returns for a split second, then vanishes again. But nothing I can ever determine, nothing I can ever get to. Once, I almost managed to grab a discarded shoe that popped into view a few feet from where I stood, but I was too slow, and just as my fingers brushed the leather, it vanished.

And then, I see that dark, limping shape silhouetted against the black and brown slope.

And this time, things are different. Because the shape lingers, has permanency. It does not vanish.

It is the shape of the boy. Unhurt, unchanged, real, and solid, and perfect.

And he is still moving towards me.

There is hope, after all!

After all these years!

I start to run, and so does he. My legs are tired, but they are spurred on by one, bright thought:

I might just make it, this time.

I might just save one of them.

Finally, gloriously, after what feels like eons of running towards each other, the boy is within reach. I grasp his outstretched arm, heave him up into my embrace.

It is the boy called Luke.

He had held my hand, and I had known him. His fingers had met mine, and I had recognised him from some previous encounter. Or was it from this encounter? I could not tell which was the right way around, anymore. Time was a close loop, knotted tight.

'Hurry!' The boy shrieks, and I can feel him flickering in my embrace, his form pulsating between solid and...something else. Something less real. Something less now.

Behind him, tall pines with strange, white trunks watch, impassive.

We run. We are going to make it. The fence is mere feet away. Then, we are beneath it, and clear out the other side.

I saved one.

I saved one!

Tears roll down my cheeks.

The tall, pale pines rustle gently around us, as if applauding.

Is this what they had been waiting for, all along?

I lie down next to the boy on the ground and hold him tightly, soothing him as he sobs hysterically.

I've got you, I think.

Then, I take him home.

54. LUKE

I brought him home to Taigh-Faire. When Rhoda saw me carry him into the kitchen, she went white as a sheet, her trembling hands covering her mouth in shock.

The boy shivered and shuddered in my arms, his eyes wide, fixed, staring into space. I carried him upstairs with enormous difficulty, never letting on how much pain I was in, and put him into my bed. Rhoda followed, and we both looked down at him with tears in our eyes.

'He doesn't look any older,' she murmured.

She was right. Ten years had passed, and you could mark every year on our faces, but Luke looked just the same age as he had been the night White Pines disappeared.

Time moves differently in the Other Place, I remembered.

The boy said nothing for weeks. He lay in the darkened bedroom, sleeping, for hours and hours of every day. Rhoda and I took it in turns to sit beside him, working in shifts so that he was never alone. He did not like being left alone. On the only occasion he woke in his room to find that he was by himself, he screamed, terrified, and didn't stop for two hours. We learned not to make that mistake again, and so we sat by his bedside, watching him twist about in sweat-sodden sheets as nightmares ate away at his sleep.

He was not the only one to dream.

I only had one dream, but it was the same dream, over and over, night after night. Matthew and I were always together in my recurring nightmare, sitting side by side on the cairn in the centre of the Island. A party was always happening in the town square below us. Tall pine trees stood to attention in a bright, distracting circle running around everything. I found it hard to tell if this scenario was a dream construct, or a memory, or both, but my brain kept taking me back there, nonetheless.

Matthew would watch me, in these dreams, studying my profile in the golden glow of a late sunset. Working up to something. A big statement of some sort. Matthew had always been good at those.

'Ever feel like you started out with the wrong person in life?' He would say, eventually, in a tone that was far too casual for the subject matter.

I would fix my eyes on the party, on the swirling people who danced through the square, and even in my dream, I could not commit to him. Even though I knew, deep down, I was about to lose him, I kept my voice neutral.

'I'm not sure I know what you mean,' I would say, for in my dreams I still had a tongue and a voice.

'Well, your marriage, and mine,' he always said. Music spiralled in the air between us. Sweet and light, but with a distinct dissonance that grew worse as our conversation continued. 'Both over and done with. I lost years of my life, years that I put into being married to the wrong person, and now, I can't get those years back. Don't you feel like that, too?'

I would face him then, and it was easier with the sun in my eyes, because I couldn't see the expression on his face.

'Do you mean that if you and I had met at the right time, before everything, we'd have married each other instead? Are *we* the right people for each other?'

Matthew would move closer still, so that I could feel his breath warm on my face. 'I feel,' he'd say, 'I feel as if you and I...' He'd stop, always carefully choosing his words.

And, when they came, they were always good words.

'Maybe they wouldn't have been wasted years, if I'd spent them with you.'

Then he would kiss me, and it would feel natural, and wonderful, and I would respond, sliding a hand up the side of his face to bring him closer. He would grab me around the waist, and pull me onto him, and I always straddled him, suddenly at the mercy of my own desire, and our clothes came away as easily as leaves falling from trees at the turn of the season, and flesh met flesh, and I closed my eyes, sliding down, filling myself up with him, and when I opened them, a three-headed pig stared back at me.

Every single time.

I would scream, and the pig heads would scream too, teeth gnashing and chomping in pain.

I slept less and less as the days passed by.

'I don't remember anyone called Matthew,' Luke said one day six weeks later, crushing my hopes with six small words.

As Rhoda had predicted, he eventually stopped sleeping as much, and began to speak instead. Only a few words to begin with. More as he relaxed into our company. We tried to make things as stable, peaceful and calm for him as possible, knowing that he had been through something so profoundly traumatic that change, no matter how small or seemingly insignificant, would set him back to the point of catatonia. So we built a new, carefully timed routine around him. Breakfast at seven-thirty, every day. It was always the same, porridge with a dollop of jam, and milk, and sweet tea. After, we would walk Murdo's dog on the beach below the house. Then lunch. Then a board game, or a book. Then dinner, then bath, then more milk, then bed. Every day, exactly the same. Day in, day out. A ritual, like walking an ancient path between piles of stone. It helped Rhoda and I every bit as much as it helped Luke.

And after a time, he began to talk.

I refrained from asking too many questions. It was hard, because with his speech came my insatiable desire for knowledge, but I knew that pushing too much and too soon would set him back.

He eventually began to offer up nuggets of information on his own. He could not remember meeting me, or Matthew. He did not remember the event, the moment White Pines vanished. He just remembered waking up on a beach, and his mother was nowhere to be seen. He never found her, after that. Never saw his Ma again.

But he did find his father, stumbling around in a daze not far from where he had woken up. Together, they found shelter behind some large rocks at the base of a cliff. They saw things that Luke couldn't, or wouldn't describe. He called them 'scary things,' and I didn't push him for more detail.

And then, Nimrod came.

Luke wouldn't talk about this at all, but he did draw a picture for me on one of our walks.

He used a stick, and traced lines in the sand. I saw long legs, a long, slender body, eyes on long stalks. A wide, open mouth. Luke drew two stick figures running away from the creature. A small one, and a big one.

Then he rubbed the big one out with his hand.

I understood from this that Luke's father was dead. Eaten by Nimrod.

Silently, I bent down, and rubbed the out- line of the giant out, too, so that only Luke's fig- ure remained on the sand.

I held him to me, then. Held him tight. He was family to me from that moment on, just as Rhoda was family. We were bound together by the Island, by loss and terror and grief, and even as I hated it for what it had taken from me, I found a new appreciation for the fresh gifts it bestowed.

Family.

After Luke, the Island gave nothing else back. The trees let me pass, but nothing ever moved in the barren wasteland inside the tri- angle.

I learned to be content with that, for a while. I did not trouble the final cairn, as much as I wanted to. I had a child to raise and do right by, and he took a lot of my time, and energy. My sense of urgency around rescuing the citizens of White Pines faded. My hope for Matthew dwin- dled along with it. I began to think of him as I thought about my Granny, my parents, my marriage, Mac, Johnny, and Fiona: dead.

Gone, beyond.

I decided to focus on the living, instead.

But still, in my nightmares, Matthew came for me.

55. EVER BURNING

The boy turned twelve. We held a small party for him, a quiet but joyous celebration with a cake and a brand new mountain bike, which Murdo had found from somewhere on our request. He uncovered it with the shaking hesitancy of a person who had seen too many unexpected things in his time, and did not like surprises very much. When the bike was revealed, he stroked the handlebars and fiddled with the gears and smiled a smile so bright I felt it pierce right through me.

After, I took him for a walk across the beach, which was the thing we liked to do most together. I noticed, as we meandered in silence, how much darker his hair was than it had been when he had first come to us. I noticed the more angular set of his jaw, and how long his legs were. The puppy fat of childhood was slowly melting away. In its place, was something leaner, and less vulnerable. I was grateful for this. He had been through so much, so much that would stay with him for life. Watching him grow and become a stronger version of himself brought me joy,

We walked along the beach, and I occasionally reached out to ruffle his hair, a thing I loved to do, but he was less keen on this now that adolescence was upon him. Sometimes he accepted my affection, other times not. Today, he could sense the mood, and allowed me to be attentive.

We stopped at our usual spot on the beach, a spot where we could see the Island the most clearly. We sat, and stared at it, and thought about the people it had taken.

'Megs,' Luke said, and I blinked, shaking myself out of a memory where a melted ball of pig flesh writhed and screamed and fell down a slope toward me.

I nodded.

'I think I would like to start calling you Ma, now. If that's alright, I mean.'

I reeled.

He repeated himself. 'I think I would like to start calling you Ma. My real Ma isn't coming back.' He pointed unnecessarily to the Island. From here it looked so small, innocuous. I felt it scratching in the back of my mind. Waiting. Always waiting.

For what?

'You look after me like my real Ma used to.'

I shook my head. I could never replace his real mother.

'And, I love you.'

I felt a hot, tight lump in my throat.

He went on, filling up my silence.

'I think she would be happy that you are looking after me so well,' he said, and I couldn't help it then. I started to cry.

Luke slipped a hand through the crook of my arm and rested his head on my shoulder. We stared at the Island, and I knew that later that night, while he slept, I would creep into his room and sit by his bed and watch him sleep, because my love was white hot, and ever burning. Luke was the fuel to that fire. He was proof that I could make things right, somehow. That there was still hope.

But that was for later. I sat, on his twelfth birthday, and enjoyed the weight of his head on my shoulder.

'I love you, Ma,' he said, again.

White hot, and ever burning.

56. THE CALL

A rumbling woke me from my regularly scheduled nightmare not long after Luke's birthday.

Giant! I thought, as I jolted upright. The rumble sounded exactly like a giant's footsteps, thundering into the ground. But then I remembered, snapping fully awake as the rumbling came again, that Nimrod was dead. I had killed the giant.

So what was happening?

It was the dead of night. Murdo's dog barked frantically from his bed downstairs. The tremor shook the walls of *Taigh-Faire* violently. Cutlery toppled and smashed in the kitchen. I heard the mirror in the hallway come free of its nail, and splinter as it hit the floor. Tiles slid off the roof, and landed with distinct thumps in the garden outside.

My head began to ache.

The rumbling stopped as quickly as it had begun, and in the aftermath I heard Luke, shouting. *'Ma!'* He yelled, his voice thick with sleep and fear.

I went to him, as did Rhoda, and we both soothed him as he shook under his blankets.

'What was it?' Rhoda said, looking confused and disoriented.

I frowned. I could see a strange glow coming from behind Luke's curtains. It was too early for dawn. I rose, and felt that familiar pounding begin to hammer at my skull, that harbinger of change that meant something on the Island was waking up.

Dry-mouthed, my knee joints swollen and painful, I shuffled to the window, pulled back the curtains.

And saw the Island in the bay, from which, a sparkling column of light shot up into the sky, piercing the night with an otherworldly glow, and I took this for a sign. A clarion call.

This light was for me. It was coming from inside the trees, from the centre of the Island, from roughly the same place as the final cairn.

Years ago, I had taken part in a ritual, an ancient, age-honoured ritual that I had never completed.

Now, it was time.

To finish what I had started.

'But where are you going?' Luke asked, as I unlatched the door to the cupboard under the stairs and began shifting boxes out of the space in front of the cellar door.

I didn't answer until the small, wooden hatch was revealed. The flashlight hung on its nail next to it as always.

'Are you going back?' He said, and his eyes were wide, and afraid. Rhoda stood behind him, rubbing his back in a distracted, soothing gesture. 'Back there?'

I nodded. My head throbbed and ached. I still had hooks in me, after all these years. There were still threads, pulling me along.

'But Ma, I love you! You can't!' Luke was beside himself, distraught at the idea of losing yet another parent.

I gathered him up in a tight hug, marveling at how tall he'd gotten. I remembered carrying him as a small, frightened little boy. I remembered how fiercely protective of him I'd always felt. How I'd felt, even when we first met, as if I'd known him a long time. He was precious to me, so precious.

And yet, the Island called.

And I had no choice but to answer.

I pointed to the ground, then, in the same way I gestured to Murdo's dog when we went walking. Luke knew what that gesture meant. It meant 'stay put.'

'But, Ma...'

I jabbed my finger downwards again, to make my point. I was deadly serious. I did not want him coming after me, because I had no idea what it was that I was walking into.

Rhoda put a hand on my shoulder. 'Don't worry,' she said. 'I'll look after him.' And I knew she would. She was old, but strong. A survivor, like we all were.

I smiled, then, taking in my family. My surrogate son, my surrogate mother. Our dog. A tight little unit. A community all of my own.

I turned my back on them, feeling sick, and cold, and yet strangely, horribly excited.

Because there was an end in sight, I could feel it.

I made for the tunnel beneath the house.

57. BENEATH

I felt the familiar tilt as the tunnel floor sloped down beneath the bay. I tried not to think of the tons of sand and water and rock above my head, bearing down. This was the first time I had been here in a long, long while. There were easier ways to get onto the Island if I needed to, ways that didn't involve dragging my sore, aching body up a series of iron rungs hammered into a rock face, and so I had neglected this route.

But now, it felt right that I should be here.

I walked, and after what felt like an eternity, I came upon the skeleton of the giant deer. Still there, after all those years. I almost impaled myself on its antlers, but stopped myself just in time. *The tunnel must branch away just beyond the deer,* I suddenly thought. I knew it hadn't come to be here from the Island, it wasn't possible. It was too large, and could never have used the ladder to climb into the cave at the end of the tunnel. It must have come from somewhere else, a second passageway, perhaps, branching out from this one. I lowered myself slowly beneath

GEMMA AMOR

the antlers, and then paused, gathered myself. From here on in, I needed to be extra vigilant. If Matthew and I had both missed the second tunnel and walked right past it the first time, it must be well hidden. I extended both arms, and used them to carefully feel the tunnel walls on either side of me as I walked, stooped like a cripple, sweeping my hands up and down and feeling for anomalies in the rock.

And, because I was searching for it this time, and because the timing was right, and because the Island had decided it would be that way, I came to it easily. My left hand trailed across the stone, and then suddenly met air. In torchlight, it would have been overlooked as a shadow, or an irregularity in the rock, which is why Matthew and I had both missed it. It was not a shadow, however, but a wide cleft, far wider at the top than it was at the bottom, easily wide enough for a giant antlered deer to fit through, but still somehow perfectly hidden, barely perceptible unless you were looking for it. No breeze came up through the fork, and there was no sense of space changing, or a shift in depth or breadth or anything noticeable at all except by touch, by absence of rock.

I knew without doubt that I was supposed to walk this way. I did not hesitate.

I went in.

Light seeped into this new tunnel. It had a strange, orange glow to it, like dawn. It reminded me of the sunset that soaked my nightmares, nightmares of love rejected and sex unplanned and screaming, mutated pig flesh.

After a time, the orange glow intensified, became a bright white pin prick up ahead at which I aimed myself. It illuminated the walls to either side of me, which were not rough like the walls of the tunnel that led to the Island. These were smooth, as if they had been polished, and looked almost glassy. They glowed with a deep, navy-blue hue. I let my fingers trail along the surface of the rock, and saw things hanging in frosted suspension beneath. They looked like fossils, only more colourful. I saw a curved shell with scalloped edges, reminding me of an ammonite, only this shell ended in squid-like tentacles, and a strange, flat, lobster-like head. I peered at it, momentarily distracted, and saw an eye nestled in amongst the tentacles, just below the mouth of the shell.

It blinked, and the tentacles retracted. A jet of something that looked like water propelled the thing forward, out of view, and I realised it *was* water, that the ammonite-creature was suspended in water, not rock, and the walls were not stone, after all. Perhaps they were crystal. They were like solid glass retainers, holding back an ocean. It was as if I walked through a giant, plexi-glass tunnel in an aquarium. As I made this realisation, something vast and grey swam over my head. A huge, primitive shark, or whale, or some distant relative of either. It moved ponderously, its huge tail swaying from side to side as it forged on through the ocean, paying no mind to the pitiful, lowly human below.

I was beneath the sea, of that much I was certain. But which sea? In which time, or space?

I walked, and the light grew brighter. The ocean around me changed, as if I were walking through a tunnel of time, and I saw fish I actually recognised, flitting in and out of forests of kelp and coral. At one point, something very like an eel snaked past, only it had a small, glowing orb attached to the front of its head on a long stalk, like an angler fish lamp. It reminded me so fiercely of Nimrod's eyes on stalks that my heart stopped for a moment. Is that what Nimrod was? Some evolutionary deviant from another reality? The landside equivalent of an angler fish? It was humanoid from the neck down, but otherwise alien. Could it be what we might have become, had nature chosen a different path? I thought of it like the fork in the tunnel. Down one trail, walked humans. Down another, our ancestral equivalent: Nimrod.

I was sending myself mad with these thoughts.

I walked on.

And found myself, eventually, beneath a great, polished, crystal archway. The light spilling out of it was now as bright as the glow of a sun. I could see a large, branched shadow against the brilliant white beyond the archway. It moved, slowly, ponderously.

I passed through the archway.

And brightness washed me away.

58. THE TREE

A cherry tree above my head sheds a single blossom.

It drifts down slowly, landing upon my cheek as I look up at the branches, watching as little birds hop and chirp and peck at seeds and preen their feathers in contented harmony.

The tree hangs, impossibly, in the air before me. It rotates, slowly, in suspension. The branches rustle gently as the birds move about within, and the roots of the tree dangle down beneath the trunk like gossamer threads, every tiny tendril and fibrous strand undulating and writhing about like the tentacles of an anemone underwater, and I have never seen anything as beautiful, nor will I ever see anything like this again.

A towering column of light shoots straight up into the sky around the spinning tree, engulfing it in a brilliant luminosity. The light sparkles with energy, and it reminds me of the waterfall that appeared above the beach so suddenly on the day I killed Nimrod, only instead of the water falling downwards, the light is travelling up, up from the roots, up along the trunk, up through the branches and out past the leaves.

And all else around me is white, white space, white air, white ground, white sky, the only thing of any colour being the tree, and the birds, and the pink blossom, and the sparkling column of energy beaming skyward from a place I cannot see.

And I know I must not touch. I know it, and yet I cannot help myself. It is so beautiful, so pure, so I reach up, place a hand upon the trunk of the tree.

And feel a sucking motion. Like a fish being reeled in on a line, the tree tugs at me, drinks me in. My hand disappears into the bark, and then my arm disappears up to my elbow, and my face comes up sharp against the tree trunk, but I let it happen, I relax into it. Soon, I am no longer flesh and blood. I am bark and sapwood, heartwood and pith. Through me flows information, sticky and rich and filled with power. Little finches peck at insects in my hair. Roots snake between my toes, reaching for earth, finding nothing.

And in the heart of the tree, embedded within like a tiny bug trapped in fossilised sap, I find the stone face of a god. It opens its mouth, but it is no longer angry with me. It welcomes me.

It sings.

And I sing with it, finding a harmony to an ancient song I didn't realise I knew, our voices mingling into a single, vibrant sound that soars up along the beacon and off into a universe unknown, for the tree is an axis, around which multiple possibilities spin, and I am a walker between worlds, a Key, a gatekeeper of the Other Place, just like my Grandmother before me, and her Grandmother before her, and hers before that, and so on, stretching back in time as far as anyone could be bothered to trace, and then beyond. I was part of something primitive and duty-bound, and my lineage had led me here, to the tree, to make music with a god.

And my arms, which have leaves sprouting from them, come up and out, for I embrace the light, I embrace my heritage. This is further than any of my ancestors have ever travelled, this is uncharted territory. This is the final stage of the ritual. I am the first, and the last, and I stretch wide, feeling power run along every part of my being, and my questing roots finally find soft, damp soil, and stones, and lichen, and heather.

The tree and I sink down towards the earth, slowly. I push my feet out with all my might, digging each of my roots into a pile of stones that I land upon, a distinctive mound of rocks packed tight to form a cairn, a carefully arranged cone on top of a sloping rise in the centre of an Island. A black, dead triangle of ash lies about the cairn, a place where once, a town called White Pines stood proud.

The beacon of light expands sideways, travelling across the bleak space until it hits the edges of the triangle, filling it up, and everything is energy, everything is song.

And the air begins to flicker, tremble.

Things that have been stolen begin to come back.

Shadows fade in and out of view, shadows that move, and speak, and huddle together in terror. The people of White Pines come slowly into view. There are less of them than there were when they had last been seen on the Island. So many have died. But these are the survivors, the ones who made it through the veil and back again, and would be forever changed because of it. They stumble about, weeping and clutching at each other, bathed in a coruscating light, and although they do not know it yet, they are safe now. There will be no more terrors for them.

One of those shadows is the shape of a man I know, a tall, slim man with salt and pepper hair. He materialises fully, a shadow no more, and drops to his knees beneath the cherry tree that has newly sprouted upon the summit of *An Eilid*, exhausted and half-mad from the things he has seen and borne. He kneels, shaking with relief, and he thinks of a woman, a woman who might be me, a woman who is no longer a woman but part of a new ecosystem, a network of possibility that spans the very breadth and depth of his known universe, and beyond.

A woman who was finally able to save him.

A woman who loved him once, and loves him still.

And if he were to look up, he might have seen me standing there, tall and wide, proud and strong, pink petals still clinging to my hair.

EPILOGUE

There is an Island, in a bay, in the Highlands of Scotland, not far from a small village called Laide.

The Island has a chequered history, as do I. It used to be home to smugglers, and rebels, and scientists, and soldiers, and livestock, and well-meaning luddites who just wanted a place to get away from it all.

But that was then, and this is now.

Now, the Island is my home, and mine alone.

My Granny would have been proud of me.

I stand anchored to a mound of rock on a hill that rises up in the very middle of a large circle of pine trees. The trees are curiously white, their bark glowing as if freshly painted. Within their confines, a fresh, green pasture now grows, where once a large, decimated expanse of ashen land lay, its shape the shape of a perfect equilateral triangle. Amongst the blades of grass, there is rubble. Stone foundations, long abandoned. Slate roof tiles, littered about like confetti after a wedding. A rusted old water pump, sprouting like a weed from the centre of a ruined flagstone square. Next to it, a collapsed sandstone bench, bifurcated by a huge crack running across the middle of it.

These are the remains of White Pines, a town that was built where no town should have been built. I watch over these ruins every single day, my face turned to the sun, my arms stretched wide to the sky. I can feel the earth beneath my feet, and the call of the Other Place, and I can feel my body, anchored in one place that is also the centre of so many places, and my roots spread wide, fraying like tiny threads, shooting across space, all of them tugging and pulling at me, demanding my attention. Every root tip sucks from a different soil, a different reality. I am in one place and all places, at the same time.

For I am the walker between worlds.

I am the Key, the Gatekeeper, the one who goes where others should not.

And I am a tree, beneath which a boy and a man with salt and pepper hair sometimes sit, sheltered by my branches, and shaded by my love.

The End.

WITH THANKS AND LOVE

This book would not be possible without the support of my wonderful backers, who funded its creation on Kickstarter. Your belief in my work is humbling, and I adore each and every one of you:

Abi Elliott, Abi Godsell, Alex Martir, Aley McCaskill, Alicia Comstock, Alicia Lynn Atkins, Alison Bainbridge, Allison Brandt, Ally Katte, Amanda Hawk, Amy Jones, Andrew Baumgartner, Andrew Peterson, Angie Plaul, Anne Maroney, Annie Malwitz, Arne Sorli, Ash Holt, Ava Dickerson, Bert, Brad Goupil, Brandon Corey, Brian Amor, Bringme Igor Engelen, Bryan Johnson, Carl-Olof Siljedahl, Cat Horn, Catherine Lacerenza, Cedric Carter, Celina Tufvegren, Christina Berry, Christina Jewett, Christopher Beard, Christopher Gauch, Claire Owens, Claudia Beck Cooper, Colton Bradburn, Courtney Taylor, Craig

Sider, Dan Hanks, Daniel Boston, Daniel Warrell, Dannika Stilson, Darrin McAlpine, David Ault (my very FIRST backer!), David Cummings (without whom especially, this book would not have been possible), David Mallory, David Stephens, Debbie Fuhr, Derek Devereaux Smith, Don Schouest, Donna Henderson, Emily Giovannucci, Emily Reed, Emma Mitchell, Erin C, Fraser McGowan, Gareth Penn, Garra Peters, Genelle Irene, Graham Rowat, Hannah Johnson, Harold Bressler, Ian Epperson, Isha Lowe, Jack Render, Jacob Houser, Jacob Schacher, James Cleveland, James Watson, Janey, Jason Kingsley, Jen Tracy, Jennifer Clarke-McKay, Jennifer Gatlin, Jeremy Carter, Jeremy Dove, Jerome Smesny, Joe Janero, Joe Sullivan, John Crinan, John Miller, Johnny Stitches, Joli Grostephan-Brancato, Jon Carmody, Jon Grilz, Jon Hall, Jonas Sværke, Jordan Kellicut, Joseph Gustafson, Joshua Demarest, Julia Brunenberg, Julia Miller, Justin Dow, Justin McCarthy, Kassidy Morikawa, Kate Flanagan, Katherine Marcucci, Katrina Rowland, Keeley Stolpe, Kenneth Skaldebø, Kirsty Syder, Krista Neubert, Kristen, Kyle Choquette, Kyle Schultz, Lauren Stephens, Lindsay Moore, Lisa Copeland, Lou Ellen Allwood, Lucinda Stillinger, Luis Delaney, Mac Zullig, Madhur Parashar, Marcos Estrada, Mark Nixon, Martin A, Martyn Drew, Mary J. Anderson, Mathieu Collenot, Matt Weaver, Matthew Karlon, Michael Armes, Michael Bent, Michael Hirtzy, Michael

Hudson, Michael R Thompson, Michael Sturgis, Michelle Crumpet, Mikael Monnier, Mike Blehar, Monserrat Molina, Nichole Sullivan, Nick Lerma, Nicolas Petit, Patrick Sant, Patrick Stanley, Paul Anders, Paul Childs, Paul M. Feeney, Pete Gibson, Peter Balog, Pètur Arnòrsson, Philip Kelly, Powell's Books, Rachael Lamb, Rachel Limna, Rachel Masters, Randall Amos, Raymond J Moyer, Réco Thomas, Richard Meek, Richard Nenoff, Richard O'Connor, Rob Greer, Robert Gaines, Robert Smith, Roman Phan, Ronald C Neely, Ross Evans, Ryan Soto, Sage Brewster, Sam Rogers, Samantha Taylor, Sarah Ealy, Sasha Hammarström, Scott Munro, Scott Uhls, Sergio Saucedo, Shawn Lachance, Shawn Yates, Silas Hyzer, Stacy Van Cleave, Stephen Hampshire, Stephen Jones, Susan Hudson, Susan Jessen, Terry Donaldson, Thomas Martini, Thomas More, Toni Forster, Tonia Winer, Tracy Nguyen, Ursula Persson, Vernon Henderson, Victoria Kelemen, Vince Hunt, Violet Castro, Wendy Hamilton, WildClaw Theatre presents Deathscribe, Will Ahrens, William Lench, Zach, Zach Hall.

ABOUT THE AUTHOR

Gemma Amor is the Bram Stoker Award nominated author of *DEAR LAURA*, *CRUEL WORKS OF NATURE*, *TILL THE SCORE IS PAID* and *WHITE PINES*.

She is also a podcaster, illustrator and voice actor based in Bristol, in the U.K.

Many of her stories have been adapted into audio dramas by the wildly popular NoSleep Podcast, and on Shadows at the Door, Creepy, and The Grey Rooms podcasts.

She is the co-creator, writer and voice actor for horror-comedy podcast Calling Darkness, which also stars TV and film actress Kate Siegel.

gemmammorauthor.com

Facebook.com/littlescarystories
Twitter.com/manylittlewords
Instagram.com/manylittlewords